RANGE WAR

CHAPTER

★ 1 ★

It was unusual for Matt Ramsey to have luck this good. Even though he had lost the last two hands, he was still up a considerable amount of money from what he had when he had entered the Texas Palace saloon and gambling hall two hours ago. His luck was so good, in fact, that he decided that after one more hand, it would be time for him to call it quits for the day.

He leaned his broad back a little deeper into the chair and swallowed a mouthful of chock beer. He was surprised again at the deep, rich taste of the chock, considering the saloon owners probably had made it here on the premises. And the town of Wentworth was not exactly one of the bigger places in north Texas.

Ramsey had been out west in Baylor County, scouting for prairie mustangs. It was how he made his living—when he was not relying on his big Colt .44 for such—catching wild prairie mustangs and breaking them for sale. The pickings had been growing slimmer and slimmer each year for such work, at least in the northern reaches of east Texas, and Ramsey had been considering leaving the old shack on the Trinity River and moving west to try his luck out there, now that the Comanches had finally been pacified.

But he had thought he might give the area within a couple days' ride of his old shack one more chance before pulling up stakes for good. Besides, the two brothers he was closest to— Kyle and Buck—were still up north in Colorado somewhere. He didn't really expect Kyle to return, but Buck ought to be back before much longer. And since Buck was his frequent partner in the horse-gathering operations, he wanted to check with the young man before moving on.

1

He had spent several weeks roaming around out in Baylor County and beyond, but had found little. He did hear talk, though, of herds of mustangs running loose out in the Llano Estacado farther west and south. He figured to head on home, see if Buck was back, and then decide just what to do.

He had hoped to make Jacksboro by nightfall on this day, but his hunger for a decently cooked steak and a few mouthfuls of chock had pushed him into town when he spotted Wentworth. It was a small, shabby place, out in the middle of next to nowhere, but it offered a restaurant and the choice of three saloons. He had eaten well at the restaurant and then gone looking at the saloons.

The Texas Palace had looked the most appealing, though its name promised a glamour that it would never have. It was small, dirty, and almost airless. Cigarette smoke crowded the low sod ceiling braced by thin poles. There were no windows and only the one set of batwing doors to let in the light. The rest of the dim illumination was provided by coal-oil lanterns all around. The lanterns lent their stench of burning oil to the rankness of the rest of the saloon—stale beer and whiskey; old chewing tobacco that had been spit out haphazardly; unwashed, sweaty men; dust.

The cards flashed around the table, dealt with easy familiarity by a would-be sharp dressed in fancy duds. Ramsey had had second thoughts about sitting at the table with such a man. But with a few minutes of watching, Ramsey had learned that the man was not the card sharp he would have people believe he was. So Ramsey had taken a seat.

Ramsey bet a dollar on the jack that lay face up before him without looking at his two hole cards. Another round of cards flew by, and Ramsey felt a surge of excitement when a second jack joined the first in front of him. But he did not let it show. Instead, he bet three dollars and stared impassively from one man to the next.

Two other players dropped out, tossing their cards away with exclamations of disgust. The would-be sharp and a hard-eyed man sitting directly across from Ramsey stayed in the game, calling Ramsey's bet but not raising him.

Ramsey bet three dollars again on his pair of jacks, when a useless three showed up. The sharp now had a pair of tens in front of him; the other man a worthless assortment of an ace, six, and nine. The sharp was impassive, but raised Ramsey's bet by two dollars. The other man and Ramsey called it.

The last up card—a five—popped up in front of Ramsey. The other man showed a pair of sixes now, and the sharp still had his tens. Ramsey still had not looked at his hole cards. He tossed a five-dollar gold piece onto the growing pile, sipped some chock, and sat back in his chair.

The bet was called again but not raised, and the last card—face down—dropped in front of the three men. Ramsey finally looked at his buried cards, just lifting up one corner of each. A deuce, eight, and jack met his gaze. He felt some relief at seeing the third jack, but he remained outwardly serene.

Ramsey tossed another five-dollar gold piece on the pot. The sharp, to Ramsey's left, put two in. He sat back with a slight grin. The other man matched it and he and the sharp looked toward Ramsey. Ramsey nodded, shrugged, and threw a double eagle into the pot, staring blankly back at his opponents.

The sharp blanched—it was one of the many ways that showed he had more ambition to be a gambler than any discernible talent. The sharp sat, thinking, trying to calm the emotions that flickered across his face. He was down to twenty dollars. To use half that to call this big, hard-looking man with the shock of black hair was foolish. On the other hand, he had three tens, and the chance of the newcomer having three jacks was small. He gulped and tossed in ten dollars.

The other man glared at Ramsey with hot eyes. He was hot under the collar; had been all afternoon. He hadn't won but two pots, and both those were small. Then this dark-eyed man with the big Colt, hard look, and broad shoulders had come along and started winning from him, too. He didn't like it one little bit. But he could not just let Ramsey walk away with this pot. The man looked at his hole cards again. He had the pair of sixes showing, and a pair of threes in the hole. He had to call Ramsey's bet—he just had to—if only to see if he had the third jack.

Reluctantly, and still glaring at Ramsey, he tossed a ten-dollar gold piece into the pot. He said nothing.

Ramsey couldn't believe his luck. Without gloating, he turned over the third jack and laid it atop the other two. He smiled ruefully, letting the other man know he was not usually this lucky.

"Son of a bitch," the other man breathed. He was angry, but the words were almost inaudible. His breathing was ragged with the anger.

Ramsey reached for his winnings, to rake the pile of gold coins into those he had already accumulated. His smile froze when the man he had just beaten said harshly, "I think there's something wrong with the way you've been winnin', mister."

Ramsey finished what he was doing. He began stacking the coins, not looking at what he was doing, but instead keeping his eyes glued to the other man. "That's mighty close to callin' me a cheat, friend," he said easily, though his voice was hard.

The three other men at the table looked interested. They glanced from Ramsey to the other man, awaiting his response.

"I didn't say that," the man retorted, without backing down. "All I said was that it don't seem right, somehow."

"I got to admit," Ramsey said lightly, trying to ease the tension, "that my luck don't usually run as well as it has today, friend." He shrugged, signifying that it was one of those things in life that defied explanation.

The sharp and the two others began to relax as the tension eased. But it rose high again when the other man said, "You sure it was just a change in luck, pard?"

Ramsey had finished stacking his coins and now folded his hands on the table just behind the gleaming piles of money. His eyes glittered in anger. "That's the second goddamn time in less'n a minute you about called me a cheat," he said coldly. "Or the next thing to it. I don't cotton to such a thing. No, sir, not one goddamn teeny little bit." He leaned back and finished off his schooner of chock. "Now," he said in icy tones after he had carefully set the mug back on the scarred table, "supposin' you either come right and out and say what you got to say, or close that flap of a mouth of yours."

Dead silence fell over the saloon as men gathered around. The other three card players looked in fear at Ramsey and then in anticipation at the other man, wondering how he would respond.

Colby Carter was not a gunman, but he was no coward either. He had fought in the big war, as he figured Ramsey had. His problem—and he knew it, though he seemed to be able to do little about it—was that more often than not he spoke before he thought out the consequences. Like he had just now. He had tried to couch his words so that a peaceable man couldn't take too much offense. But still, a touchy hardcase could read what Carter meant, as this powerful-looking man had.

Carter finally managed to regain control over his mouth. "I didn't mean nothin' by it, mister," he said. There was no regret in his voice. He had made his point known and now could safely back off without seeming to back down. "It's just that I ain't seen a run of luck like that in a long spell."

"Such things don't come often," Ramsey said, lightening his tone a trifle.

The saloon patrons began turning back to their cards or their drinks. The other men at the table with Ramsey and Carter relaxed and looked forward to another hand.

"Well," Ramsey said brightly, "I got a far piece to travel yet, so I reckon I'll just take my leave of you boys. I'm obliged for this," he added as he scooped his coins into a buckskin sack.

"You're leavin'?" the card sharp asked, surprised.

"That was my thinkin'," Ramsey said. He stood and shoved the buckskin pouch of money into his shirt, which was stretched across the wide chest and back.

"That ain't very neighborly, mister," Carter said. The others at the table nodded agreement. "Such a thing ain't done."

"What ain't done?" Ramsey asked, the coldness back in his voice.

"Leavin' with such a big pile of winnin's."

"You never said such when that other feller left—when I took my seat here," Ramsey said calmly.

Others in the saloon were beginning to pay attention again.

"He didn't win near as big as you," the sharp said.

"And he wasn't no outsider," Carter tossed in recklessly, his mouth getting the better of him again.

"If you didn't want no outsiders winnin', you shouldn't let an outsider sit to your gamin' table, boy," Ramsey said harshly. "But you was willin' enough to take an outsider's money, though, wasn't you? That's why you didn't say nothin' about all this before." He paused a moment. "Well, boy, I'm a Texan through and through. You ain't. Neither is he." Ramsey pointed to the sharp. "You're goddamn Yankees is what you are, no matter how long you've lived in this hellhole of a town. And where I'm from, a man takes his losses in stride, just like he does his winnin'. He don't sit there, pissin' and moanin' about how poorly he's been treated of late."

He glared from one man to the next. "But I reckon y'all wouldn't understand that. Now, I won this money fair and square, and I got me a load of travelin' ahead. Like I said, I'll be takin' my leave."

He looked up at the bartender, who stood watching as intently as his patrons. "Supposin' y'all buy these boys here at the table a bottle of whatever it is they're drinkin'." He pulled a double eagle from his shirt pocket and flipped it toward the bartender. It was the last one he had left of the money he had arrived with.

"That ought to be more than enough to cover it. If I'm due any change, buy everyone else—includin' yourself—drinks till the money runs out."

He looked back at the men at his table. He touched the brim of his hat. "*Adios,* boys." He shoved the chair back with his legs and began striding toward the door.

Carter's chair scraped along the rough floor as he stood and turned to face toward Ramsey's back. "That's far enough, mister," he called.

CHAPTER

★ 2 ★

Ramsey stopped at the sound of Carter's voice. His right hand moved slowly toward the big Colt at his right hip as he turned back to face the table. The other men in the saloon had backed off, creating a lane. At the one end of the lane stood Ramsey, at the other, Carter and the would-be card sharp.

Ramsey sighed. There would be gunplay here, and death. He would wind up killing—or being killed by—men whose names he did not even know. He didn't much like such things. He sighed again. Such was the way of things. It would not be the first time he faced men he did not know; nor, he hoped, would it be his last.

"You got somethin' to say, boy, best come out with it."

"I've done all the talkin' I need to do, mister," Carter said. His hand streaked for his Colt pistol.

Ramsey yanked out his own Colt, crouching and lifting the pistol at arm's length in a single, smooth motion. The Colt barked twice.

Carter jerked under the impact of two bullets. His hand clenched in a spasm of death, and his revolver fired. The bullet slapped into the floorboards as Carter fell sideways. He hit a table, rolled off, banged off a chair, and then hit the floor. He felt none of it, since he was dead when he fell.

Ramsey did not pay any more heed to Carter. He knew instinctively as soon as he had fired the first time that his opponent was dead. After firing the second time—insurance, he liked to think of it—he turned slightly, still crouched.

The would-be card sharp had pulled a navy Colt from under his suit coat but seemed to be having trouble thumbing back the hammer. It was evident that he also was no gunman. But at this point, Ramsey didn't much give a damn. Even a nongunman could

7

be deadly given enough time and opportunity. He calmly fired, plugging the sharp in the brisket. He fired again, the bullet ripping though the sharp's throat.

Ramsey slowly straightened. He scanned the room but no one else was going to make a play. He hastily ejected the spent shells from the Colt and reloaded it before dropping it back into the holster. He eyeballed the room one more time before backing up the five steps to the door. He spun and slipped outside.

Hurrying, without seeming to do so, Ramsey moved toward his horse. The big, black stallion was one he had caught and broken himself several years before. The horse had proved to be such a fine animal that Ramsey could not bring himself to sell him, so he kept the steed instead. The animal had a powerful chest and strong legs. He had good wind and Ramsey had never found another horse with as much stamina or heart.

Ramsey mounted up and swung the horse around. Home was east, but he rode out of Wentworth heading south, figuring to throw off any pursuit that might be mounted. He didn't see any, and after an hour's easy ride southward, he turned east, eventually heading northeast on a line that would bring him to Jacksboro.

Dusk was just beginning to color the sky ahead of him, and Ramsey swore. Making it to Jacksboro before darkness was impossible now. He had started playing poker in Wentworth with the idea that he would spend the night at the hotel there, until those two damn fools had decided to throw down on him. He sighed in resignation. There was nothing he could do about it now, and to fret over it would serve no purpose.

He found a thicket of small oaks and cedars bunched up along a small, rippling stream and pulled in, though there was still some daylight left. He was not in that much of a hurry, and there was no reason for him to push on.

He unsaddled the black. Pouring some grain into a feed bag, he hung it over the horse's muzzle. He began rubbing the horse down, checking the animal over as he did so. The horse had been ridden long hours the past couple of weeks, and Ramsey wanted to make sure the horse was suffering no ill effects from that. He found nothing out of the ordinary.

When Ramsey finished currying the horse, he tied one end of a short rope to the horse's left foreleg and the other end to one of the oaks. It gave the steed enough room to roam a bit and graze on the grama grass and bunch grass once Ramsey removed the feed bag.

Ramsey began gathering wood and then started a fire. With a look of some distaste, he set salt pork and beans cooking. He pulled a small bottle of whiskey from one of his saddlebags. He sipped from the bottle while he waited for his supper to cook. He sipped from the bottle after he finished his supper, too, until it was gone. He flung the bottle off into the gathering darkness.

He wished Buck or Kyle was with him. He was not by nature an outgoing man, but either of those two brothers was a pleasure to travel with. Being kin, they were close, but they also knew when to keep their mouths shut. There was nothing worse than a blabbermouthed traveling companion.

His thoughts drifted from the wish of having one of those two brothers with him to wondering what they were up to in Colorado. He grinned when he thought of what Kyle must have thought when Luke, yet another brother, rode in with Buck to pay a visit. Kyle had been almost as bored a few months ago as Matt was now, and so had written asking Matt and Buck to come up for a visit to break the monotony. Matt had been recovering from the effects of one of his "jobs," and so Luke had gone along in his stead.

Though it was not full dark, Ramsey began to spread out his bedroll. He figured that he could be up and on the road again early. For some reason, he decided he wanted to be back either at his shack or the family homestead with oldest brother Amos. The want of family was strong on him these days, and he was not sure why.

Just before he unbuckled the gunbelt, he heard the sound of a buggy from far off. He left the belt on and melted into the shadows beyond the ring of firelight. He waited, listening to the clattering of the coach and the other sounds of the night—the bark of a coyote, the hooting of an owl, the rustle of the wind in the leaves overhead, the ripple of the stream, a nighthawk's cry.

The carriage grew closer and closer. Then the sound stopped. "Hallo, the camp," someone called.

"Ease on in, mister," Ramsey answered. There was a warning, but no threat, in his voice.

A few moments later a small carriage pulled by a blocky, high-stepping bay edged into the thicket, stopping in the only clear area large enough to accommodate it. A man in his fifties, well dressed despite the trail dust on his clothes, surveyed the seemingly empty camp from his buggy seat. "I don't mean any harm," he said into the night.

"You alone?" Ramsey called out from his spot in the shadows.

"You can see that I am."

"No one's follerin' you?"

"No, sir." The man waited.

Ramsey stalled, thinking. It was obvious the man was alone. At least here. No one could be hiding in the wagon. But a dozen could have been following along and could be sitting out in the rapidly coming darkness. On the other hand, the man looked rather harmless himself. He wore no pistol in sight. He appeared to Ramsey to be a rancher. Ramsey shrugged to himself. He didn't figure Wentworth even had a marshal, and if the town did, he doubted he would find enough interest in chasing after a drifting gunfighter who shot two gamblers down in self-defense.

Ramsey stepped out into the light. "Set to the fire, mister," he said politely. "Rest your horse."

"Thank you, son," the man said. He wrapped the reins around the brake handle and stepped down. He stood a moment, stretching, feeling his age. He reached into the carriage, making Ramsey tense momentarily. But when he turned, he had only a tin cup in hand. He finally came up to the fire and squatted, holding out the mug. He gratefully nodded when Ramsey filled it. He sipped.

Ramsey kept an eye on him as he poured coffee for himself. "Hungry?" he asked.

"I could do with a bite."

"Ain't much left, but help yourself to the beans and salt pork there." He handed over his tin plate, cleaned not long before by a dose of sand and then a quick dunking in the stream.

The stranger took the plate and fork, too, nodding. He scraped the remaining beans and meat onto the plate and then sat heavily on his rump. Then he began shoveling the food in, stopping only long enough for a gulp of coffee on occasion.

He finished quickly and set the plate aside. He refilled his mug with coffee and pulled out a cigar. After lighting the cigar with a burning stick from the fire, he sighed in contentment. "Thanks, mister," he said. "I never did get a chance to sup back in Wentworth." He watched Ramsey closely.

Ramsey stared back levelly, showing nothing of the irritation that arose in him. He somehow thought he was being set up. But he would wait and see how all the cards played out. "You leave there in a hurry?" he asked, indifferently.

"Something of a hurry," the man said with a disarming smile. "I was following you."

"Oh?" Ramsey shifted subtly, making sure his Colt was accessible. His ears perked up, hoping that he might pick up the sounds of anyone trying to sneak up on him. But all he heard were the night sounds of before.

"I saw what you did back there in the Texas Palace," the man said. Seeing the hard, almost desperate look leap into Ramsey's eyes, he said hastily, "Hold on, there, mister. It ain't what you're thinking."

"And what am I thinkin'?" Ramsey asked tightly.

"That I'm following you to bring you back there."

"Ain't you?" Ramsey's voice had not softened any.

"Hell, no," the man said with a nervous chuckle. He shuffled his broadening behind on the dirt. "Maybe I'd better explain."

"Might help," Ramsey said drolly.

"I was in Wentworth on business. My name's Jasper Pomeroy. I own the Sitting P Ranch, northwest of Jacksboro."

"So?" Ramsey said. He was still wary.

"I was just about to head into the saloon there when I saw what happened. As you left, I slipped out of the way. I watched you get on that big black of yours—and, I might add, that's one hell of a horse—and ride out. I had heard you saying you planned to go to Jacksboro, so even though you headed south, I went east, hoping you'd eventually swing around that way. I was beginning to think I'd lost you when I saw the fire. I wasn't sure it was you, of course, but I had to take a chance that it was."

"Could've been some outlaws," Ramsey allowed. "There's a passel of 'em in these parts."

"Don't I know it." He chuckled again.

Ramsey looked at Pomeroy. The man was in good shape for someone his age. His steely gray hair under the black derby and the heavy mustache were neatly cut. His string tie was neatly tied and his clothes under the dust were expensive. He was maybe five foot eleven and running to fat a little, but his face was clear.

"That still don't tell me why you're followin' me, friend." Ramsey was tense, wary, waiting for something to happen.

"In addition to running the ranch, I'm also head of the Jack County Cattlemen's Association. We've been looking for someone like you of late. We've had us a few problems we'd like to have taken care of, and you seem like the kind of man to do it."

The explanation was short and simple. And it made sense to Ramsey. He wasn't sure, still, if it was true, but he had to think it probably was. "What kind of troubles?"

"Rustlers." It was said simply, but the heat rushed to Pomeroy's face at the mere mention of the word.

"You fixin' to hire me?" Ramsey wasn't very interested in taking the job, but he had learned a long time ago that one should hear folks out first. He had nothing better to do these days, and, while he might have pocketed one hundred and twelve dollars from the poker game in Wentworth, it wouldn't last forever. A man had to work for a living, and Ramsey was always willing to listen when a job was in the offing.

"If you're of a mind to throw in with us."

"Tell me about these rustlers."

"Ain't much to tell," Pomeroy said with a shrug. He stared at the lighted end of his cigar for a moment. The darkness had come on fully now. "There ain't many of 'em, as far as we can tell, but those bastards've been keepin' mighty busy. It took us a while to catch on to them, since they're pretty smart. They hit all our places, but they make off with just a few head at a time." He shrugged again.

Ramsey sat thinking. He didn't have anything against rustlers. Most of them he had come across were poor men just trying to make their way in the world. Men who had gotten a poor hand dealt to them by life and were trying to even the odds a little. But not all were that way. Some were trying to become rich at someone else's expense. The Ramseys had never had any money, but they had always had aspirations. And they had always had a great capacity for hard work—usually designed to reach those aspirations. None of the Ramseys might have achieved any of those aspirations, but there still were none of them who would be willing to take shortcuts like rustling to try to improve their chances.

Pomeroy had watched Ramsey while he thought. He could see Ramsey calculating whether this would be worth his effort and time. Pomeroy thought he had the gunslinger now. "Pay's a hundred a month for three months. I figure you should be able to clean this little matter up in that time. You'll get the full three hundred, even if you handle it faster than that. Or," Pomeroy added pointedly, "we can pay you fifty dollars a head."

Ramsey had been about ready to accept, but the last statement gave him pause. "I ain't no hired killer, Mr. Pomeroy. You want somebody to come in and backshoot a bunch of goddamn rustlers, you got the wrong man."

Pomeroy cursed inwardly. He had been a fool. He should have stopped at the first offer and seen if Ramsey had taken that. "It ain't necessary that you kill them, Mr. . . ?"

"Ramsey. Matt Ramsey."

Pomeroy nodded. "It ain't necessary that you kill them, Mr. Ramsey," he said with sincerity. "Just as long as you run them off—permanently. I don't want those sons of bitches showing up again the day after you leave." He thought of questioning Ramsey's courage, until he remembered Ramsey in action back there in the Texas Palace. "Of course," he added cautiously, "some gunplay might be needed. . . ." He trailed off.

"I ain't above killin' when there's a call for it, as you should know," Ramsey said evenly, though he was angry at the insinuation. "I just ain't the sort of man to be hired for straight-out killin'. Not if there's another way."

"That's all I ask of you, Mr. Ramsey."

"Then you got a deal, Mr. Pomeroy." They shook hands across the fire.

CHAPTER

★ 3 ★

"One man? You hired only one man for the job?" Calvin McIlvaine asked, jowls flapping in agitation. McIlvaine was one of the cattlemen, the biggest rancher of all the members of the Jack County Cattlemen's Association. Even so, he thought it ostentatious to lead the group. Instead, he preferred to sit in the background, directing things from that vantage point.

"Calm down, Cal," Pomeroy said, almost smiling.

"Hog shit," McIlvaine snapped. "We wanted to hire an army to wipe out these pestiferous bastards, and you come back with one man?"

Matt Ramsey stood to the side, leaning against the wall. His arms were crossed over his big chest. None of the anger that bubbled within him showed on the surface.

Pomeroy was not afraid of McIlvaine. He was used to dealing with the fat, pompous rancher. "He's good, Cal," Pomeroy said soothingly. "Hell, I saw him take down two men in a couple of seconds down there in Wentworth. Four shots, two in each man, any one of them fatal. I've never seen anything like it." He chuckled softly.

"He better be good, Jasper," McIlvaine growled, though he had been mostly assuaged. "We've got to get this problem cleared up. Soon."

"It will be."

McIlvaine looked at Ramsey. "You think you can handle this, boy?" he asked. Condescension dripped from his voice.

Ramsey said nothing. He simply stared hard at McIlvaine, who wilted under the gunman's hard, dark eyes.

"I've got to be sure, you know," McIlvaine said lamely.

"I could shoot off your ears from here, if that'd convince you," Ramsey said dryly.

McIlvaine blanched, as the five other members of the association—Pomeroy, Tobe Walker, Oscar Baron, Howard Crowell, and Blaine Yates—chuckled or snickered. They were a typical lot for ranchers. Wealthy, well dressed in wool suits and fresh shirts, and pompous for the most part. Pomeroy and Yates looked like they had worked cattle at some point, but were now in their fifties and long past such menial labor. The others looked as if they had never worked a day in their lives.

"Then perhaps you'd better get on with it," McIlvaine said stiffly.

"It's about time," Matt answered sourly. He pushed away from the wall. "Do I get supplies from you folk? Or do I get 'em at the general store here in Jacksboro and put 'em on your tab?"

"The store," Pomeroy said. "I'll arrange it with Flanagan, who owns the place."

Ramsey nodded. "There any fringe benefits to this job?" he asked with a wink.

The other men laughed and Pomeroy said, "Don't see why not. I'll arrange it. Just make sure you do your job. We ain't paying you to spend all your time here."

Ramsey nodded again. He turned and headed out of the big room and through the ornate building in which the Jack County Cattlemen's Association had its headquarters. The office, as the cattlemen called the big room, took up most of the back of the building.

The Jacksboro Social Club was a combination men's club, saloon, and high-class brothel. It was set off the main street, sitting in rich splendor but away from the beaten path. The girls who worked there—in the rooms on the second floor over the office—were, as a rule, young, pretty and well versed in their arts. They were scantily dressed, as befitting their profession, but the things they did wear were made of the finest silk and satin; their jewelry was real.

The long bar in the spacious saloon was made of hard-carved mahogany, as was the back bar. Plenty of glass and mirrors decorated the back bar, and huge paintings of nude women in various states of repose hung from the walls. There were gaming tables, billiard tables, and other diversions.

Ramsey considered stopping at the bar, or even one of the rooms upstairs—he had spied a shapely, raven-haired beauty on his way back to the office that he wanted to meet, if only briefly. But then he decided not to stop. Not now. Pomeroy would not have had time to set up a tab for him, and Ramsey was loath to spend any of his own money in such pursuits, knowing he would have it free soon.

He stepped outside in the blistering heat of the July afternoon. It was too late in the day to really do anything as far as the rustlers were concerned. He mounted the black and rode slowly down the livery stable at the western edge of the town. He left the horse there with a warning to the liveryman about caring for him. Ramsey tossed his saddlebags over his left shoulder. Holding his Winchester in his left hand, he strolled back toward the center of town, taking in the sights.

Ramsey had not been in Jacksboro for several years, but the city had changed little. It had grown some and seemed to have more hustle and bustle. A few of the buildings were fancier than he remembered, and there were more houses and stores lining the streets of the town.

Ramsey suddenly stopped. He had no place to stay in Jacksboro. "Damn," he muttered. He decided he'd have to head to one of the hotels in town and pay for his own room. Since it probably would be only one night, he was not too put out at it. But he was annoyed that he had not thought of it earlier and mentioned it to the association members.

He shrugged. It made little difference now. He planned to be on the trail at first light, heading out to scout the cattlemen's ranches and try to find the rustlers' hideout. He mostly likely would have to spend several weeks at it, most of that time sleeping under the stars, since he couldn't make it back to Jacksboro every night.

He was about ready to enter the Royal Hotel when he met Jasper Pomeroy. "You ain't going in there, are you?" Pomeroy said.

"You got something else in mind?" Ramsey asked dryly.

"The Social Club." Pomeroy grinned.

Ramsey's opinion of the cattlemen inched upward. "Reckon I could accept such a thing," he allowed.

"I thought you would," Pomeroy said with a laugh. "Everything's all arranged. Just go on over there and talk with Wilkins. He'll get you a room—and keep you supplied." Pomeroy winked lecherously.

"Thank you, Mr. Pomeroy."

"It's the least we can do, Mr. Ramsey." He turned serious. "However, we do expect results in return."

"You'll get 'em." He moseyed on up the street and a few minutes later entered the Jacksboro Social Club. He found Wilkins, one of the Social Club's top servants.

The tall, thin man led Ramsey up to a room in the corner overlooking an alley. With exaggerated dignity, he opened the door and let Ramsey in. "Anything else you require, sir?" Wilkins asked less than sincerely.

Ramsey was tempted to shoot the man, just for the hell of it. Instead, he just sighed and said calmly, "A bottle of your best sippin' bourbon, and that little raven-haired belle."

"Veddy good, sir," Wilkins said in obvious distaste.

"And soon," Ramsey said, cheered a little by having punctured Wilkins's pomposity just a bit.

"Yes, sir." Wilkins's usually acid disposition turned even more sour. He left, and Ramsey grinned as he shut the door. He never did understand people like Wilkins, people who seemed to think the whole world was there for the sole purpose of antagonizing them for some reason or other.

Ramsey tossed his gold-coin-laden saddlebags in a corner and leaned the Winchester against a wall. He poured some water into the basin and cleaned his face. He was just rubbing dry on a rough towel when he heard a soft tapping at the door. Gliding easily to the side, he rested his hand on the butt of his Colt .44 and said, "Come on in."

A vision in a white silk shift entered. In her right hand was a bottle of bourbon; in her left, two glasses. She stopped just inside and looked around. As always, she had felt some trepidation when she knocked on the door. Though usually only rich, important men came to the Jacksboro Social Club and partook of the amenities there, occasionally there were men who were not so nice. She felt some relief when she saw Ramsey. Indeed, she smiled. Yes, she realized, there was a hard, dangerous look about this dark-haired man, but he was tall, strong, and rather handsome. He would be a good companion for a while, she decided. Unless he was one of those men who got their enjoyment from hurting women. But she had become a pretty good judge of men, and she did not think that the case here.

"Howdy, ma'am," Ramsey said, almost shyly.

The perfectly sculpted head nodded, and the full, deep red lips parted in a welcoming smile. "My name's Lucy," she said.

The voice sent a shiver down Ramsey's back. He knew what kind of woman she was—what she did for a living. But he still found himself attracted to her more than he should. There was something compelling about this tiny, beautiful young woman. Something more compelling than just the overt sexuality of her.

"I'm Matt Ramsey," he said politely. "Come on in and set."

Lucy sashayed in, every movement of her small, supple body sending a shiver of anticipation through Ramsey. She set the glasses down on the table before the window and then poured bourbon into each. She turned, holding one of the glasses out toward Ramsey.

He took it, nodded thanks, and gratefully chugged the liquor down. It was good—he had thought that like most other saloons, the Jacksboro Social Club might water down their drinks. But such was not the case.

Lucy sipped her drink, eyeing Ramsey over the rim of her glass. She pretty well liked what she saw. When Ramsey put his glass down, Lucy did likewise. She shrugged out of her shift and waited for Ramsey to come to her. She did not have long to wait.

Though it was still early morning, the heat was oppressive as Ramsey rode out of Jacksboro the next morning. He headed north. Just after dawn, Ramsey had risen from his bed—reluctantly, since the delectable Lucy was still there, sleeping quietly. Ramsey looked down at her for a few moments, remembering the past night's delights. He ate downstairs in the saloon, then headed over to Flanagan's general store, where he picked up several sacks of grain, some jerky, salted beef, flour, cornmeal, smoked chicken, coffee, and sugar. He also bought two boxes of cartridges for both the Colt and the Winchester. He got a mule at the livery stable to carry the supplies. Soon after, he was riding out of town.

Howard Crowell's ranch was the smallest and the one closest to Jacksboro. Ramsey checked that one first, riding over the open prairies, through the dips and over the swells.

The land was almost devoid of trees, and there were few places, Ramsey found, that could be used to hide rustled cattle. Ramsey spent that night out in the open, making a cooking fire of buffalo and cow chips. The dried dung made a short, hot fire and gave an added tanginess to the salted beef.

He rode northwest the next day, onto Oscar Baron's spread and searched it for the next three days. It took nearly a month to cover all the land owned or claimed by the six who made up the Jacksboro County Cattlemen's Association. He still had found little that would provide a hideout for rustlers, so he rode all the way on up to the Red River.

He rode on a line straight north from Jacksboro, which brought him to a wide, hard-angled crook in the river. He patrolled west up the river several miles, checking for possible hideouts. There were several.

Then, with a feeling of nervousness, he turned eastward along the river. He stopped at a flat, sandy stretch of beach and stood looking out over it for some time. It no longer held the terror for him that it once did, but there remained in his heart a sadness at his losses there.

More than two years ago now, he and two wrangler friends of his had been attacked by Comanches on this very spot. The two wranglers had died at the hands of the Indians, and Matt had come mighty close to doing so himself—until his brother Buck had come along and saved him. Ramsey shuddered involuntarily at the remembrance.

He eased the big black stallion into the river and swam across. The two graves were still there, the poorly made markers already faded by the elements. Ramsey said a silent prayer of memorial for his friends.

Then he shook off the gloom and swam the horse back across the Red River. He rode through the thicket of trees that lined the small stretch of sandy beach, making haste. He wanted to be away from here.

As it had half a dozen times in the past month, rain started. It was not hard, but it was steady. And chilling. The wind kicked up little pools of water into fine spray. Ramsey turned westward along the river and after an hour's ride pulled into another thicket of cedar and ash.

It was as comfortable a camp as he could expect. He ate without much hunger, sick of his normal fare after a month of bacon and beans or salted beef and beans or jerked beef and beans. He finally leaned back, sipping coffee, thinking.

It seemed like the Red River area was the most likely area for the rustlers to head to with their stolen cattle. Nowhere else closer to Jack County would be safe. It might be possible that the men were crossing the Red River into the Indian Nations to hide, gather enough cattle, and then sell the beeves. It would be easy to sell them up there in the Nations.

He decided he would just have to go out and find the rustlers and then follow them a spell. See what that brought. He rolled into his blankets under a small piece of canvas tarp tied to two trees. He fell asleep.

CHAPTER

★ 4 ★

Ramsey finally rode back into Jacksboro and spent a few nights in the Social Club. He relaxed, filling his stomach with good food, his bed with Lucy, and his time with thoughts about his situation.

He also spent some time fending off the curious members of the Jack County Cattlemen's Association. Ramsey stayed mum, much to the annoyance of the cattlemen.

"We could hire someone else, sonny," Calvin McIlvaine snapped, his fat cheeks flapping with indignation.

"Makes me no never mind," Ramsey retorted calmly. "You can just hand over the month's pay you owe me and I'll be ridin' out."

"I'll do no such thing," McIlvaine said. He was indignant at the very suggestion.

"I will be paid, Mr. McIlvaine," Ramsey said. His voice was even but contained more than a hint of menace.

McIlvaine stared at the gunman for a moment, sweat beading on his flaccid face. He wiped at the beading perspiration with a handkerchief.

Ramsey figured the cattleman had suffered enough—for now. "If there's no more questions," he said quietly, "I've got some things to tend to." He did not wait for an answer. He simply turned on his boot heel and strolled out of the office and headed up to his room.

But he figured three days was plenty enough to rid himself of the trail weariness. With one last good meal under his belt, and one last fling with Lucy, he saddled the black in the morning and trotted out of Jacksboro.

He headed south, across the emptiness of the north Texas

21

plains. He needed to go north, but he wanted to see if anyone other than the Cattlemen's Association was interested in his movements. Half a day out, he decided that no one was, and he swung to the west and curled upward toward the north. The next day he rode onto Yates's ranch.

During his long ride, he passed little, save for scattered, small farms. The occupants turned hate-filled eyes on him, if they even looked at him at all. It was bothersome to Ramsey, who did not know why they should be so cold to him. He had done nothing to them. He shrugged. He had seen it before. Such people were always afraid of men like him. Men who made their way in life with a heavy pistol. It could not be helped.

It took Ramsey several more weeks—until well into August— to get a handle on the rustlers. There was so much land to cover, and he never knew when or where they would strike, Finally he decided that he would just linger on McIlvaine's ranch. He knew the rustlers would get there sooner or later.

He took up the watch near a small, free-roaming segment of McIlvaine's vast herd. He followed the herd at night, moving silently not far away from the stock. He holed up in brush along almost nonexistent streams or in grassy arroyos during the day.

Nine days after he had taken up his silent, dark watch, the rustlers came. The arced sliver of a moon, combined with the dotted bowl of stars, provided some light. It wasn't much, but it was enough for Ramsey to see the three dim figures scurry out of the shadows, rope three longhorns, and tug the cattle off.

Ramsey followed them quietly. As expected, the big black cooperated in providing silence, and much to Ramsey's surprise, so did the mule.

A mile northeast, the three men pulled up. Ramsey edged as close to them as he could, nodding. They were good at what they did. It showed in the way they rustled the stock, taking only a few at a time so as to not anger people too much. And it showed in their stealthy, sure movements.

And it showed in the fire they built to mar McIlvaine's brand with their own running brand. Ramsey had never seen the fire; did not know it was there until he caught the dim glimmer of a red-hot branding iron. Then he realized that the rustlers had built a small fire in a hole dug in the sod in a slight dip of the prairie. They had covered maybe three-quarters of the hole with a flat rock and let the flames burn down to coals. As such, it was unseen at anything more than a few feet, and that only in one direction.

Ramsey was rather impressed with the rustlers. Not so impressed that he wouldn't do what he was being paid to do, but impressed enough to have some admiration for the rustler's competence.

Within minutes, the men had slapped their hot running brand onto the sides of the bawling cattle and turned them out with half a dozen others nearby. The men conferred as they sat sipping coffee, continuously looking around nervously. Bits of their conversation drifted up to Ramsey, who had left the black and the mule ground-staked back a ways and had crept up until he was lying on his stomach barely ten yards away from the rustlers.

He heard one say, "I don't like it, boys. Sure don't. I got me a spooky feelin' tonight."

Another started to josh him about it, until a third barked at the second man, saying, "This here ain't nothin' to make light of. I got the same damn feelin'."

"Think somebody's watchin'?" a voice asked.

"Might be," another answered quietly. "But I ain't seen no sign of such."

Ramsey nodded, satisfied that he had been doing well. He had made the rustlers nervous but had not given them anything definite, just a spooky feeling.

"Let's ride on," one of the rustlers said. He flicked his wrist, and the fire sizzled a moment as coffee danced in it. The five hurriedly dumped their coffee into the fire and kicked dirt over it. In a few minutes, they had packed up their few supplies, tightened their cinches, and mounted up. They rode north, driving the nine steers ahead of them.

Ramsey followed at a discreet distance. He began to hang back farther and farther, though, as he saw dawn threatening in the east, until he was several miles behind. Just after daybreak, he found a trickle of water supporting a lone, stunted cedar. He tended the black and the mule before sitting to chaw down a meal of cold jerked beef and stale biscuits. He wanted coffee, but could not risk starting a fire and being detected, so he did without.

Before darkness had fallen, Ramsey had eaten another cold meal, had saddled the black, packed the mule, and was loping along the rustlers' trail. He could follow the track all right now, but night was coming and the dark clouds spread out overhead as far as he could see would obscure most of the moonlight. He would never be able to follow their trail at night, so he needed to close the gap before they got too far ahead. He stopped every half-mile or so and listened intently. He was finally rewarded by the sound of the rustlers' movement.

Just to make sure it was them, Ramsey hurriedly but cautiously closed the distance. A break in the dark, bunched clouds provided enough light momentarily so that Ramsey, who was less than an eighth of a mile behind, could make sure it was indeed his quarry ahead of him. He dropped back again until he was riding a quarter of a mile or so behind the rustlers.

They rode through the night, and Ramsey could feel the boredom hanging heavy on him. He fought off sleep, helped by the wind, which whipped sand at his face.

Ramsey sensed more than saw that the rustlers had stopped. It was an almost unconscious judgment, seeing as how the blackness of the night was giving way ever so reluctantly to the grayness of predawn.

Ramsey found a gently sloping arroyo. He pulled into it and looked around, satisfied. Even the horse could not be seen while they were in the arroyo. There were no trees and no water. But buffalo and cow chips were plentiful. Ramsey decided he could risk a fire—if he was careful.

Once again he tended the horse and mule, keeping a wary eye out on the sky. It was still cloudy, but he doubted it would rain any time soon. He gouged a shallow hole into the side of the arroyo wall at the base. He built his fire in the hole and cooked salted beef, hot biscuits, and best of all, hot coffee. He ate it with relish, having decided such fare was not bad when compared with a cold camp. As the sun rose, Ramsey stretched out in his bedroll and slept.

They went through the strange ritual again the following night, making an odd-looking procession strung out along the prairie.

Ramsey cursed silently into the darkness as he crossed the shallow, narrow Wichita River less than half an hour after pulling out. Well after midnight, they veered northeast. As dawn approached, Ramsey could smell water. He figured it to be the Red River.

Ramsey closed the gap, wanting to see if the rustlers were planning to stop for the day. They weren't. He could see them drift off into a heavy thicket of brush, oak, and cedar lining the river. He followed cautiously.

The trail was barely discernible, especially in the pitch darkness that was usual just before dawn. But Ramsey found it and followed. The thicket began thinning out. Not far ahead, Ramsey could see the five rustlers. They were just easing the cattle into the wide, sluggish river. Ramsey sat there, gnawing on a strip of jerked beef, watching.

Ramsey waited another hour after the rustlers and their booty had made their way with herky-jerky efforts up the fairly steep bank across the river before he moved. He moved the black into the water. The mule balked, but then followed docilely along. Ramsey worked up the bank and stopped. He could see a small cloud of dust off in the distance.

"Reckon there's no sleepin' for us today, boy," he said to the horse. He moved forward, taking his time.

He followed the trail to the lip of a puckered gash of a canyon running off to the northwest. He sat for a few moments, wondering if he should enter what he expected was the rustler's haven. He had no idea of who or what or how many men were down there. Maybe only the five men he was trailing. But it could be that rustlers had gathered from miles and miles around, and he was not being paid to clear out the rustlers from all of Texas and maybe Colorado, the Indian Nations, and New Mexico, too. He was being paid to rid Jack County of rustlers, that was all.

Ramsey scratched his nose, irritated, calculating the odds. He was tired, and the heat of the day emphasized that. He decided it was not worth it to head into the canyon. He was certain he would find things there that were better left alone by him. It would be, he thought, much easier for him to wait somewhere back along the trail and stop the rustlers out there. They might be amenable to talking then.

Somewhat reluctantly, he backed the black away from the lip of the crumbling canyon. He turned the animal and found himself face to face with three men. They did not look friendly.

"Howdy," Ramsey said. He had attempted to inject a note of lightness into his voice, but he did not think he had succeeded very well.

"Lookin' for somethin', mister?" the man in the center asked with a sneer.

"A way around this goddamn canyon," Ramsey answered, still trying to achieve lightheartedness. "I kind of lost my bearin's somewhere back down the trail a bit. I thought maybe once I crossed the Red, I'd be able to find my way again." He shrugged as he so-very-slowly edged his right hand toward the Colt. "Reckon that didn't do me much good."

"That story's full of cow shit, mister," the same one said. His tones were flat and harsh. "And so are you."

Ramsey sighed. "All right," Ramsey said harshly. "I come lookin' for some rustlers."

"You found some," the man said. He grinned evilly.

CHAPTER

★ **5** ★

I'm too goddamn old for such nonsense anymore, Ramsey thought as he threw himself to the ground. The three rustlers had wasted no more time on words; they simply had gone for their pistols. At the same instant, Ramsey had flung himself off the horse, to his right. He figured the move would do two things: first, it would put the big black stallion between him and two of the rustlers; and second, it would confuse them, since he was right-handed. If he was going to dive off the horse, he would be expected to do so on the left, keeping his gun hand free.

He hit the ground hard, grunting with the impact, and rolled. All the while, Ramsey hoped the black would not be caught in the gunfire. The horse was too good to lose.

Ramsey came up on one knee, Colt in hand. He ignored the dull pain in his right shoulder. His pistol spit fire four times. He wanted to keep one shot left, just in case.

But it was not necessary. The three rustlers jerked off their mounts as bullets slammed into them with deadly certainty. Their horses whinnied and then bolted. One of them dragged its rider along. The body bounced in the hard dirt, kicking up puffs of dust as the body flapped wildly. Ramsey's mule tried to run, too, upset by the roar of gunfire, but could not. The black held steady, though its eyes rolled in his head. The rope dallied to the saddlehorn kept the mule from moving.

Ramsey slowly stood. With Colt cocked and held skyward, he edged up on the two rustlers lying in bent awkwardness. Both were dead. He looked around, listening intently. He heard only the three horses still running away. There was no pursuit. Yet. But he figured it would not be long before someone came

27

to see what had happened. He had not recognized any of the three as the men he had been following, so there must be other rustlers about.

Quickly, without flourish, Ramsey ejected the spent shells from the Colt and reloaded the revolver with cartridges pulled from loops in his gunbelt. He dropped the gun into his holster. He stood for a moment, absently rubbing his sore shoulder. He rolled it several times, and decided that it might give him some pain, but it was not hurt too badly and would not affect his movements. With a last look around, he pulled himself onto the black and rode off. He got five yards toward the river and then stopped.

They would be expecting him to go that way, he figured. He turned east, following in the rough tracks left by the third rustler's horse. He loped along easily, the mule clumping stoically in the stallion's smooth path.

An hour later he passed the rustler's horse, which was cropping the sparse bunch grass in the dusty soil. The rustler was still hung up in the stirrup. Ramsey shrugged and rode on. He eventually passed the other two rustlers' horses, too, but ignored them.

He did not slacken his pace for a half day. Then he finally stopped. He loosened the black's saddle and the mule's packs, letting them breathe. He stood, looking back the way he had come. Out here, with the dry soil, pursuit would be obvious from the cloud of dust. But Ramsey saw nothing. With a nod, Ramsey unsaddled the horse and unpacked the mule. He poured grain into the nose bags and fed the animals. He chewed on jerky and sipped from his canteen, sitting in the sparse shade of a stunted cedar, watching his back trail.

After eating, Ramsey tested his shoulder again. It was still somewhat sore, but not too bad. Just a dull ache that would ease with time. Finally he pulled his dark Stetson down over his eyes and napped for two hours. It was late afternoon when he awoke and stood. He stretched and yawned, feeling the tiredness and tightness of too many days in the saddle, of too many nights sleeping on the hard prairie sod, of too many hours riding through thundering rainstorms.

Ramsey scanned the horizon, but he still saw no pursuit, and he began to relax a little. He felt secure enough now to build a small fire, heat coffee, and cook up a mess of bacon and beans. He ate the meal without relish, enjoying only the coffee. After cleaning his cookware in the sand, he stomped out the fire and packed the mule. Then he saddled the stallion, who seemed refreshed and strengthened. He pulled himself into the saddle and headed south, toward the river. He had to skirt some thickets, moving eastward half a mile, but he finally pulled down onto the beach where he had buried his friends Marcus Book and Jamie Cotter.

"Damn," he muttered as he waded the black into the swift river. This place, with all its horror and bad memories, seemed destined to become a second home to him. This was the third time he had been back since Book and Cotter had been killed. His chest, where he had taken a Comanche arrow and bullet, ached in remembrance, but he shoved the thoughts out of his mind.

It was growing dark by the time he pulled up on the sandy beach on the south bank of the river, but he was determined not to make camp here. Besides, he told himself, the nap had refreshed him. He pushed on, through the thick tangle of trees and brush that bordered the beach. Then he loped steadily across the prairie.

In two days of hard riding, he was back in Jacksboro. He turned the black and the mule in at the livery and wearily carried himself back to his room at the Jacksboro Social Club. Lucy heard right off that he was back, and she quickly got rid of the customer she was with and headed toward Ramsey, with expectation.

She knew it was not wise for her to have the feelings she was having for this man. For any man, for that matter. It just plain was not a smart thing, considering her profession. It would make her job more difficult after a while, and would bring her only heartbreak. But she seemed helpless, and she didn't know why. All she knew was that this big, hard gunman held an attraction for her that no other man had ever had. She just accepted it for the time being. Now was not the time to worry about what might be or what could be. She went with her feelings and intuition, and usually would let the chips fall where they may.

A bare-chested Ramsey whirled, snatching out his Colt as Lucy entered the room without knocking. She yelped and froze, her mouth forming a circle of fright. Ramsey drew in a raggedy breath. He was too tense. He dropped the pistol into his holster. "Sorry, Lucy," he mumbled. He unbuckled the gunbelt and dropped it on the bed.

"That's all right," Lucy said, recovering some. She was still frightened, but she had dealt with enough men like Matt Ramsey that she was almost used to such things now. She came close to him and brushed her fingers across the bruise discoloring his shoulder. She shuddered, telling herself it was because of his proximity, and not because of the old bullet wounds and scars that marred his broad chest. "What happened?" she asked quietly.

"Fell off my horse," Ramsey said with a little grin.

"Shoot," she muttered, grinning at him. But she felt weak at the knees in his presence.

"Well, actually, I flung myself off him." The grin dropped, and he described what happened, using a flat, dull voice.

"Oh," she said when it was told. She rested her small, dark-haired head on his chest.

Ramsey was struck again, as he was every time he was standing near Lucy, at just how small she was. The top of her head barely came to his chest, and he could encircle her waist with his big, callused hands. He was fighting—as he had been since he had first seen Lucy—feelings for her that he did not want to admit to himself. Those feelings swept over him anew now, and his eyes narrowed in anger at himself for his weakness. He had sworn long ago that no one would ever replace Kate Silcox in his heart. And yet here this woman—this fallen angel—was weakening that vow.

He growled softly, low in his throat, startling Lucy a little. But then he encircled her slim shoulders and held her close. She relaxed and breathed hotly on his chest.

The next morning, after a hot, filling—and leisurely—breakfast in the company of Miss Lucy Tillman, Ramsey strolled into the office at the Social Club. The five members of the Jack County Cattlemen's Association were waiting, impatient and irked.

"Well?" Calvin McIlvaine asked, flab bouncing in indignation.

"Well, what?" Ramsey asked ingratiatingly, biting back a grin. He could not resist needling the corpulent cattleman, even though McIlvaine would not recognize it as such.

"Goddamn it!" McIlvaine exploded, flab on fire with his anger.

"Calm down, Cal," Jasper Pomeroy said easily.

"No, goddamn it! We've paid this jackass too much with too little results. I . . ."

"Best watch the way you talk, pus gut," Ramsey snarled. He bristled with rage. "There's a number of folks who talked to me in such a way that're now worm fodder."

"But . . ."

"Shut up, Cal," Pomeroy snapped. "Let the man talk. You ain't even given him a chance to tell us whatever news he has." Pomeroy turned to look at Ramsey. "I do hope, though, that you have some good news for us, Mr. Ramsey."

Ramsey glared at him a moment, then grinned. "Reckon it's good news for you folks. Can't say it's the same for the rustlers." He paused a moment, seeing the eager expectation in five pairs of eyes looking at him. "There's three boys ain't gonna be rustlin' no more cattle from you fellers," he said with a hard grin.

"Now, that's what we wanted to hear!" Oscar Baron said gleefully.

"Damn right," Tobe Walker added.

"How many more are there?" the ever-practical Pomeroy asked.

"Ain't sure. At least five that I know of. Could be just a couple more. Could be a couple dozen." He paused, rubbing absently at his healing shoulder. "I expect it's closer to the first than the second though, judgin' by what they've been takin' from you boys all along."

McIlvaine still was not happy with it. "Well, then, sir, when will you finish the job?" he demanded.

"When I get 'round to it," Ramsey said coolly.

"Damn it, Ramsey, we ain't paying you to sit around the Social Club, poking the girls and eating high on the hog."

"You ain't payin' me to sit here and listen to you babble, neither, but I've done that, too. I've been out scoutin' your ranges for most of two months now. I've slept in the rain, on hard ground. I've ate beans, bacon, and salted beef till I'm about to puke from it. My ass hurts from sittin' a saddle. I figure a couple days of high livin' ain't gonna hurt nobody."

"You seem to forget that you're being paid to protect our cattle."

"I ain't forgettin' a goddamn thing," Ramsey snapped. "But after your losses the past couple years, or however long it's been that these rustlers been workin' these parts, a few more head ain't gonna make you no difference." He sucked in a deep breath, trying to settle his anger. "And you seem to forget that in addition to just plain desirin' a few days of comfort, I also got to come back here for supplies. I was about down to eatin' cactus."

"But, you . . ."

"Enough, Cal," Pomeroy said, his own patience grown short. "Mr. Ramsey has rid the area of three of the rustlers and . . ."

"So he says," McIlvaine snapped.

Ramsey shoved away from the wall and took a few threatening steps forward. "You callin' me a liar, you fat-faced son of a bitch?" he said menacingly.

McIlvaine turned the color of new snow and fear-sweat trickled down his blubbery face. He squawked a few times, but no real words would form.

"Didn't think so," Ramsey said. Sarcasm dripped from the words. He glanced at each of the other men in the room before settling his gaze back on McIlvaine. "I may be a lot of things, Mr. McIlvaine," Ramsey said softly. "But a liar generally ain't among 'em. Had I not found any rustlers this time out, I would've offered to leave your employ—without bein' paid."

He glanced out the window, then looked at McIlvaine again. "I'm a prideful man, Mr. McIlvaine. Maybe too prideful at times. It's a trait of the Ramseys. Every damn one of us is prideful almost to a fault." He shook his head, seemingly trying to shake himself back from the world he had entered briefly. He smiled a little. "Just don't ever doubt my word again, Mr. McIlvaine. It ain't nice. Nor healthy."

McIlvaine was still sweating. His head bobbed in acknowledgment.

"How long will you be staying in Jacksboro, Mr. Ramsey?" Howard Crowell asked. He seemed shy, almost afraid to speak. Ramsey assumed it was because he was the least wealthy of the six cattlemen.

"Two, three days at most," Ramsey comment. "Just long enough for me to stretch out my trail-weary bones, get me a bellyful of decent redeye and good food. And my fill of some other things." He grinned lecherously.

The ranchers laughed with easy camaraderie. They were all men of the world, and they accepted such things with understanding and rough good humor. A man like Matt Ramsey would be expected to think along such lines; to do less would be to make him seem unmanly to these rich, though still frontier-hardened men.

Ramsey was reluctant to leave, considering the quality of his accommodations at the Jacksboro Social Club and the charms of Miss Lucy Tillman. But three days later, he knew it was time to get back on the trail. There was much work to be done yet, and he would not get it done sitting on his rump in the Jacksboro Social Club, no matter how pleasurable that might be.

CHAPTER

★ 6 ★

There was a sharp chill in the night air, reminding Matt Ramsey that it was September. Winter would be coming soon. He was glad he had brought a good wool coat from Jacksboro.

Ramsey sat on the cold ground atop a small hillock watching the scattered cattle—part of Tobe Walker's herd—grazing on the rolling prairie and moving into the brushy arroyo fifty yards away. The fat, bold glob of full moon spread a silvery, ghostly light over the landscape.

Ramsey's patience was finally rewarded when he saw five riders ease into the arroyo from the northwest. They moved swiftly but silently and surely, not disturbing the longhorns.

Ramsey had been fairly certain the rustlers would strike here next. He had ridden from Jacksboro to the Red River, where the rustlers would cross, taking three easy days to make the trip. The canyon the rustlers used as a hideout was directly across the river from him, and several miles north. Ramsey had kept concealed, and waited. Two days later, five rustlers—two of them he had seen before, the others he had not—waded into the cool Red River and began making their way across. Ramsey silently moved farther back into the trees and brush. Grain bags over the muzzles of the horse and mule kept the two animals quiet.

He had followed the rustlers through that afternoon and into the night. But then they had split up. He picked one trail to follow and kept at it as best he could in the darkness. Eventually he had lost the trail, but he was close enough to Walker's ranch now that he figured it was where the rustlers would strike. Only trouble was, Walker had cattle scattered over several thousand acres. Ramsey roamed, growing more tense. He feared that the longer he took looking for a likely spot for the rustlers to strike, the more likely

34

it was that they would have hit before he got there.

So it was with no small amount of satisfaction that he saw the five men—reunited somewhere in the past day or so—heading into the shallow arroyo. Ramsey stood and brushed off his pants. He walked to the other side of the hillock and checked on the horse and mule, making sure their reins were firmly tied to the picket rings and that the iron pickets were still fast in the ground.

As he marched up the hill, he checked his big Colt as well as the extra one he had tucked in the back of his gunbelt, under his coat. He had bought the extra weapon before leaving Jacksboro. It had suddenly occurred to him that he might be facing a lot of rustlers, and he needed some extra firepower. In a gunfight with six or seven or more rustlers, one six-shooter would not be sufficient. He was by no means certain he would need the extra pistol, but he had long ago learned that caution was wise in such matters.

He crouched as he neared the crest of the knoll, and then sprawled out. Cautiously he crawled over the grassy pinnacle and then slid on his behind down the side nearest the arroyo. Within moments he had trotted to the arroyo and moved into the ditch.

He could hear men talking softly a little ahead of him, around a crooked turn in the arroyo. Then he smelled the acrid odor of a cow-chip fire. The rustlers were preparing for their night's work. As Ramsey moved forward silently, he hoped that the men were preoccupied enough to be lax in their watch.

Brambles and thorns clutched at Ramsey as he stalked forward. He froze once at the sound of a snake slithering away at his approach. He wasn't fond of snakes, but he was not afraid of them, either. Still, he would hate to run into one here and now.

The voices grew a little louder as the brush thinned out. Ramsey moved even more cautiously forward. Finally he stopped. He could see four men, their shaded faces gleaming in the glow of the fire. Ramsey waited, wondering where the fifth man was. He smiled when he heard the sound of urinating. A few moments later, the fifth man appeared, joining his companions standing or squatting in a semicircle before the fire built against the north wall of the arroyo.

Ramsey knew it was as good a time as any. At any moment at least some of the five rustlers could head off to rope some cattle. Ramsey did not want to chance that. He eased out his familiar Colt. Holding the pistol at arm's length against his leg, he stepped away from the brush. "Howdy, boys," he said politely, though his voice was hard. "I'd be obliged if you all were to put your hands up and make no sudden moves."

Five heads turned as one. Most of the men registered surprise. But five sets of eyes glittered hard. "Who the hell are you?" one rustler asked. His voice was rough, but he was smiling.

"Name's Matt Ramsey. The Jack County Cattlemen's Association has asked me to make every effort in increasin' the number of beeves they got in their herds."

"How're you fixin' to do that?" the same man asked. It was clear to all what Ramsey had meant; however, he thought that perhaps by keeping Ramsey occupied with talk, he might find an opening to escape. Or, better yet, remove the stranger and then get back to work.

"Well, the cattlemen seem to think the easiest way'd be to keep their beeves from bein' took off by those that ain't supposed to be doin' such a thing," Ramsey said lightly. But his vigilance had not relaxed any.

"You callin' us rustlers?" the man asked in aggrieved tones, though the grin remained.

"I am," Ramsey said bluntly. He paused a heartbeat. "You got a name, boy?" he asked.

"Smiley Whickham." The man continued to show why he had that name.

Ramsey suspected the man had some facial damage rather than a propensity for smiling. "Well, Smiley," Ramsey said without humor, "supposin' you and your *compadres* drop your gunbelts— one at a time—nice and easy."

"And if we ain't of a mind to?" Whickham asked, still grinning.

Ramsey thumbed back the hammer of the Colt. The soft click was loud in the dead of the night.

Whickham shrugged. "No need to get nervous, Mr. . . . er . . . Ramsey," he said, the stupid-looking grin still plastered over his face. "Logan, y'all go fust."

Ramsey looked relaxed, though his eyes flickered from one man to the next. This was a touchy business, and Ramsey did not much like it. But he could think of no easier way to accomplish it.

As the man named Logan began slowly unbuckling his pistol belt, Whickham asked, "What're y'all fixin' to do with us, pard?"

Ramsey was well aware that Whickham was trying to divide his attention, making it more difficult for him to concentrate on all the men at once. "Take you back to Jacksboro and turn you over to the law there."

Whickham nodded in understanding, the smile never leaving his face. "Reckon that'd be hard doin's for boys like us," he said thoughtfully. "As I recollect, they usually hang rustlers."

Logan dropped his gunbelt in the dirt, and another of the rustlers began to unhitch his.

"You should've thought on that before you started stealin' other men's stock," Ramsey said coldly.

Whickham nodded again, as if agreeing. Then he said, "But I reckon I can't let you do that, pard." He went for his pistol. His two still-armed companions followed suit as Logan and the other unarmed man dived for cover, scrabbling to snatch their pistols from the ground.

Ramsey fired. But even as the bullet was knocking Whickham spinning to the ground, Ramsey had flopped down onto his belly. He rolled twice to his right, bullets from the two other men's guns kicking up pieces of earth where he had been. He came to a stop, Colt cocked.

He drilled one man twice and then the third man once. The two fell, groaning, in heaps. Ramsey fired off the last round in his Colt. The bullet whined off into the darkness after clanging on Logan's pistol. It sent the rustler's weapon skittering away across the dirt.

As Ramsey stood, he shifted the empty revolver to his left hand and pulled the extra one from behind his back in his right. Thumbing back the hammer, he waved the new pistol at Logan and the other man. "I wouldn't keep reachin' for them pistols, boys," he said harshly, "less'n you want to join your pals there."

Logan Hinckley and Vint Cookson looked up at Matt Ramsey and saw the hard set of his jaw and the unwavering pistol. The muzzle was aimed directly between them. Each knew that a mere flick of the wrist and a fractional amount of pressure and he would be dead. They clapped their hands atop their heads and pushed awkwardly to their feet.

"Turn around," Ramsey ordered.

The two did, nervous at having their backs to this deadly man.

"Link your hands behind your heads and kneel," Ramsey barked. When the two had done so, he added, "Now, lean forward till your foreheads are restin' on the ground. Make any other move, and I'll put a bullet in your spine." He watched cautiously as the two men gawkily did as they were told.

Ramsey relaxed fractionally. The two would not be able to do anything the way they were. At least, not with any speed. He checked Whickham and the two others. Whickham and one of the men were dead; the third was clinging to life by a thread, a bloody froth bubbling over his lips. The smile was gone from Whickham's face, surprising Ramsey a little. To be on the safe side, Ramsey picked up Hinckley's gunbelt and tossed it into the brush. He did the same with Cookson's.

Keeping an eye on Hinckley and Cookson, Ramsey squatted, laying the new Colt on the ground within quick reach. Then he hurriedly reloaded his old Colt and stuck the newer one back in his gunbelt. He stood, looking around. The third man who had drawn on him had died. He sighed. He did not relish killing, but there was little he could do about it. He took each dead man's pistol and threw it after the others, and then he quickly checked them for other weapons. He took their knives—and the derringer he found on Whickham—and pitched them into the darkness, too.

The rustlers' horses, loosely hobbled nearby, looked at him in wide-eyed nervousness. Ramsey walked to them, talking softly to soothe them. On two he found small shovels. He took them.

"Stand up, Logan," Ramsey said, "and then turn slowly."

Hinckley did, until he was facing Ramsey.

"Strip down to your longhandles and socks," Ramsey snapped. "Or your birthday suit, if that's all you're wearin'."

"What'n hell fer?" Hinckley asked. When Ramsey just glared, Hinckley shrugged. He peeled off his crusty shirt, leather stovepipe chaps, and filthy trousers, tossing each item to the side. He sat to pull off his boots and threw them atop the clothes. He stood again, shivering a little as the chilly wind cut through his faded, threadbare longjohns.

"What's your pal there's name?" Ramsey asked, pointing the Colt at Cookson.

When Hinckley told him, Ramsey said, "All right, Vint, your turn."

When Cookson stood there naked—except for socks and his hat—Ramsey grinned at them. "Didn't your mamas teach you boys to wear good underwear all the time?" he asked mockingly.

"Piss off," Hinckley snarled.

"I see your mamas didn't teach you no manners, neither." Ramsey shrugged. "It's your affair. But best learn to control your tongues or . . ." He didn't need to finish the sentence. Ramsey took the shovels he held in his left hand

and threw them on the ground in front of the two men. "You boys look cold," he said sarcastically. "I bet diggin' graves for your pals there will warm you up directly. Get to it."

The men reluctantly went to work. They soon picked up the pace, though, as the wind blew up the arroyo and chilled them. While they did so, Ramsey rummaged through the rustlers' saddlebags—keeping an eye on Hinckley and Cookson. He made sure there were no extra weapons in them. He found a coffeepot, coffee, beans, a cook pot, and salted beef. He filled the coffeepot from a canteen and put it in the fire. He began cooking beans and boiling the salted beef in the cook pot. Then he went back and got some rope from one of the horses.

Hinckley and Cookson were making pretty good progress on one large grave when Ramsey figured the food was done. He took a mug of coffee and a plate of beef and beans and sat on the lip of the arroyo, where he could watch over the grave diggers. The two talked softly to each other, and Ramsey could hear an occasional curse directed softly at him, but he didn't much care. The two men could do nothing—it was why he'd had them strip. They were vulnerable that way.

Soon enough they were finished. Ramsey, who had completed his meal, watched carefully as Hinckley and Cookson rolled the three bodies into the grave and then hastily covered them up. They had been sweating while they worked, and the brief let-off had them racked with chills.

"Christ, pard," Cookson said as he and his companion smacked the dirt down over the graves with the shovels, "how's about you let us get dressed and fill our bellies?"

"Put the shovels down and have at it," Ramsey said magnanimously.

The two raced for their clothes. Then they hurried to their horses and dragged out tin plates, cups, and spoons. They argued almost amiably as they got grub. Then they sat to eat under Ramsey's watchful eyes.

"You really gonna take us back to Jacksboro?" Cookson asked, chewing greedily on the food.

"Yep."

"They'll hang us for certain."

"Yep." It was only right, too, Ramsey thought.

"Shit, ought to jus' kill us now," Hinckley said angrily.

Cookson elbowed him in the ribs. "Shet up," he snapped quietly, hoping Ramsey could not hear him. "Hell, it's two days down to Jacksboro. We might get us a chance to jump this jasper along the way. Now eat."

Ramsey heard him, though he did not have to. He knew what the men were thinking.

CHAPTER

★ 7 ★

They stopped not far outside Jacksboro. Ramsey was tired and just a little irritable. But he wanted information from the two rustlers, and he thought this might be the time and place to get it.

After Cookson and Hinckley had finished their meal in the arroyo, Ramsey had tied each man to his horse. Then he strung the five rustler's horses together—one horse, then Cookson, another horse, Hinckley, and the last horse. Leading the caravan, he walked back to the big black. He tied the mule's rope to the last horse. He mounted the black and, with the rope to the first horse dallied around the saddlehorn, he rode off.

They had ridden through the night at a sure, steady pace. They stopped at midmorning the next day and Ramsey made a meal. He ate, then untied his two prisoners, one at a time, so they could eat and relieve themselves.

As he was tying them back onto their horses, Cookson tried to kick him in the face. Ramsey managed to sidestep most of the short kick, and the man's boot only grazed his chin. But it send a blinding flash of anger through him. He reached up, grabbed Cookson's shirt and he pulled Cookson down, slamming the rustler to the ground. The Colt leapt into his hand. "Give me one goddamn reason I shouldn't just blow your goddamn brains out here and now," he snarled, furious. He rubbed his chin lightly with his left hand.

Cookson gulped and licked his suddenly dry lips. He tried to speak, but the lack of saliva made it difficult. Adding to his problem was the fact that he didn't really have much to say.

Ramsey had his own reason for not killing Cookson now, though—he wanted information. His brain battled the thought—

41

one side telling him that he could get his information from Hinckley just as easily; the other side telling him that Cookson, being the slightly smarter of the two, might be the better source.

He decided he needed as many chances of getting information as possible, so he forced himself to relax. He uncocked the Colt and slid it away. He yanked Cookson to his feet roughly and practically threw the small, wiry man onto the horse. He tied the rustler on, sharply jerking the ropes tight.

"Hey, go easy on them ropes, pard," Cookson snapped, trying to sound a little lighthearted. Since Ramsey had not killed him right off, he thought he had the upper hand. He figured either that Ramsey wanted something from him, or that Ramsey was reluctant to kill in cold blood. Either way, he figured he had gained some measure of control.

"Best mind your mouth, boy," Ramsey snapped.

"Or?" Cookson smirked.

"Or they won't have to hang you in Jacksboro," Ramsey said. His voice was filled with menace.

Cookson gulped, realizing that he had not really gained any advantage over Matt Ramsey.

They rode on. By late afternoon, they were within a half hour's ride of Jacksboro. Ramsey stopped in a small copse of cedar and cottonwood. A dribbling rivulet passed for a stream, feeding the trees and brush. Ramsey untied the rustlers' feet, but left their hands bound. He hauled them none too gently off their horses, one at a time. He propped Cookson against a tree trunk and Hinckley against a boulder.

"What're you gonna do?" Hinckley asked, nervous.

"I need some information, boys. Information you two can provide."

"We ain't sayin' a goddamn word to you," Cookson snapped. He was tired, angry, and frustrated. "So save your breath." He spat defiantly, but had too little saliva to make it very effective. "Goddamn. You're gonna bring us in and hand us over to the marshal in Jacksboro, you bes' jus' go on and do it,'cause ain't neither of us gonna tell you jack shit."

"Damn, boy, you don't even know what the hell I'm gonna ask."

"Don't matter the least goddamn little bit," Cookson snapped. "That's all there is to it."

"All I want to know is how many of you boys are workin'

together. Ain't much to ask of you, is it?" He was trying to maintain his voice of reason.

"Goddamn, you jus' don't get it, do you, Ramsey?" Cookson said, shaking his head in wonder. "We ain't gonna tell you a goddamn thing. Nothin'."

"You know, I might be obliged to tell the marshal how you helped me out, boys, if you tell me what I want to know," Ramsey said.

"Go to hell," Cookson snapped. "The only thing I'm gonna tell you is that you ain't gittin' shit from me or Logan."

"Come on, Vint," Ramsey said reasonably, "how much is it gonna hurt anybody for you to tell me how many of you boys are workin' together?"

"Enough," Cookson growled.

Ramsey was squatting in front of the two rustlers. He rubbed his chin, thinking. Suddenly he grinned in understanding. "You think that if you tell me how many of you there are that you might blab too goddamn much and wind up tellin' me where your hideout is? That your problem, Vint?"'

Cookson said nothing, but the venomous look he suddenly wore let Ramsey knew he had scored a hit.

"Don't let it trouble you, boy," Ramsey said, almost gleefully. "I know where the hideout is."

"Sure," Cookson sneered.

"How long've you boys been usin' that canyon up there a couple miles from the north bank of the Red? Six months? A year, maybe? It don't look none too safe to me. Someday the law's gonna . . ."

Both Cookson and Hinckley looked at Ramsey in horror. A chill ran up Cookson's back. *The son of a bitch does know!* he thought.

"How'd you find out? . . ." Cookson stopped, sudden dread in his eyes. "It was you who killed Otis, Artie, and Tole, wasn't it?"

"I never did get names, you understand," Ramsey said dryly. "But if you're talkin' about them three damn fools I come across just outside the canyon, yep, it was me made worm fodder of 'em." He grinned nastily.

Cookson began to sweat. This man had faced three men at the hideout and had killed them all, getting away without a scratch. Then he had faced the five of them last night in the arroyo. He had gunned down three there, too, and gotten the drop on him and

Hinckley. Respect for Ramsey began to grow in Cookson's dim brain. Cookson knew he was not the smartest man in the world, but he understood gunplay, and knew now that Ramsey was not a man to trifle with. He swallowed hard, realizing how really close to death he had come several times in his foolish arrogance toward Ramsey.

"You'll speak to the law?" Cookson asked nervously. "Tell 'em me and Logan was a help to you?"

"I'll talk to 'em." Ramsey looked from Cookson to Hinckley and then back. "Can't promise it'll do any good, though." He shrugged. Hanging was all a rustler could expect, and was better than many of them deserved.

Cookson knew that as well as Ramsey, but he had to take the chance. To continue giving Ramsey a hard time would ensure that he and Hinckley would be the guests of honor at a necktie party. Even if Ramsey killed them as soon as he got the information, it would be better than a hanging. Cookson almost soiled his trousers just thinking about the noose tightening around his neck, and that fateful plunge through the trap door.

"There was eighteen of us, all told," Cookson said, the fight gone out of him. "With the six you've put in the boneyard, plus me and Logan here, there ain't but ten left."

"They all at the hideout at any one time?"

"Occasional. Boys come and go."

"Who's the leader?"

"Lark Coleman."

"What's he look like?"

"You mind if I wet my whistle some?" Cookson asked nervously. "There's some redeye in my saddlebags."

Ramsey nodded. He had found the bottle last night after the gunfight and noted it. He stood and walked to the horse, grabbed the small bottle, and came back. He pulled the cork and held the bottle for Cookson to take a drink. He did the same for Hinckley. He squatted back in front of the two men and took a sip of the powerful, foul whiskey himself. "Tell me about Coleman," he ordered.

"He don't look like nothin' special," Cookson said truthfully. "Maybe five ten, one fifty or so. Like I said, ain't much to distinguish him. Except the eyes. He's got one blue and one brown. Goddamn strange lookin', you ask me. But nobody calls him on it. Lark can be a mean cuss, pushed too far."

"I once saw him gun down a man in a saloon down in El Paso

for makin' light of his eyes," Hinckley offered. "He never said anything to the damned dude. Just bore up under the man's insults a few minutes and then, pow, shot his ass dead right there."

Ramsey looked at Cookson with a question in his eyes.

Cookson shrugged. "I wasn't there that time, but it sounds like Lark, all right. He's a crazy bastard sometimes, and I wouldn't put it past him to do such a thing." He licked his lips.

Ramsey took the hint and tilted the bottle up so Cookson could get another drink of whiskey. He went through it with Hinckley and then went back to his position.

"Lark favors a vest at all times and wears a bandanna tied around his left arm all the time. That's how you can tell him from a ways off."

"He the toughest *hombre* of the bunch?"

"No. That'd be Elmo Dinkins. Elmo's a half-wit. He ain't too tall, but he's near as big around as he is tall. Goddamn lummox. He's somethin' of a guard for Lark. Bastard'd kill his own ma for a nickel. Maybe less. Loves killin'."

Ramsey snorted at the depravity of man. It never ceased to amaze him how little some men cared for life, of how they could kill without compunction, regret, or any feeling—except perhaps joy. He often worried that, because of the path his life had taken, he was turning into such a man. He hadn't, at least so far. But the thought was still with him.

"Anything else you'd like to tell me about your *compadres?*" Ramsey asked.

"Not that I can think of."

"You, Logan?"

"No, sir." Hinckley sighed. "But if I've caused harm to folks, I'd like 'em to know I didn't mean it."

Cookson snorted in disgust. "Goddamn, Logan," he said with a sneer, "don't start whinin' and pulin' now. Shit." He looked at Ramsey. "He's just lookin' for some goddamn sympathy."

"He ain't gonna get none from me," Ramsey allowed. He rubbed his face, feeling the tiredness settling over him. Once again he wished that Buck or Kyle—or both—were with him. It'd make his job a lot easier. But they weren't, and he would have to do what was necessary.

"All right, boys, time to ride," he said. He stood and got Cookson and Hinckley on their horses again.

Twenty-five minutes later, they rode into Jacksboro. Ramsey stopped them in front of the county sheriff's office. Sheriff R. J.

Laybe—who also was doubling as town marshal, at the pleasure of the cattlemen—stepped outside. Looking into the fading afternoon sun, he asked, "What you got here, Matt?"

"Couple of rustlers. We buried three of their pals back in an arroyo on Tobe Walker's place."

"Cal and the others're going to be pleased."

"I expect." Ramsey had dismounted and was untying the two men. He hauled Cookson down and pushed him forward. "Vint Cookson, Sheriff."

Laybe grabbed Cookson's shoulder. "Welcome to Jacksboro, son," he said, a hint of glee in his voice. "The jail ain't much, but I reckon you ain't gonna be here long, anyway."

"This one's Logan Hinckley," Ramsey said, pulling the second rustler forward and up onto the wooden sidewalk.

"Thanks, Matt." Laybe started to turn away.

"I promised these boys I'd put in a good word for 'em, since they give me some information that's likely to help me rout the rest of the damn rustlers. I told 'em I didn't know as it'd do much good, but . . . Well, I've told you now. I'd be obliged if you was to take it into account when the trial comes."

"I'll do so," Laybe said solemnly. Everyone there knew it would have no effect on the outcome of the trial—or what would follow it.

"I'll bring the horses over to Burkhardt's and leave 'em there. I reckon the city can sell 'em and use the cash."

"Obliged," Laybe said. He shoved Hinckley. The two rustlers shuffled forward, beaten, broken men with the end of their lives looming before them.

Wearily, Ramsey mounted the stallion and rode slowly toward Burkhardt's livery. He ignored the people who watched him. After dropping the horses off, he slowly plodded up the street toward the Social Club. Tiredness clung to him like burrs to a saddle blanket.

He felt somewhat more human after he had a bath—in which he was aided by Lucy Tillman—a fine beefsteak with the trimmings, several shots of bourbon, a session with Lucy, and a good night's sleep.

The morning after the next day Ramsey rode out of Jacksboro, making a beeline for the Red River—and the rustlers' hideout just beyond it.

CHAPTER

★ 8 ★

Ramsey left the mule tied to a stunted, wind-whipped cedar and then edged the black mustang down into the canyon. It wasn't much of a canyon here. Just a ragged gash in Mother Earth angling northwest. It was maybe twenty-five feet deep, with steep walls of crumbling dirt, stones, and tenacious little bushes that clung to a precarious life.

The horse picked its way gingerly down the angular trail leading to the canyon bottom. Ramsey gave the horse its head, not pushing it. Ramsey had implicit faith in the steed.

Clouds chugged by, darkening the afternoon sky, bringing with them the heavy scent of impending rain. Ramsey had been flirting with the rainstorm since he had left Jacksboro. Lucy had tried to convince him to stay another day, and he had been sorely tempted. But he knew he had to move—to act fast—lest the other rustlers catch on and scatter. So he had moved on out, feeling things for Lucy that he had not felt for a woman in a long time.

In addition, once the members of the Jack County Cattlemen's Association heard what had happened, they were anxious to bring the entire episode to a conclusion. Ramsey was just an eager to do so, since it would get him his three hundred dollars and get him out of the clutches of the cattlemen. It's not so much that they were insufferable, just overbearing. And Matt Ramsey was not the type of man to suffer such things too long.

Ramsey was down on the canyon floor now and he pushed up the gulch, following its crooked, twisting route northwest. The walls were only four feet apart here, widening as they rose. The black's hooves kicked up small, powdery puffs of dust, and the occasional hoof step on bared rock produced a dull, ringing echo.

Ramsey assumed they would not be heard, especially after he
caught the sounds of cattle lowing and horses snorting. He slowed
almost to a stop as he edged around another of the innumerable
curves, wary lest he be found out. Surprise, he figured, was his
only edge when he would be facing as many as ten men.

The sounds of the cattle were getting louder. Ramsey stopped
and glanced up at the sky. Down here in the canyon, there was
little of the wind he could see whipping the grasses and shrubs
near the top of the gorge. But the temperature had dropped,
and he knew the sky would open up soon. He pulled his long
slicker from behind the saddle and shrugged it on and moved out
slowly again.

He rounded another rocky protuberance jutting deeply out into
the trail and saw that the canyon opened up into an almost circular
corral. He froze and then hurriedly but calmly backed the black up
so that he was behind the promontory. He dismounted and peered
around the rock.

A small spring dribbled down the crumbling wall at the far end.
About twenty longhorns and a dozen horses chewed placidly on
bushes, brush, and the nearly nonexistent grass. The rest of the
area had been beaten down by hooves until it was nothing more
than dust.

Three small canvas tents sagged against their ropes near the
right-hand wall of the circle. Several men wandered around.
Ramsey scanned the walls but saw no one. He did the same
for the top of the canyon and still saw no one. With the number
of horses, he figured there were more men in the camp than were
visible, and he assumed they were asleep in the tents. On the other
hand, it could be that they were out rustling horses, too, which
might mean there were only four or five men in camp.

The rain started with a rush and a roar. There was no easing
into it. One minute it was dry and quiet; the next there was a
thundering deluge. The men in the canyon camp ran toward their
small herd, afraid that the thunder, lightning, and heavy downpour
would stampede the steers.

Ramsey stayed behind his rock, watching, ignoring the rain that
pelted down on him, the thunder that ricocheted off the canyon
walls, and the streaks of lightning that sizzled downward from
the gunmetal gray sky.

After an hour, the thunder quieted considerably and the lightning flashed less frequently. The rain eased off to a steady,
drenching downpour. The men in the camp began to relax as

the cattle and horses settled down. Ramsey stood there still, trying to decide just how to go about capturing the men in the camp. It would not be easy; not if they were all here. If there were only the four he had seen, he might stand a halfway decent chance of getting out of here with his skin—and with the rustlers captive.

After another half hour, a man popped his head out of the biggest tent and shouted something. Three of the four men visible across the way trudged toward the tents, their steps picking up as they neared the shelters. The one left out in the rain hunched deeper into his coat. The set of his back showed Ramsey that he was not happy at having been chosen to cow-sit.

Ramsey decided it was time for action. He checked to make sure the black was still securely tied to a shrub growing straight out of the side of the canyon wall. Satisfied that it was, he moved around the jutting stone and slid his back along the canyon wall toward the tents. The only wrangler left out in the rain was looking away from him and Ramsey thought he was fairly well hidden by the gloom of the day and the dusty color of his clothes. But he kept an eye on the man nonetheless.

He made the tents and crouched outside, listening. He determined four voices after a quarter hour's worth of listening. He nodded and was about to move when one of the men stepped out of the tent. The man moved just to the side of the tent and started to relieve himself.

Ramsey waited until the man was done, then quickly popped up from behind the tent right in front of the man. Before the man could react in any way, Ramsey had whipped his pistol out and cracked the man across the temple. The man started to topple. Ramsey dropped his pistol and caught the man, easing him down. He figured the man would be out a while, even with the rain pounding him in the face. Ramsey grabbed his revolver and dropped it back in the holster under the slicker.

He moved faster now, figuring the men left inside the tents would begin to miss their friend before long. He backed up against the canyon wall again and moved around it to a point almost directly opposite the man who was watching the herd. The man seemed miserable, and seemed to be making a point of keeping his back toward the tents, showing his displeasure. Ramsey moved quickly at an angle that would bring him up on the man's blind side while still keeping him out of the line of sight of the tents until the last moment.

Ramsey wasted no time. He simply walked quickly up behind the man and buffaloed him, too. The man slumped with a groan. Ramsey turned and took a few steps toward the tents, figuring to take direct action.

Three men came out of the shelters. One was poorly dressed, another was nearly as big around as he was tall. The third wore a vest and a bandanna fluttering from his arm. The three men and Ramsey stopped at the same time, frozen in a moment of time that seemed both surreal and at the same time crystal clear in reality.

Ramsey and Lark Coleman moved at the same time. Coleman, unhampered by a slicker, had his pistol out first. He fired, and Ramsey felt a bullet tear through the flying end of his slicker. Another bullet ripped through a sleeve of the long, waterproof garment. But by then Ramsey had his own Colt ready. He crouched and fired twice. The bullets punched Coleman back into the tent.

Ramsey winced as a slug from one of the other men's pistol burned a slight trail up his arm. "Shit," he muttered. He fired again, winging rotund Elmo Dinkins, who had just shot him. But the third man was firing, too, and Ramsey heard bullets splattering in the puddles on the ground, tearing through the cloth of his slicker, and buzzing past his head.

Angry, Ramsey straightened. He figured that if the two men he faced hadn't hit him by now, they most likely never would. He fired with calm deliberateness, knocking down both. He jammed the Colt away and grabbed the spare.

The man he had wounded last was still down, but Dinkins had struggled back up. He stood weaving. Ramsey aimed and squeezed the trigger. Dinkins' head was jerked backward by the impact of the bullet.

After taking a quick glance around, Ramsey headed toward the tents. He checked Dinkins. The man was dead. Then he checked on the other man and Coleman. They both were dead too. Ramsey looked inside each tent in turn. They were empty.

With a sigh of relief, Ramsey stepped inside the largest tent. He tossed his hat on a bedroll and pulled off his slicker. He sat, thankful to be out of the rain for a bit. He could not stay in here forever, he knew, but he needed to look at his arm.

He unbuttoned the cuff of the shirt and rolled the sleeve up. It was amazing, he thought. The bullet had gone under the cuff of the slicker, then slid up his arm from just above the wrist to the elbow and then had torn out of the garments. It was not a bad wound—Ramsey had suffered much worse in other melees. But he figured he should tend it as best he could out here. He searched around the tent. It wasn't hard to find a bottle of whiskey. He took a few swigs and then poured some of the amber liquid on the wound.

Ramsey sucked in his breath as the whisky burned across the wound. Taking another quick swallow of the redeye, Ramsey corked the bottle. Without haste, he pulled down the sleeve and buttoned it. He sat, still loath to leave the dry comfort of the shelter. He chewed a piece of jerked beef.

He finished the food. With a sigh, he pulled on his slicker. A length of rope was lying in the back corner of the tent. He grabbed it and stepped out into the drenching rain. He tied up the first man he had knocked out, cutting off the rope he needed with the knife carried in his boot top. Then he tied up the second man.

He found tack stacked in another tent and saddled two horses that appeared to be plodding beasts with little spirit. It took only a few minutes to hoist the two unconscious men onto the horses, hanging across the saddles. He walked them out through the narrow neck of the canyon onto the trail, where he stopped and mounted the patiently waiting black.

Getting out of the canyon up the steep trail was an adventure. The track up to the canyon rim was slick with mud and running water. But the black made it, and used his great strength and endurance to help haul along the two animals with their unconscious riders.

Ramsey gave the horses a few minutes to breathe, got the mule, and then moved on. At the river's edge, he worked his way into the brush as far as he could and set up his tarp, tied to several small cedars. He hauled both prisoners down off their horses and tied them to trees. Both men were still unconscious, though they were showing signs that they might wake up before too much longer.

He unsaddled the black and cared for it. When he was done with that, he gave the sturdy animal a nose bag full of grain. It was the last of the grain, but he figured the black deserved it. Then he unsaddled the other two horses. He brusquely rubbed them down, not taking much time at it since they had been used little. Then he unpacked and cared for the mule.

Ramsey managed to get a fire started under the sparse cover of another cedar. He made coffee and boiled some salted beef.

The hot food warmed him and gave him strength and energy. The coffee pleased his palate.

By the time he finished, his captives were awake. They were groggy and their heads throbbed, but they were conscious and mostly alert.

"Your pals're dead," he told them bluntly. "You'll join 'em if you give me any shit. Understand?"

Both nodded, their heads hurting too much to argue.

"Good. I'm gonna get me some sleep. I'd be in one hell of an ill humor was I to be disturbed. Understand?"

The two men nodded again, and Ramsey spread out his bedroll under the tarp and turned in.

The rain had stopped by the time he awoke. It was, as best he could judge by the cloud-hidden moon, about two in the morning. He stretched and yawned. His two prisoners were asleep, slumping uncomfortably against the tree trunks. Ramsey stirred up the fire, drank more hot coffee, and ate boiled salted beef.

His rustling around woke the prisoners. Ramsey made up a little more of the stew. One at a time, he allowed the men to eat and drink, then take care of personal needs.

"What're you gonna do with us?" one asked.

"What in hell do you think, damn it?" the man's friend snapped, not expecting an answer.

The two shut up.

Ramsey looked at them. The one who had asked the question was young. Ramsey judged him to be about seventeen. The other was older, scrawnier, more dissipated and hard. Ramsey began to feel bad about having captured the younger one. The youth looked out of his element, and Ramsey wondered about the young man's having been forced to stay out in the rain. Maybe he hadn't gone completely bad yet, Ramsey thought. He figured he should have just left the youth back at the camp, with maybe a note of warning in his pocket.

Ramsey sighed. It was too late now, though he decided that if he found the right opportunity, he might still arrange it so that the younger man could "escape."

"What's your name, boy?" he asked the youth.

"Grover Haynes," the young man said shyly.

"You?" Ramsey asked, looking at the other man.

"None of your goddamn concern."

Ramsey shrugged. "Reckon I can just call you cow shit. How's that suit you?"

The man glared. "Bastard," he spat. "Name's Rufus Jennings, goddamn it, and I'd be obliged was you to use it."

Ramsey nodded. It was time to move. There was a day and a half to two days' worth of traveling before he could get to Jacksboro. And there were still three rustlers unaccounted for. He stood and moved toward the horses.

CHAPTER

★ **9** ★

The rain-swollen Red River roared around the sharp curve of the bend. It sailed along the sluice of its muddy banks, rippling and boiling in foamy fury. Even in the darkness of the gloomy, cloud-cluttered night, Ramsey could tell there was no way he would get across the river safely.

"Hellfire and damnation," Ramsey snapped, frustrated.

Rufus Jennings, the older prisoner, chuckled, the sound full of phlegm and harshness. "Well, go on in there, boy, why don't you?" He chuckled some more, the sound nauseating to his young companion, Grover Haynes.

"Well," Ramsey snapped. He turned in the saddle and glared at his prisoner, whom he could barely see. "I'd make it across on this here big, strong black of mine. But I ain't so sure about you."

Jennings spat. He jerked his body, trying to loosen the ropes that bound his hands together, his arms tight to his sides, and his feet to the horse. He made no progress, and his efforts served only to tire him.

"Go to hell, you sonabitch," he gasped.

"I expect I will," Ramsey allowed. "Eventually." He faced the river again and sighed heavily. It was hopeless. They had no chance of getting across now, and sitting here wishing it were different would not change it a bit.

He backed the black up and then turned it. He tugged on the rope that led to Haynes's horse, which in turn tugged the rope to Jennings's horse, and finally the mule. They moved slowly past the dripping bushes toward the campsite.

Ramsey went through the ritual again—pulling his two prisoners off their horses and tying them to the stunted trees; unsaddling

54

the black and the two other horses; unpacking the mule; finding a bit of dry wood and preparing a fire. Ramsey was sick of it, but he had no choice.

While Ramsey worked, Jennings jabbered almost constantly, offering a continuous stream of profanity-laced commentary on everything from Ramsey's parentage to his method of unsaddling a horse.

Finally, Ramsey had enough of the man's chatter. He suddenly whirled, yanking out his Colt, and then fired.

Jennings shut up in a hurry, mouth agape, when the bullet plowed into the thin trunk of the scrawny cedar less than an inch from his head. He gulped, his Adam's apple jerking rapidly up and down.

"I am in rather poor spirits, boy," Ramsey said in a voice that backed up his words. "I'd suggest you button that spit-sprayin' flap of yours and dwell on your fate." He paused to let the words sink in. "I've got no trouble with the idea of takin' you back to Jacksboro across the saddle rather than ridin' in it."

Ramsey glanced over at Haynes, who looked at him in fear. Ramsey nodded. He holstered the Colt and went back to his work in blissful silence.

They were stuck there throughout all that day and that night. But by the following dawn, Ramsey could not bear to sit any longer. He just had to move on. He was never blessed with as much patience as some of his brothers, a failing in himself that he often tried to hide. But rather than go through all the work first, he saddled only the horse. He was too much of a horseman to walk a hundred yards; not when there was a horse available.

He left his prisoners tied to the trees and rode down to the river. The flow had lessened and the water level had dropped a couple of feet. He sat on the horse, knee hooked around the saddlehorn, and studied the river for ten minutes or so. He finally nodded. Straightening in the saddle, he swung the horse around and rode back to the camp.

"All right, boys," he said almost cheerfully, "it's time to leave."

"Again?" Jennings asked sourly.

"You know, Rufus," Ramsey said, beginning to enjoy Jennings's plight, "it's gonna be plumb interestin' to see how well you float." He offered a gloating smile.

Jennings growled in anger as Haynes stifled a high-pitched chuckle.

Within an hour they were on the trail. Ramsey stopped at the river, having second thoughts.

"We gonna be able to make it 'crost?" Haynes asked. The youth was nervous. He never had any inclination toward water under the best of circumstances; watching the swift-flowing river here filled him with anxiety.

"Easy as fallin' off a log, boy," Ramsey said lightly. But he felt nowhere near as confident as he sounded.

"Well, move on then, goddamn it," Jennings snapped in his whiskey-ruined, phlegmy voice. "Less'n you're scart."

Ramsey smarted at the challenge. He started to retort, but then decided it would be wiser just to plunge ahead and do what needed to be done. He kicked the black and softly talked to the horse, urging it into the swift water.

The black entered the water fearlessly. Water whipped at him, and swirled forcefully around Ramsey's legs. The bottom soon dropped off, but the horse's powerful legs propelled him slowly, steadily, surely across the river as the current tried to push him downstream. But the horse fought on, even when Haynes's horse entered the river, then Jennings's, and finally the mule. The pack animal brayed and fought against the rope and the current.

But still the black pushed on, despite the drag of the other animals. Ramsey sat on the horse, worriedly trying to watch everything—the far bank, the current, the floating debris, the two men, horses, and the mule.

Suddenly the black's hooves scrabbled on the river bottom, seeking a purchase. He jerked and bucked out of the water and up the bank. The other horses had followed along, seeming more relaxed once they hit solid ground.

The current had succeeded in shoving the animals downriver, and the small party came out more than a quarter of a mile east of where it had entered the Red River.

Ramsey pulled up a few yards from the riverbank, in a clearing amid the tangled brush off the barely discernible trail. He dismounted and carefully checked the ropes holding Jennings and Haynes to their horses.

"How's about you let us down fer a spell?" Jennings asked. He sneezed and then hunched up so he could wipe the result on the shoulder of his shirt.

"No," Ramsey said flatly.

"Hey, goddamn it, I got to make water."

"Go 'head," Ramsey said cheerfully. "I don't reckon anybody'll know the difference." He was speaking truthfully, considering how wet Jennings was from having just come across the river—and also taking into account the rancid, foul odor that emanated from Jennings at all times.

Jennings scowled, but then relieved himself where he was. He looked pleased as he sighed with relief.

"Jesus," Ramsey breathed. Jennings was a disgusting caricature of a human being, and Ramsey would be plumb grateful to be shed of the offensive, shriveled stalk of a man.

Satisfied that the prisoners were still secured, Ramsey mounted the black and moved off without another word. He set a fairly quick pace. The stallion had a smooth gait, and the lope was not uncomfortable. But he knew the rustlers' horses and the mule could not match the rhythmic, easy movements of the black. He grinned, thinking of the jouncing the prisoners were undergoing.

He kept going till long past dark, stopping only occasionally to give the horses a breather. He chewed a little jerky as he rode, but he would not permit the rustlers anything. That would mean loosening their hands, and he was not about to do that.

But at last he figured they had had enough and he stopped. He pounded two picket rings into the ground and tied all the horses and the mule to them. He helped Haynes down. The boy's legs buckled as they hit ground, and Ramsey grabbed him. He held the youth up until enough feelings had returned to Haynes's legs to support him. Only then did he ease Haynes onto the ground, where the youth sat.

Then Ramsey helped Jennings down. The older outlaw's legs would not hold him either, but Ramsey let him fall to the ground.

"Goddamn sonabitch," Jennings screeched. "Goddamn punk sonabitch, got no . . ."

"You remember what happened last time you started up with such foul-mouthed rantin's?" Ramsey asked. "If you do, you'd best think back on the consequences. You don't remember, I'll be more than happy to provide you with a reminder."

Jennings shut up.

Ramsey cared for the horses and the mule. Then he gathered cow chips and built a small fire. He boiled coffee and cooked up a mess of bacon and beans, as well as some biscuits. He ate, enjoying the food, sopping up grease with his biscuits. He could feel the tiredness clinging to him like morning fog on the trees. But he figured that with one more good day of riding, they'd be in Jacksboro and he could turn over the two rustlers, get a good meal, and spend some time with Lucy.

After that, he figured he'd collect his money and head back toward Fannin County. He suspected the cattlemen might argue some over paying him his money—especially if they heard there were still three rustlers unaccounted for. But Ramsey figured the three would soon learn what had happened to their companions and head for parts unknown as fast as their horses could carry them. Ramsey did not worry about them.

Ramsey finally untied Haynes. He let the young man eat, then attend to personal needs before tying him up again. At last he did the same for Jennings, who said nothing, but scowled continuously. Ramsey grinned at him ingratiatingly.

Before going to sleep, Ramsey tied Jennings's hands behind him. He tied the man's feet together and then bent Jennings's legs up behind him and tied the rope to that holding his hands. Jennings would be going nowhere.

Ramsey did the same to Haynes, though did not make the knots so tight. Then he looped a rope around the black's neck and tied the other end of the ten-foot length of rope to his left wrist. He stretched out in his bedroll and fell instantly asleep.

The black's snuffling snort of warning awoke him. He lay there a bit, listening to the sounds of the night—trying to catch whatever it was that had alerted the horse. Then he heard hooves approaching, and the soft lowing of a longhorn steer.

In an instant, Ramsey was up and checking his Colt .44. He grabbed the spare revolver from where he had set it on the blankets and jammed that into the back of his gunbelt. Then he swung silently up onto the black, thankful for the clouds that obscured the moon. That cover wouldn't last long, but Ramsey figured he didn't need too much time.

The horse moved forward like a shadow, as Ramsey guided him gently with his knees. The sound of moving cattle was a short distance to the southwest, but Ramsey rode mostly south for a bit, until he thought he was about even with the slow-moving stock. He turned due west, heading for the sounds. He heard a man's voice, and was certain that rustlers were coming. Any self-respecting cowboy moving a herd would have been bedded down long ago.

He came up on them from the east. The clouds had drifted off, allowing the moon to bathe the slightly undulating landscape in shimmering silver light. Knowing he was getting close, Ramsey drew the Colt and rode ahead, holding the pistol unobtrusively on the flat upper part of his right thigh.

Since Ramsey was on the lookout for a herd and some men, he spotted them well before they saw him. There were three of them in a small semicircle around a dozen plodding longhorns. The rustlers did not see Ramsey until he was within twenty feet of one and said, "How do, boys."

Three men's heads whipped around to face him. They stared blankly for a moment before the two who were farthest off trotted up to the nearest man. "Who the hell are you?" the one who had been at the far end asked. His voice was nasal, whiny, distorted by a deviated septum.

"The man who's come to put an end to your thievery, boys," Ramsey said almost cheerfully. These were, he figured, the last three of the rustlers' group. Once they were taken care of, his job would be finished. And he was beginning to like the idea of wrapping this up very much.

The three men laughed, but they did not sound amused. They sounded dangerous, angry.

"You talk tough for a man 'bout to get his ass planted," the same man said, his voice reminding Ramsey of a saw. He laughed again and rubbed a hand across the lower half of his face. He breathed through his nose as he laughed, the sound of mucus thick and disgusting.

Ramsey shrugged nonchalantly. "I didn't have no trouble with your mangy pals back in the hideout," he said quietly, getting a rush of pride when he saw the shock on their faces. "Reckon I ain't gonna have no trouble with you damn fools neither."

"Y'all best haul your ass outter here," the same one said, his words coming out angry and sharp.

"Afraid not." Ramsey waited, figuring he had the upper hand since his revolver was already out of his holster.

The one who had spoken looked in rage at Ramsey. Then he glanced at his two companions. He nodded ever so slightly.

Ramsey saw the nod and tensed.

CHAPTER

★ 10 ★

The three rustlers had little chance, considering that Ramsey was expecting trouble and was ready for it. At the first sudden move made by one of the rustlers, Ramsey's Colt popped up from its resting spot on his leg.

Ramsey fired. Two bullets slammed into the chest of the rustler who had done all the talking. The sickly sounding man fell backward over the horse's rump and landed with a loud splat in a fresh pile of droppings left by his own horse. Ramsey noted it in the blink of an eye and thought such an end was appropriate for the outlaw.

But Ramsey was not really paying attention to the dead man. As soon as he fired his two shots at the man, Ramsey whirled and fired again. The man in the middle jerked as one bullet tore into his arm. He dropped the pistol he had only halfway out of his holster.

"Don't shoot!" the third rustler screeched as Ramsey swung the Colt toward him.

"Give me one good reason not to, boy," Ramsey said tightly.

"I ain't caused no trouble," the man said weakly.

"Bullshit," Ramsey snapped. "You're runnin' the range with this goddamn rabble," Ramsey said, easily waving the pistol at the wounded man and the dead outlaw. "And you're herdin' a bunch of stolen beeves."

"I ain't *gonna* cause no trouble," the man amended hastily. "That's what I meant to say."

"What's your name, boy?" Ramsey asked, voice hard. He was looking at the man to whom he was speaking, but with his peripheral vision, he was keeping a watch on the wounded rustler.

"Leroy Waterman."

"Well, Leroy, supposin' you drop your gunbelt to the ground. Usin' your left hand, of course."

"Yessir," Waterman said glumly. The young, hollow-eyed man did as he was told.

Ramsey turned to look at the wounded man. "And you are?"

"Vern Dumars."

"You gonna give me any more trouble, Vern?"

"No, sir."

"Good. Now suppose you both mosey on ahead of me. Northeast. And keep your hands where I can see 'em. It gets to a point where I can't—even if you just got to scratch your stones—I'll plug you. I got no problem with shootin' a rustler in the back. You can count on that."

Dumars scowled but his voice was calm as he asked, "What about Cobber there?" He jerked his chin at the body.

"The wolves and coyotes can have him," Ramsey said. He felt a little odd about leaving the man lying out there for the elements. He would have preferred burying the man, as he would have preferred burying the men he had slain back in the canyon. But now—as then—such a thing was out of the question.

"That ain't right," Dumars snapped.

"Neither's stealin' cattle," Ramsey said reasonably. "Now move out," he ordered.

Dumars took a last look at his dead companion. Then he shrugged. They all knew they could end up this way. It was the biggest of the many hazards in this business. He rode past Ramsey. He was holding his wounded right arm with his left hand. His reins were entwined in his right fingers.

Waterman kicked his horse, and the horse jumped a few feet forward, and started prancing. The young man fought to get the animal under control and then rode alongside Dumars. His face, as he had ridden past Ramsey, was pasty white.

Ramsey rode along behind the two, staying within ten feet of them. He had quickly reloaded the Colt within the first few steps and then kept the pistol resting on his thigh again.

He directed the two with an occasional word, aiming them toward his camp. Then, finally, "Hold up, boys."

The two rustlers stopped and looked around. There was little to see in the dim moonlight—a few horses, the faint glow left by an old fire, and two people.

"Rufus? That you?" Dumars asked.

"Yah."

"Who's that with you, Rufe?"

"Little Snot Face."

"Grover?"

"It's me, Vern," Haynes answered rather meekly.

"Where's the others?" Dumars asked, the beginnings of a chill snaking up his backbone.

"Dead—'ceptin' fer you two. What about Cobber?" His voice was more gruff than usual, barely masking his fear.

"Dead, too." The chill ran full out up Dumars's back, and he shuddered visibly.

Four pairs of hard, flat eyes turned toward Ramsey as he dropped the Colt into his holster and slid off the bare back of the black mustang. He ignored Jennings and Haynes. Instead, he looked from Dumars to Waterman. "Light and tie," he said quietly. "One at a time. But go easy, lest you make me jumpy." He saw no need for adding add the "or . . ."

Dumars climbed down from his saddle. He faced his horse, hands behind his back, when Ramsey ordered him to do so. He winced from the pain in his wounded arm when Ramsey tied his hands behind his back. Then Ramsey led him a few feet away, helped him onto the ground, and tied him like he had the other two rustlers. Moments later, Ramsey did the same to Waterman.

"Best get some shuteye, boys," Ramsey said, tossing his extra revolver down on his blankets. "We got us a long day ahead of us." He lay down and closed his eyes.

"What about my arm?" Dumars asked, the pain intense.

"It'll keep," Ramsey said. It took a little while to get to sleep this time, especially with the sounds of wolves and coyotes growling as they gnawed hungrily at Cobber's body out in the darkness.

Ramsey was so tired that it took dawn's light to wake him. He stood, feeling only a little refreshed. He glanced at each of his prisoners and smiled to himself. Life wasn't so bad after all. Before nightfall, he would be in Jacksboro with his prisoners. A good meal and a few stiff jolts of bourbon at the Jacksboro Social Club, an hour or so with Lucy Tillman and a good night's sleep in a soft bed, and he would feel as good as ever. By this time tomorrow, he would be riding out of Jacksboro, his pockets packed with cash. He grinned inwardly one more time, as he adjusted his thinking. Perhaps he would leave the morning after that.

He stretched and yawned, his mood souring when he realized that he would have to make breakfast not only for himself but for the others. He looked at Haynes with sudden inspiration. "You know how to cook, boy?" he asked.

Haynes glanced at him in surprise, as if he was not sure Ramsey was talking to him. Then he nodded his head tentatively. "Some," he allowed.

Ramsey nodded, mind made up. "Then you can make us all some grub." He moved toward the youth and began untying the bonds. Done, he stepped back and watched warily.

Haynes lay for a few minutes, letting the blood flow back to his arms and legs. Then he ventured upward. He surprised himself when he found he could stand.

Ramsey pointed at the fire pit.

Haynes nodded and took two uncertain steps. Then he stopped. Looking sorrowfully at Ramsey, he said plaintively, "I need to go, Mr. Ramsey. Make water, ya know."

Ramsey nodded and pointed. Haynes walked on wobbly, uncertain legs a little away across the prairie from the others. Ramsey followed. Haynes had trouble, what with knowing that Ramsey was standing there watching. The others were probably watching, too. Haynes's neck felt hot from the embarrassment, but he finally accomplished his task.

With relief, he turned and shuffled toward the fire pit. He knelt gingerly and placed some kindling in the pit. A sulphur match appeared over his shoulder. He glanced up, looking at Ramsey.

As Haynes took the match, Ramsey said quietly, "I'm puttin' a certain amount of trust in you, boy. But not all of it. You make one stupid move and I'll blow out your spine. You got that?"

"Yessir." There was a tremor in the youth's high-pitched voice. He scraped the match on a rock and held it to the kindling.

Ramsey moved back a little, and stood, watching.

Haynes got the kindling going and then began stacking cow chips on the low flames. While the fire began licking greedily at the new fuel, Haynes turned his attention to the food supplies Ramsey had set out.

Ramsey sat back about ten feet, keeping an eye on Haynes. He was close enough to the rustler to shoot him easily if the need arose. But he was far enough away to prevent Haynes from trying something foolish like flinging a hot pan of beans or coffee at him.

"Hey, what about us?" Jennings ask nastily. His spit-thickened voice was worse than usual. "That fancy-ass little sonabitch ain't the only one's got to drain his pizzle."

"You've pissed yourself before, Jennings. You got to go that bad, you can do so again."

"You goddamn sonabitch, you," Jennings snapped. "You . . ."

Ramsey glared at him, and the man shut up. Ramsey grinned. "You really are something, you mangy old fart. Your knowledge of words is mighty impressive."

Waterman and Dumars laughed; Jennings scowled.

But Jennings did have a point, Ramsey knew. He looked at his two newest prisoners. "You boys got to go?" he asked. When both nodded eagerly, Ramsey stood and walked toward them. "Best listen, though. I ain't gonna risk my neck on you boys. You try anything and I'll backshoot you without a second thought. Clear?"

The two nodded. "And, just because I'm tryin' to treat you folks decent don't mean I've takin' a likin' to you. So don't think you're gonna get loose and sweet-talk me into lettin' you stay loose. Since I can't watch you both—and Grover there all at the same time, I'm gonna let you loose one at a time and then tie you back up."

He went to Dumars first. He untied the man and then checked the wound. It was superficial, and most likely would cause little trouble. Both Ramsey and Dumars knew it meant nothing anyway, considering Dumars's likely fate in Jacksboro. But Ramsey cleaned the wound and bandaged it before taking Dumars a few feet away to relieve himself.

By the time both men had taken care of their business, Ramsey was softening a little. He decided it would not hurt to show Jennings a little decency. He allowed the malodorous twig of a man to relieve himself, too.

With the three tied up again, Haynes announced, "Food's ready."

"Damn," Ramsey muttered in annoyance. He was glad he had only the one day of traveling with four prisoners. He didn't think he could take all this tying and untying and constant watchfulness for more than a day or so. "You eat first, Grover. Just make sure you save enough for the rest of us."

Ramsey tied Haynes back up after the youth had eaten. Ramsey finally relaxed, able to eat in peace. He savored the beans and bacon, even though he was sick of such fare. He enjoyed the coffee even more. But as much as he enjoyed just sitting here sipping the strong coffee, he knew he had to get moving. It would take a considerable amount of time to feed the three men since he would have to free them one at a time and then retie them after they had had their fill. The sun was already an hour up, and the longer he lingered here, the longer it would take to get to Jacksboro. He hoped to be there before dark, and he figured he could still make it—if he got his butt moving.

It took the better part of an hour to get it all done, but Ramsey finally managed. With rapidly souring disposition, Ramsey turned to the rest of his work—saddling five horses, tying all the horses together, packing the meager supplies on the mule, helping each prisoner onto a horse, and then binding him to the animal.

At last he was finished, and he sat down heavily on the ground. Another hour had gone by. He took several sips of water from his canteen, before pushing wearily to his feet.

"You gonna take all day, Ramsey?" Jennings asked raggedly.

"You in a hurry to hang?" Ramsey asked, glaring up at the mounted Jennings.

"Better'n sittin' out here in the goddamn sun all day long, watchin' you make an ass of yourself, you sonabitch."

"Reckon I could try to find us a tree somewhere and hang you right out here," Ramsey said helpfully. "Save you the trip, save the folks of Jacksboro the expense of a trial and all. That suit you, Rufus?"

"I 'spect I kin make the trip all right," Jennings allowed.

"I thought you might see it that way." He pulled himself into the saddle and moved on out. He let Haynes take the lead. Since Haynes's horse and all the others were tied together, he was certain the prisoners couldn't escape. And by riding behind the rustlers, he could keep an eye on them, lest they try something.

Along about midday, Ramsey trotted up alongside Haynes. "The animals need a rest, son. Let's call a halt."

As much as he hated the work, Ramsey knew that the horses needed the break. So he pulled the prisoners down, loosened all the saddles, helped the captives drink from the canteen, and half an hour later tied the men back on their horses. Ramsey mounted the black and pulled up to Haynes. "Best pick up the pace a tad, son," he said evenly. "Don't push the horses, though. But we need to move a little faster."

Haynes gulped. He did not like the idea. The faster he got to Jacksboro, the faster he would be put on trial. And the sooner he would be hanged. But he knew that if he stalled, he would die out here on the prairie, and his bones—like those of Coleman and Cobber and the others—would be left out here to bleach in the glaring autumn sun. He shuddered.

CHAPTER

⋆11⋆

Ramsey caused a little stir when he trotted into town just before dark leading four prisoners. Curious people watched from the sidewalks, doorways, and windows. Ramsey even admitted—to himself only—that he felt a touch of pride in showing off.

He stopped in front of the county sheriff's office. A hatless Sheriff R. J. Laybe stepped out of his office, using a hand to shade his eyes against the sunset. "What do you have there, Matt?" he asked, certain he knew.

"The last of the rustlers." Ramsey slid off the horse, once more feeling the tiredness sweeping over him.

"You mean that's all there were?" Laybe sounded doubtful.

"It's all there *are,* Sheriff."

Laybe nodded. He was no fool; Ramsey did not have to explain further. "Well, help me get 'em inside with the others you brought in." There was no humor in the man—or at least none that showed. "It'll be a tad crowded, but I reckon since these punks were workin' so close together, they won't mind. That right, boys?" He glared balefully up at them.

None of the prisoners said anything. All of them—even the crusty reprobate Rufus Jennings—were pale and subdued as the realization of their predicament settled in over them. They were in a town run to a great extent by ranchers and they were charged with rustling cattle. They could expect no mercy or sympathy here, only a hangman's noose.

Ramsey cut the rope tying Jennings's ankles together under the horse. He pulled Jennings down. "Best keep an eye on this one, R. J. He don't look like much, but he's a pesky little bastard. I expect he wouldn't hesitate a moment to slip a bowie into you the minute your back was turned."

"Y'all wouldn't do such a thang, now, would you, Rufus?" Laybe asked in his thick drawl.

Ramsey was surprised. He had not seen the usually garrulous, profane Jennings so quiet. He glanced at Laybe, and thought he knew why. Laybe was not a big man, nowhere near as big as Ramsey. But his eyes were deadly; they held not just a hint of death, but the promise of it. Laybe also carried himself in a way that led men to believe he was capable of doing anything he put his mind to. He was impressive, even to the hardened Matt Ramsey.

"Nah, sir," Jennings said softly.

"Didn't think so." Laybe winked at Ramsey over Jennings's shoulder. The sheriff had enough sense to know not to turn his unprotected back on any of these men. "Now, come on, Rufus. Your new home awaits." He shoved Jennings toward the gaping maw of the office door—and the deputy standing next to it—and then waited for the next one.

Ramsey quickly slit the ropes for Haynes, Dumars, and Waterman, pulling them down as he did. They stood on weak, wobbly legs before lurching forward to their doom.

"Need any more help, R. J.?" Ramsey asked as the last of the rustlers moved into the office.

"Nope. Me and my deputies can handle it from here." He paused. "Y'all done the folks here a big favor, Mr. Ramsey."

Ramsey shrugged. "Only doin' my job. Just like you."

Laybe nodded. "Y'all goin' to stick 'round Jacksboro for the trial—and the hangin'?"

"Hadn't thought that far ahead. When's the trial?"

"Circuit judge is supposed to be back through here day after tomorrow. I'd expect he won't wait a hell of a long time befo' he gets down to business."

Ramsey nodded. "I expect I can wait around that long. You might need me to testify."

"That's likely."

"But I've seen hangin's before. Never have taken to 'em much, though."

Laybe spit a stream of tobacco juice flecked with bits of plug. "Tell the God's truth, I ain't either." He shrugged. "Comes with the job, though." He spit again.

"Reckon it does. What do you want me to do about these horses?"

Laybe walked up to each one and examined the brand. "Those

goddamn dudes weren't content with stealin' longhorns," Laybe said as he came back up onto the wooden sidewalk. "Those're rustled horses, too. Had runnin' brands used on 'em just like the cattle." He shook his head. "Hell, best take 'em down to Burkhardt's—if y'all don't mind."

"I expect I could do that."

"Thanks. I'll get 'round to lettin' their owners know about 'em directly." Laybe almost grinned. "Well, see y'all 'round town, Mr. Ramsey."

"Sheriff." Ramsey mounted the black and turned the horse. Leading the mule and the other horses, he headed toward Burkhardt's Livery. He explained to Rudy Burkhardt about the rustled horses. Wearily he began to unsaddle the black.

"I can do dot for you, Mr. Ramsey," Burkhardt said. He had little accent; it was evident only with a few words here and there.

"Reckon I should do it."

"Looks like you've had a long day already . . . Matt. I'll see to that black like he was my own."

"I'd be obliged," Ramsey acknowledged. He rubbed the denim trousers over his buttocks. "Reckon I would appreciate restin' my weary ass soon."

"Then go on. *Schnell.*"

"*Danke,* Rudy." Ramsey pulled his saddlebags off the horse and hung them over his shoulders. With his Winchester rifle in his hand, he headed, slumping, for the wide mouth of the stable door. Just before he stepped outside, he squared his shoulders. He didn't really strut down the streets as he headed for the Jacksboro Social Club. But he did move with a certain amount of swagger. He was a big, strong, self-confident man, and it showed in the way he moved.

The Social Club fell into silence as he entered. Unlike a cheap saloon, the Social Club had real doors, with real glass in them. And there were plenty of lanterns inside. Ramsey was used to people staring at him, but he never liked it. Still, the people gaping at him now would never know how he felt about that.

He walked straight to the bar. Since the place was ostensibly a private club, the bar was small. Many of the men who came here to drink did not stand at the bar for it. They sat at tables and had servers bring their food and drink to them. The back bar also was little, but it was very ornate.

The bartender on duty, McCafferty, had seen him coming and had a shot of bourbon poured and waiting. Alongside of it was a mug of foamy beer. Ramsey nodded his thanks and jerked the shot down. He set the glass on the bar and lifted the beer. While he did that, McCafferty refilled the short glass with bourbon.

Ramsey gently placed the Winchester on the bar. With eager anticipation, he poured the bourbon down his throat, enjoying the warm trail the liquor made as it sluiced down into his stomach. "Ah," he said fervently. "That does cut the trail dust."

"Yes, sir."

Ramsey reached for the beer and drained almost half the large mug at one time. "That ain't so bad, either," he commented.

"Yes, sir." But McCafferty's usually wooden facade was cracking, and he came down close to smiling. Then the reserved look was back, and he said, "Mr. McIlvaine and Mr. Pomeroy await your pleasure in the office."

"They can await my pleasure a wee bit longer."

"They're not used to being kept waiting."

Ramsey winked. "Then I expect it's about goddamn time they learned, ain't it?" He finished off the beer slowly. As he grabbed the Winchester, he said, "I'd be obliged if you could see if Lucy's around and . . ."

"I'll see she's in your room directly, Mr. Ramsey," McCafferty said blandly.

"Thanks. And I'd be obliged for a tub with some hot water."

"Everything will be ready, Mr. Ramsey. I'll have Wilkins see to it."

Ramsey nodded and marched toward the door at the rear. He considered ignoring the cattlemen's "invitation." But he decided that he might as well get it over with. He could demand his money, too, while he was in there, and then he would be free to go whenever he got the urge to do so. He rapped on the thick wooden door with the muzzle of his Winchester. A voice growled at him, telling him to enter, so he did.

"Welcome, Matt," Pomeroy said. The man smiled warmly and stepped forward, hand outstretched.

Ramsey shook his hand and then sat in one of the heavy leather chairs in front of the desk at which McIlvaine seemed to have been permanently installed. He dropped the saddlebags on one side of his chair and the rifle on the other.

"Your report?" McIlvaine asked without preliminary.

"He always this much of a joy to be around?" Ramsey asked, looking at Pomeroy, who had taken the chair next to him.

"You caught him on a good day," Pomeroy said with a grin.

"Just give us your report, Mr. Ramsey," McIlvaine said. He sounded aggrieved.

"Back off, Cal," Pomeroy snapped. "Christ, the man just come off the trail after a time." Pomeroy stood, shaking his head in irritation. "And, damnit, I'm getting to be as bad as you, for Christ's sake. Ain't even offered Mr. Ramsey a drink. My apologies, Mr. Ramsey."

Ramsey nodded and waved the slight away as if it had no meaning.

"You take bourbon, if I recall?"

"Yep."

Pomeroy filled a decent-sized glass with amber liquid and carried it to Ramsey, who took it with a nod. All the while, McIlvaine stewed, his flabby face fluttering with indignation. After Ramsey had taken a healthy slug, McIlvaine said impatiently, "Tell us."

"Ain't a whole lot to tell, Cal," Ramsey said more than a little sarcastically. "I found the rest of the rustlers. Some of 'em chose to debate me—with Mr. Colt's help—and paid the final price for it. The others're sittin' over in Sheriff Laybe's jail waitin' to have their necks stretched."

"And you're sure there are no others?"

"Not in this bunch, there ain't. Lord knows, there's enough goddamn outlaws runnin' around north Texas, a new bunch might move in next week." He grinned, trying to lighten McIlvaine's jowly arrogance and remoteness. It had little effect. "But this bunch is done for."

"You're absolutely certain?"

"Listen you pork-faced idiot," Ramsey said, his temper flaring, "I've been on the trail too damn long, have been in several gunfights and carted four prisoners across a good chunk of Texas land. I'll be damned if I'm gonna sit here and listen to you call me a liar." His words were cold.

McIlvaine blanched. "I was not . . ."

"Like hell you weren't."

"But I must know for certain if they have all been accounted for."

"One of those boys was kind enough to talk with me," Ramsey said dryly. "He told me how many of them there were. I found that many."

"Could he have been lying?" McIlvaine seemed anxious, worried.

"I suppose he could've been." Ramsey paused for a sip of bourbon. "But I've found it's pretty damned hard to lie when you've just damned near shit your trousers from fright."

McIlvaine looked considerably relieved.

Ramsey polished off his glass of bourbon. "Now, Mr. McIlvaine, if you'd be so kind as to fork over the cash you owe me, I can haul my weary ass up to my room and take my leisure for a spell."

McIlvaine stared at him from hooded, frog-like eyes for a minute. Ramsey was not sure the cattleman really saw him. Then McIlvaine pulled a small iron box from the interior of his desk. He reached inside and started counting out the cash.

"I want hard money," Ramsey said. "I don't want any of that worthless paper shit."

McIlvaine scowled, but he tossed the paper dollars back into the box and began counting out double eagles. With several neat stacks in front of him, McIlvaine closed and locked the box and put it away.

Ramsey nodded. He grabbed his saddlebags and rifle, tossing the bags over his shoulder. He stood and took the two steps to the desk. As he reached for the money, McIlvaine looked up at him. "A moment, Mr. Ramsey." Ramsey was not sure it was a question or an order. He straightened and glared down at McIlvaine.

"One of the reasons I was so insistent in my questioning, Mr. Ramsey," the fat man said, "was that I was sounding you out, to make sure . . ." He paused. "Well, we have another job for you—if you're interested."

"I'm always interested in makin' a dollar, Mr. McIlvaine," Ramsey said slowly. "But right now I'm dirty, tired, hungry, and . . . lonely." He half grinned. "I'd expect that whatever it is you want me to take on can wait a day or two." He questioned McIlvaine with his eyes.

"I suppose," McIlvaine said. Doubt had edged into his voice. He was the type of man who, once he had made up his mind, wanted to push on with something right away. He disliked it when obstacles were placed in its path.

"Of course we can wait, Mr. Ramsey," Pomeroy said jovially. "Go, get cleaned up, relax. Have some supper. Are all your needs being attended to?"

"So far."

"You need anything?"

Ramsey shrugged. "McCafferty told me there'd be a tub with water waitin' in my room. Also, some bourbon and . . ." he grinned, ". . . a companion."

"Supper?"

"That wasn't mentioned."

"I'll see to it for you."

Ramsey nodded. "Well, gentlemen," he said after he had scooped up the coins and stuffed them into his shirt pocket, "I'll see you in the morning." He paused. "Or the mornin' after."

CHAPTER

★12★

Ramsey went directly from his meeting with the two cattlemen to his room in the Jacksboro Social Club. He walked swiftly, with a sense of anticipation building inside him.

Lucy Tillman was waiting inside, sitting nervously on the quilt-covered brass bed, watching the door expectantly. She smiled tentatively as he entered.

Ramsey returned the smile warmly, feeling a rush of excitement and enchantment. The latter was disconcerting, since to Ramsey it came disturbingly close to love. It could not be that, though, he told himself firmly. For him to love someone like Lucy would be to dishonor the memory of Kate Silcox, and that was something he would never do. No, after loving—and being loved by—Kate, he could never love a common prostitute like Lucy Tillman. Then again, he thought, Lucy was not all that common.

His face had darkened and hardened with the thoughts. Lucy, sitting on the bed, felt a gnawing pang of fear at seeing it. She had come to love Matt Ramsey in the short time she had known him. It was odd for her to have done so, since she thought she had hardened her heart long ago, considering her profession. But Matt Ramsey was unlike any other man she had ever known, and she had unconsciously—almost unwillingly—given her heart to him. She seemed incapable of preventing it, and so she had adjusted her thinking and accepted it as inevitable. She would give herself willingly to him, in any way he would want. And she would hope that he would come to reciprocate those feelings. She knew she had no right to expect such a thing, but to live without hope of it would be to die. And she was too full of life for that.

He had seemed genuinely pleased to see her, and her breath had quickened at that. But in the next several heartbeats, he seemed to have grown angry, and Lucy was tied in knots inside, worried that he was displeased with her for some reason. She felt like crying.

Ramsey saw Lucy's look of fear and he felt guilty, knowing that some of his thoughts of Kate had been reflected on his face. He did not want to hurt Lucy. He closed his eyes a moment. Kate had been dead almost a decade. He could not carry a torch for her forever. He might not—no, he told himself angrily—*would* not ever forget her. Her memory would always be special to him. But maybe, he decided, it was time to put her aside and get on with life. There were other women in the world, other women he could find happiness with. Maybe even settle down some; give up this life of the gun and start a home and family.

Lucy Tillman might not be the woman he would want to do that with, but he sure as hell ought to give her the chance, he thought. She was beautiful, warm, and giving. And he was certain she loved him. That, in and of itself, struck him as odd, considering what she did. But that bothered him only a little. If his brother Kyle could have loved a prostitute—and a half-black, half-Cherokee one at that—then he sure as hell could do so, too.

He pushed the lingering thoughts of Kate away. Kate was gone. Lucy was here, warm and full of life and love. Ramsey walked farther into the room and leaned his Winchester against the wall next to the bureau. He turned and smiled at Lucy again. "Well," he said softly, "ain't you gonna come over here and welcome me back?"

Relief burst through Lucy like a geyser. She jumped up and ran to him and threw her arms around him. She looked up at him, her love evident in her eyes. Then she turned her head and rested her right cheek on the dirty, stained shirt over his chest.

Ramsey smiled over her and closed his eyes, feeling a surge of tenderness for the raven-haired little beauty. He enveloped her in his big arms and squeezed. The top of her head barely reached his broad chest. Ramsey lightly grasped the back of Lucy's head and tugged. Her face came away from his chest, and her head tilted back. She looked up at him, desire smoldering in her eyes. He bent his head, lips heading for hers. Lucy stood on tiptoes, mouth achingly reaching for his.

They eventually broke apart and stared tenderly at each other for a few minutes. "I missed you, Matt," Lucy said quietly.

Ramsey grinned. "I felt the same." He surprised himself with the ease with which he said it. But he didn't care.

Lucy's heart rushed with emotion. "You want a bath first?" she asked. "Or food? Or? . . ."

"There's plenty of time for the last," he said with another grin. "I'd like a bath, but I'm hungrier than a wolf. If you can stand bein' near me a while longer, I'd as soon eat first and then have that bath."

"I can stand it," she breathed. She thought, but didn't say, "I can stand anything as long as you're around."

"Good. Mr. Pomeroy was supposed to arrange it. You hungry?"

"A little." She walked away and pulled the bell rope near the bed. In the few minutes before Wilkins appeared, Ramsey pulled his pay from the cattlemen out of his shirt pocket and added it to the money he had won in the poker game down in Wentworth, stored in his saddlebags. He set them in a corner out of the way.

Wilkins arrived, knocking and then entering. "What is your pleasure, sir, ma'am?" he asked in his cultured, stentorian voice.

"Two steaks, plenty of taters, biscuits and butter, peas, maybe some carrots, milk, coffee."

"Yes, sir. Mr. Pomeroy said you would be ordering."

Ramsey hated the man's voice and pretentiousness. "And don't be all goddamn night at it, either."

"Yes, sir," Wilkins said in his usually droll manner. "Anything else, sir?"

"Not for the moment."

"Veddy good, sir." Wilkins turned and strode out, thin shoulders squared and stiff.

"Where in hell did a bunch of roughnecks like the dudes in the Cattlemen's Association ever find a British servant to work here?" Ramsey asked after the door had closed behind Wilkins.

Lucy giggled and then laughed, the sound pleasant and refreshing to Ramsey. "He ain't no more British than you and me," she said. "He's from Pennsylvania. Coal-mining area, I think. He just likes to put on airs, tryin' to make everybody think he's somethin' special."

Ramsey laughed. "I'll be damned."

Ramsey and Lucy chatted about inconsequentials as they waited for their supper. Neither would dare to mention what was on his or her mind, but somehow each knew. Lucy's heart soared as she realized the depth of Ramsey's feelings. He might not harbor as deep a love for her as she wanted or as she held for him, but there was substance and reality to it, and that was enough for her right now.

The food finally arrived, carried by two black youths. The ever-officious Wilkins directed the laying out of the table and then shooed the young men out. "Will there be anything else, sir?" he asked.

Ramsey considered teasing Wilkins about his humble upbringing, but he decided he was too hungry. "No, Wilkins," he said, holding a chair out for Lucy. He noticed with a flash of anger the reproof that furrowed Wilkins's brow at his act. It was another telling point about the servant. But Ramsey decided to let that pass for now, too. "But in half an hour, I want hot water for the tub, and plenty of it. We'll be finished suppin' by then, and you can clear the supper things away, too."

"Veddy good," Wilkins said stiffly before walking out.

"Pompous ass," Ramsey muttered. Lucy giggled.

They ate quietly. Lucy was not very hungry. She had ordered food more to be doing something with Ramsey than anything else.

But Ramsey had not lied about being hungry. He had had nothing in his stomach save for a few pieces of jerky since late in the morning. He had not wanted to stop any more—or any longer—than was necessary while transporting the rustlers back to Jacksboro. He had stopped several times, but only long enough to give the horses a few minutes' rest. He was not about to waste all kinds of time in gathering fuel, building a fire, cooking, feeding the prisoners one at a time, and then cleaning up. He figured his captives would eat at the jail, and he could eat here at the Social Club.

So he chowed down, too busy with filling his belly to talk much. But at last he sat back, sated with the food. He checked the clock on the mantlepiece. Still fifteen minutes before Wilkins returned. Too much time to do nothing; not enough time to . . .

He smiled at Lucy again. She smiled back but looked chilly in her thin silk wrap. "You cold?" he asked. He had not noticed that it was cool in the room, but he was wearing longhandles and a long-sleeve shirt. It was, he remembered, September, and while real winter might be a ways off yet, autumn was here and the north winds brought with them a hint of the cold weather to come.

"A little," Lucy admitted.

"I'll have Wilkins start a fire when he comes back." He smiled. "Unless you rather I did it now?"

Lucy stood and walked around the table to him. "It's his job," she said, staring into Ramsey's dark eyes. She perched gingerly on Ramsey's lap, then wriggled closer into his lap, resting against his torso, half fearing that he would reject her. "And I'd rather get warm this way for now," she whispered, waiting for his reaction.

Ramsey closed his eyes and wrapped his arms around her. "My pleasure, ma'am," he said softly. He ran his hard, callused hands along her arms, back, flank, anything he could reach. It would warm her, but it also warmed him. Lucy snuggled comfortably against him, her heart bursting with pleasure.

Far too soon for either of them, Wilkins and his helpers returned. Each youth carried two buckets of steaming water. They poured the water into the tub, grabbed the empty pails in one hand and some dirty dishes in the other. They left.

"How about you start us a fire there, Wilkins," Ramsey said.

"The boys will do it when they return," Wilkins said pompously.

"Can't wait that long," Ramsey said, voice hard.

Wilkins caught the inflection—and the implied warning. "Veddy good, sir," he said. He knelt stiffly at the fireplace and began piling kindling in it. He used a match taken from the tin on the mantlepiece to light the fire. He patiently nursed it along as the youths returned, went through the same ritual, and left again.

As Wilkins began piling firewood on the growing blaze, Ramsey asked innocently, "Wouldn't it be better if you was to use some coal there instead of that wood?"

He felt a rush of satisfaction as the sight of Wilkins's suddenly stiff back. Lucy saw it, too, and giggled.

Wilkins finished what he was doing. He stood and turned, looking for all the world like someone had added too much starch to his pants. The black youths, who had come and gone twice more, entered again and poured more water into the tub. The copper tub was more than half full of hot water. Ramsey waited until they had gone again, taking with them the last of the supper plates. Then he said, "A damn dude like you ought not to go puttin' on airs, pretendin' to be somethin' he's not, Wilkins."

Wilkins stared blankly across the room, refusing to respond, or even to look at Ramsey.

Ramsey grinned. "After all, you're a servant. All you do is perform services for the likes of folks like me and Lucy. It ain't like you own the bank or something."

Wilkins deigned to look at Ramsey then, and the gunman was taken aback by the pain in the man's eyes. "You ever been a coal miner, Mr. Ramsey?" Wilkins asked tightly.

"Can't say as I have," Ramsey responded, feeling badly that he had insulted the man. Wilkins might be pretentious, but he was not a bad man.

"Though I might have to wait on gunfighters and whores," Wilkins added in a voice that was flat with the man's roots and far harsher than the cultured tones he usually used, "it's a goddamn far sight better than breakin' my ass in a hole in the ground." He held himself with dignity.

Ramsey felt even worse. He nodded. "I didn't mean no disrespect, Mr. Wilkins."

The butler's eyes widened. No one had ever called him Mr. Wilkins. He was shocked, though it brought a flush of pleasure.

Ramsey had paused when he saw Wilkins's reaction. It took a moment, but he finally realized the reason for it. Then he went on. "There's nothin' wrong with your job. It's good, honest work. But so's bein' a miner—whether he's diggin' for gold or for coal. You ought to quit all this puttin' on airs, though. Just 'cause you get to wear a fancy suit in your job and not a miner's dirty overalls don't make you better'n anybody else. Be your own man, Mr. Wilkins. You'll get far more respect bein' true to yourself than you'll get while tryin' to pretend you're some goddamn British royalty."

Wilkins almost cracked a smile. "Perhaps you're right, Mr. Ramsey," he said. His voice still was without the put-on cultured tones. "But I suppose I've come too damn far in all this play acting to change back now. It'd disappoint the hell out of most of the Social Club's regulars." He did smile, then. It made him look younger, more common.

Ramsey nodded, laughing. "Reckon it would throw these folks into a tizzy."

"Yes, sir," Wilkins admitted. "But I . . ." He shut up when the two young men returned with more water.

"Just set them pails on the floor there by the tub, boys," Ramsey said. "And bring up one more load of 'em. I'll add to the tub when I see fit."

Ten minutes later, a naked Matt Ramsey was easing himself into the tub, luxuriating in the hot water that eased his aching muscles. When he was settled in, Lucy asked, "Want a cigar?"

"You got one?" he asked, surprised. Ramsey did not smoke cigarettes, but like all men, he enjoyed a good cigar of a time.

"Of course. Several boxes are kept in all the rooms." She smiled and walked to the mantlepiece. From a wooden box, she selected a small, slim cheroot. She grabbed a match from the mantlepiece. Handing Ramsey the cigar, she waited until he stuck the cheroot in his mouth. She held the match out. Ramsey lighted the cigar and leaned back, puffing. He was content.

CHAPTER

★13★

It was the third morning after getting paid by McIlvaine and Pomeroy before Ramsey got back to the two cattlemen—a time during which he never left his room at the Jacksboro Social Club.

After his hot bath, in which he was ably, willingly, enthusiastically assisted by Lucy Tillman, he had dried off and then carried Lucy to the bed.

Afterward, he found the sleep of the sated. He slept out the tiredness of too many days on the trail, too much violence, too much tension. He awoke long after the sun had risen, feeling rather guilty for it. But Lucy, who had been sitting at the table sipping coffee, smiled at him. She stood, shucked her silk wrap, and slid under the covers with him. Ramsey forgot his guilt in the passion that followed.

Ramsey and Lucy cleaned themselves up and then rang the bell. Ramsey was rather surprised to see that Wilkins responded. "Ain't you ever off duty, Mr. Wilkins?" he asked.

"Yessir." Wilkins smiled wanly. "It should be Southfield here now. But . . ." He paused, embarrassed. He cleared his throat and proceeded. "Well, Mr. Ramsey, you treated me like . . . like . . ."

"Like a human being?"

"Yes, but more than that. Like regular folks." He smiled a little again. "One of the reasons I started putting on airs was to get a little dignity. I act like that, and folks give me a little respect—even if it's false respect. It's kind of hard to explain, but most folks look down on servants, and when I can pretend to be something a bit special, they don't treat me so poorly. But you're the first to treat me like I was just folks. I have a job to do, and you expect me to do it." He stumbled to a halt. "I guess

81

not much of that makes sense, but because of the way you treated me, I wanted to show my respect for you."

"So you sat downstairs in your rooms waitin' for me—us—to call so you could wait on us?" Ramsey asked, surprised. "While you were supposed to be on your own time?"

"Yes, sir." It was said humbly. Wilkins hung his head.

"Well, I'm obliged, Mr. Wilkins," Ramsey said truthfully.

Wilkins's head came up and he stared at Ramsey. He wanted to smile but was not sure it would be appropriate. He felt relieved, honored that there had been no condescension and no mockery in the gunman's voice. "Thank you, Mr. Ramsey." He looked around the gunfighter. "And you, Miss Lucy."

It was Lucy's turn to be shocked. There was respect in Wilkins's voice. It had never been there before when he had addressed her or any of the other women who worked at the Social Club. To Wilkins, the women were simply whores and therefore not to be treated with any consideration.

"Now," Wilkins said, regaining his composure, "What will be your pleasure this morning?" He was back on the job, as efficient as ever.

"A mess of eggs," Ramsey said. He realized he was very hungry again. "With some chili sauce on 'em. Coffee—hot, black, and plenty of it. Maybe some biscuits."

"Yes, sir. Anything else?"

"You can have some of the boys start emptyin' the tub and haulin' the dirty water off."

"Would you like the tub left?"

"I expect it wouldn't hurt nothin' to leave it there. And maybe some buckets of water. We can heat 'em up ourselves, should we get the hankerin'."

"Veddy . . . Very good, sir."

In due time, the tub was emptied, the room cleaned, the food delivered, and Ramsey and Lucy were eating their meal. They ate in silence. Neither felt a need to talk—at least, not now. There was much that needed to be said between them, but they knew they would find the time and place to say it all. Or those things would become so unimportant that they would no longer need to be said. Either way, now was a time for silence, for gazing into each other's eyes, for letting the troubles of the world pass them by.

They spent the rest of the day enjoying each other's company. They talked—much of it of little import; some that they felt a need to bring out into the open.

Ramsey enjoyed himself immensely that day and that night, but by morning, he knew he ought to be getting back to life outside the tasteful room in the Jacksboro Social Club. After breakfast, he kissed Lucy. "I've got to go meet with the boys of the Cattlemen's Association. You'll wait for me?"

"Yes," Lucy breathed in relief. She had been scared to death that he was about to walk out of her life forever.

"Good."

"I need to go to my room for a bit, though," she added. "Just to get some clothes and such." The words faded. She wasn't sure if her words had gone too far.

"Oh?" Ramsey said in mock severity, "So you're plannin' to just up and move in here with me without even askin' my permission? Lord, you women're all alike—just . . ." He clamped his mouth shut as he saw tears beginning to well up in Lucy's eyes.

He knelt beside her chair and touched her tiny, high cheek-boned face with a big finger. "I was only funnin' you, Luce," he said softly. "That's all. If I didn't want you in here, I wouldn't have asked if you were gonna wait for me."

"I know," Lucy blubbered. Her emotions had gotten the upper hand. She knew she was being foolish, but she seemed unable to help herself. Still, Ramsey's words were comforting, and the tears slowed until they stopped. She dabbed at her runny nose with a handkerchief and wiped a hand across her reddening eyes. "Lord, I must look a fright now," she said. "I'm surprised I ain't scared you off."

"Hell, even with your red eyes and your hair mussed up from our lovin', you're still the best-lookin' gal north of San Antone," Ramsey said gallantly though truthfully.

Lucy's face brightened like the August sun coming out from behind the clouds. Ramsey might be lying to her, but she wouldn't care. He had said it, and he sounded like he meant it. That was good enough for her.

"I won't be gone long," Ramsey said as he stood. "I expect you to be here from wherever it is you got to go, when I get back," he added gruffly.

"I'll be here."

Ramsey nodded. He strolled out. As he walked down the stairs, he began to worry. He wanted to get home to Fannin County soon. Buck and Luke ought to be getting back from Colorado soon, if they weren't back already, and he wanted to see them. He also wanted to see Amos, though he and the oldest Ramsey brother were not as close as he and Buck or Kyle. Still, it would be good to be back in familiar surroundings, with family and friends around.

The problem arose from wondering what he should do about Lucy Tillman. He could admit to himself now that he liked her more than a little and that he was even considering a permanent relationship with her. Therein lay the rub. He could either stay here in Jacksboro until he made up his mind to marry Lucy—or ditch her. Or he could force the decision now and drag her back to Fannin County with him—if she consented to go.

He didn't think he wanted to hang around Jacksboro. At least, not too long. Now that he wasn't working for the association any more, he doubted the cattlemen would let him live here in the Social Club for nothing. He might be able to get a few more days out of them, but that would be about all he could expect. Then he would have to find another place to live. He didn't mind that so much, except that his Scottish heritage made him wince at the thought of having to pay money for it.

He had not expected this while he was out chasing the rustlers. All he had figured to do was complete the job, get his pay, and ride on out. His feelings for Lucy confused him and complicated his life.

The problem was still plaguing him as he entered the office. He was a little surprised to see that all six of the cattlemen were in attendance. Then he realized the judge was due back in town today. He figured that McIlvaine or Pomeroy had spread the news of his completion of the work and that the others had flocked to Jacksboro for the trial and hanging.

"Come in, come in," Pomeroy said graciously. "Sit."

Ramsey shrugged off the uncomfortable feeling that had come to rest on his shoulders. He didn't know why it had come, and he did not have the time or energy to try to puzzle it out right now. He sat and took the tall glass of bourbon Wilkins handed him. Wilkins winked and stepped back, his old reserved self in front of the cattlemen.

"I thought you were to visit us yesterday, Mr. Ramsey," McIlvaine said reprovingly.

Ramsey shrugged and sipped the bourbon. "I was occupied," he said flatly.

Pomeroy laughed and all the other cattlemen save for McIlvaine joined in. "Ah, yes," Pomeroy said, "Miss Lucy. A most impressive choice, Mr. Ramsey." He was about to say more, but he saw the darkness of anger clouding Ramsey's eyes, and he said nothing. He had realized the danger he suddenly was in, and he thought with a shock that there might be more to the relationship between Lucy and Ramsey than simply a whore and her pleased client. It made him wonder. Ramsey would not be the first man to fall in love with a prostitute. Indeed, Pomeroy had seen many instances where a prostitute married and became an upstanding member of the community.

"Thank you," Ramsey said coldly.

"The other members of the association rode through the night after you arrived so they could be here by yesterday morning, Mr. Ramsey," McIlvaine said, half in anger, half in annoyance.

"My apologies, gentlemen," Ramsey said, looking from one cattleman to another.

"There's nothing to apologize for," Oscar Baron said. "I think I speak for all the others here when I say that we are most appreciative for what you've done for us."

There were growls of assent from all but McIlvaine.

"Glad to be of service," Ramsey said glibly. He drank more bourbon. "Well, I'm here now. I believe you said you had another proposition for me?" He looked at McIlvaine questioningly.

"That's right." McIlvaine's breathing was labored as air fought to make its way past the fat nostrils and down the airway that was encompassed by corpulence. He paused, resting his laced fingers across his blubbery stomach. "It seems we have been running into another problem of late."

"Oh?" Ramsey was only half-interested. A large part of his mind was still wondering what to do about Lucy; another hefty segment dwelled on the woman's delights. He sipped whiskey and waited.

"Sodbusters, Mr. Ramsey. Sodbusters."

"What about 'em?" Ramsey asked. McIlvaine missed the harshness and sudden sharpness in Ramsey's words.

"They are growing in numbers and strength, Mr. Ramsey."

"So?" Ramsey's humor was plummeting.

McIlvaine looked at him like he was an idiot. The corpulent cattlemen was blind to the rage growing inside Ramsey. He sighed nasally. "What's the first thing sodbusters do, Mr. Ramsey?"

"Build a house," Ramsey said sarcastically. The others did not think it funny.

"No, they don't," McIlvaine insisted. "They put up fences. Goddamned barbed-wire fences. You have any idea of the damage barbed wire does to cattle?"

"You have any idea of the damage cattle do to a garden patch? Or a farmer's field?" Ramsey snapped.

The cattlemen were shocked. "You seem to have a rather surprising attitude concerning this, Mr. Ramsey," Pomeroy said.

Ramsey shrugged. "You're the ones started playin' guessin' games with me," Ramsey said. He was touchy, and did not like the way this conversation was heading.

"All right," McIlvaine snapped, eyes flashing from the piggish face. "I'll be blunt, Mr. Ramsey. The goddamn sodbusters are gettin' to be a godawful nuisance. They're putting up fences all over God's creation—on our land. Our land! We want them removed, Mr. Ramsey."

"I don't remove fences," Ramsey said dryly, finishing off his bourbon.

McIlvaine's fat face flushed red. When his choler had eased minutely, he said angrily, "There is no humor in this situation, Mr. Ramsey. We've solved one problem, with the rustlers. But we are losin' cattle—and land—to the damned sodbusters. You remove them, and the fences will come down. I can assure you of that."

"Have your ranch hands do it." Ramsey shook his head as Wilkins strolled up with the bottle of bourbon in hand. Wilkins faded into the background again. "It ain't like chasin' rustlers, who're outlaws and often vicious. You're talkin' about a bunch of farmers, is all."

"Our ranch hands are paid to punch cattle," Pomeroy said. "Not run rustlers to ground or rid the area of sodbusters."

The others agreed, nodding. "You showed us in taking care of the rustlers, Mr. Ramsey," Tobe Walker said, "that you are a man of your word. And a man who knows how to handle tough situations. It's why we thought of no one else once we had decided to do something about this growing problem."

"I'm obliged for the kind words, Mr. Walker. All of you. But I reckon I'll turn you down this time."

The six members of the association reacted with surprise and disgust.

Ramsey shrugged, not caring.

CHAPTER

⋆ 14 ⋆

"But why not?" a flabbergasted Howard Crowell asked. He, like the others, had thought Ramsey would jump at the chance to earn more money. Indeed, that had been the largest bone of contention among the cattlemen—how much to pay Matt Ramsey. After considerable argument, they had decided on five hundred dollars. But no one had expected Ramsey to just flat out refuse to help them.

"Mainly," Ramsey said evenly, "I've been away from my home and family a long time and would like to get back to see 'em."

"Family?" Pomeroy asked, surprised. "I didn't know you were married and had a family, Mr. Ramsey."

"I ain't married." The mentioned of it reminded him of Lucy. He shoved that thought away before it grew into unwieldy proportions. "I meant my brothers and such. We have a close family, Mr. Pomeroy. Even though some of us drift a bit, we're still close. I ain't seen my brother Kyle in quite some time, and I'm considerin' takin' a trip up into Colorado to visit him. A couple of my other brothers already have done so, and ought to be back by now. I'd like to see them. As well as my nieces and nephews and such."

"A reasonable thing," Blaine Yates said. "I've got an even dozen brothers and sisters myself. Ain't seen most of them in a long, long time, since a great many of them live back in the East. But . . ."

Ramsey nodded, understanding. "Anyway, I've spent a far longer time around here than I had planned, and so I'd like to mosey on back."

Pomeroy looked at him with hard, unforgiving eyes. "There's more to this refusal than just a desire to get home, isn't there? After all, this ain't like chasing down rustlers, who were always on the move. These people are settled—on our land, I remind you—so they ain't going anywhere, unless we—you—make them. You could have this wrapped up in a couple of weeks at most. Therefore, there must be more to your reasoning."

"Smart thinkin'," Ramsey said with an easy smile. "And you're right, of course." He glared at McIlvaine. "You ought to watch that fat mouth of yours around folks, Cal. Ain't everyone you meet is a rancher. There's other people in the world."

"What in hell's that supposed to mean?" McIlvaine asked in a snarling voice. He was angry. He wanted things a certain way, and when they did not go exactly as he wished—like now—he grew ill humored in a hurry.

"It means, you big, fat bag of wind, that my folks were sodbusters, goddamn it." He was angry now. He pushed up from his chair and leaned forward, hands on the desk. He virtually loomed over McIlvaine. He ignored the others. "My pa broke his ass every goddamn day to make that farm work. And he did, goddamn it. He never got rich, but, by Christ, he raised him a fine family. Five boys who don't ask nothin' from the world for free, a daughter who was as fine a person as you could meet. Don't you sit there on your big, fat ass and start railin' about sodbusters as if they were some kind of bug you want to crush under your foot. They're people, goddamn it. And most of 'em are good people, too." He glared.

"I'm sorry, Mr. Ramsey," Pomeroy said solicitously. "We didn't know."

Ramsey swung toward him, his face darkened like a sky covered by lowering clouds. "I don't expect you to know, damn it," he snapped. "I don't even care that you asked me to do the damned job. What put the burr under my saddle is lard ass over here talkin' down about sodbusters for no goddamn good reason 'cept he don't like anybody who don't stand here and kiss his ass."

"Those are hard words, Ramsey," McIlvaine said angrily.

Ramsey whirled, death in his eyes. He slammed his paws on the desk and leaned over, getting as close to McIlvaine as he could. "Listen to me, you blubbery goddamn toad," he roared into McIlvaine's face. "You open your flappin' mouth again and I'll put a bullet in you. I ain't sure it'll find a vital organ inside that fat carcass of yours, but I'll be interested in findin' out."

Silence hung heavy in the room. McIlvaine sat there with beads of sweat rolling down his pasty, obese face. The ticking of a clock was very loud. Finally Ramsey straightened and turned.

"You others have a problem with me turnin' this job down?" he demanded.

"Of course not," Pomeroy said soothingly. "Like I said, we didn't know. And I reckon you're right. Cal should've kept his big mouth shut and just asked if you'd run the sodbust . . . those farmers off our land. No hard feelings, I hope, Mr. Ramsey?" He stepped forward, hand outstretched, his face open and regretful.

"Reckon not," Ramsey said, trying to calm down. He shook Pomeroy's hand.

"How long're you planning to stay in Jacksboro?"

"Just till the trial, which ought to start soon, seein' as how the judge is due back today." He hoped it would allow him a little more time to decide what to do about Lucy.

"Oh, haven't you heard?" Pomeroy asked. When Ramsey looked blank, Pomeroy said, "We learned this morning that Judge Baldwin has been delayed a few days."

"No, I hadn't heard."

"Do you know where you'll be staying?"

"Hadn't thought on it too much. I was kind of hopin', though, that I could just keep my room here."

"But . . ." McIlvaine started. He shut up when Pomeroy glowered at him.

"We'd expect you to pay, Mr. Ramsey," Crowell said almost apologetically.

Ramsey raised his eyebrows at the rancher. "Seems to me," he said reasonably, "that testifyin' at the rustlers' trial is still part of the job you boys hired me for. Now, I know I've been paid my cash money for the job, but the room and all that comes with it was part of the deal. Seems like it still ought to be."

"He's got us there, boys," Pomeroy said. While McIlvaine wanted to think of himself as the power behind the Jack County Cattlemen's Association, it was really Jasper Pomeroy who held the reins. And the others knew it. He got no argument on the statement, especially when he stood glaring at McIlvaine again. "Besides, maybe it'll make up in some small way for the insult to your parents."

Ramsey nodded his head, surprised but pleased at the turn of events.

"So, it's agreed." Pomeroy smiled. "But only until the trial's done." He paused. "You're not staying for the hanging?" He was surprised.

"I've seen hangin's before. I've got no reason to watch another."

Pomeroy nodded. "Never a pleasant thing, but often necessary. All right, Mr. Ramsey, the room is yours till after the trial. With all food, drink and . . ." He winked in a spirit of manly lechery.

"Good. Well, gentlemen, if you'll excuse me." Ramsey smiled tightly. "I have a lady waitin'." He marched out. He felt the anger build again as he climbed the stairs. His anger fled for the most part when he entered his room and Lucy was waiting for him, smiling and warm.

Her joy turned to fright, though, when she saw the scowl on Ramsey's face. "What's wrong?" she asked, worried. She came to him and took his big hands in her own tiny ones and pressed her cheek to them.

Ramsey told her quickly. When he finished, he looked down at her. Lucy's face was hard to read and he wondered. "You got a problem with the fact that I turned them down?" he asked, voice low and rough.

"Well, no," she said slowly. "I'm just surprised, is all."

"Why?" he asked.

"I don't know." She dropped his hands, turned and walked away. "I just figured that if . . . well, if the Jacksboro cattlemen asked you to do a job for them, that you'd . . ." She trailed off.

"I ain't beholden to these folks," Ramsey said harshly. He walked up to her, placed his big hands on her small shoulders and turned her to face him. "And neither are you."

"Yes, I am," Lucy whispered. For the first time, the shame of her profession overcame her.

"Why?" he asked.

"They hired me. They . . ."

"Hell and damnation, woman," Ramsey snapped. "They don't own you."

"Where would I get money to live on and such?" She had some money put away, but she was reluctant to let Ramsey know that just yet.

"You can do what you do anywhere," Ramsey said, feeling guilt for throwing such a thing in her face.

Lucy blanched, but it firmed her resolve. "You're right, of course," she said softly, though her voice was firm. She looked around the room, as if seeing it for the first time. She was crushed, her heart ground to a pulp by the harsh, unforgiving words of the man she loved. She would have to move her few things back to her small, cramped room in the building next door again.

"Of course," Ramsey said through a suddenly dry mouth, "continuin' to follow such a life would cause me to tie you up someplace where you wouldn't be able to . . ." He knew what he wanted to say, but the words would not come to him just now.

She glanced at him again, eyes piercing as they searched his. "If you got somethin' to say to me, Matt Ramsey, just come out and say it." Her heart was in her throat. "I ain't ever took you for a man to mince words and not say what's on his mind." She thought she would not be able to breathe.

For the first time since he had come back from the war, Ramsey was totally unsure of himself. His tongue felt like it had thickened until it filled his mouth. "It ain't necessary that you do that no more," he said in what he hoped was a firm, strong voice.

"It ain't?" Lucy asked. She was skeptical, but hope bloomed in her breast.

"No," Ramsey muttered.

"You gonna make an honest woman out of me?" Lucy asked. Though she didn't mean to, she had given it an overtone of sarcasm.

Ramsey gulped. "I ain't said that exactly," he commented hastily. "But I reckon it's a bit little early for thinkin' of such a thing anyway. Isn't it?"

Lucy had not really hoped for a proposal, and was fairly certain that Ramsey would not offer one. But she had wanted him to make some kind of commitment, and he had done so. "Reckon it is," she allowed, relief making her legs rubbery with weakness. "But what're we gonna do?"

"I'd like you to stay with me a spell," Ramsey said in a strangled voice. "I . . . and well, I ain't sure of what . . . how . . ." He shut up and cursed himself silently for being a fool and a tongue-tied one at that.

"I'll stay with you, Matt," Lucy breathed. She rested her head on his chest. He had asked her to stay; that was all she needed—for now. She pulled back and looked up at him. "But where'll we stay?"

"Right here," Ramsey said with a grin. He was beginning to relax again. He still had no idea of what the future would hold where he and Lucy Tillman were concerned. But they were set for now, anyway, and that was a step.

"How? I thought you said. . . ."

"All I said was I turned them down and that I was angry at the way they talked about folks such as my parents were."

"And they're gonna let you stay here?" Lucy was incredulous.

"A few days." He explained about the trial.

She nodded as he spoke. When he finished, she said, "It still surprises me that Mr. McIlvaine would allow it, though."

"He didn't have much to say about it, Luce." Ramsey walked to the table and poured a shot of bourbon.

Lucy's surprise seemed to know no end today. "He didn't?" she asked. "He's the biggest rancher in all Jack County, has the most money, and has always been generous with me . . ." She stopped, a sickly look plastered over her face.

"He's been comin' to you regular, hasn't he?" Ramsey tossed down the shot of liquor. It did little to quell the sickly, sour feeling growing inside.

"Yes." Her voice was hardly a whisper.

"Still?"

"Up till you come back the other day." Lucy thought she would vomit from shame and self-disgust. Tears coursed down her soft, pale cheeks and dripped unheeded off her small, rounded chin.

Ramsey stood, sick at knowing. The very thought of that ponderous, fat beast lying in the same bed with Lucy twisted his entrails into knots. He had never given any thought before to what Lucy did. He knew, of course, and accepted it, as long as the men were faceless, nameless, unknown. But knowing that Calvin McIlvaine was bedding Lucy regularly—and probably doing so in a spirit of belittling Ramsey of late—revolted Ramsey.

He poured and swallowed another drink. He set the glass down softly on the table. He wasn't sure he was doing the right thing, but he said, "He won't do it no more, understand?" He was not sure why he had made the statement, or even if he really wanted to, though he did mean it. He hadn't decided whether he loved her, and thus wanted to take her away from this soiled life. Or whether he was just being obstinate.

"Why?" Lucy sobbed.

"I won't let him," Ramsey said firmly. Now that he had made up his mind and said what he had, the tight knot in his stomach began to unravel.

"But he's the head of the association. He's the most powerful man in Jack County."

"I'll tell you a secret, Luce," Ramsey said calmly. "He ain't the man he thinks he is. The real power of the association is Jasper

Pomeroy, who lets McIlvaine *think* he's the big shot." He smiled
at Lucy. "I'll tell you somethin' else, too. It wouldn't matter none
to me if McIlvaine was the power behind the association. I still
wouldn't let him bother you no more. I ain't afraid of Calvin
McIlvaine nor of the association. Now come here."

CHAPTER
★15★

As pleasing as the thought was to him, Ramsey knew he could not stay in his room—or even the Jacksboro Social Club—forever. He needed some fresh air, sights and sounds and smells that were a little different. He also decided he needed some new clothes, and figured it wouldn't hurt much to part with a bit of his new cash to buy them.

"Want to come with me, Luce?" Ramsey asked after he had made up his mind.

"Nah, that's all right." She smiled. "I've got a couple of things to do here. . . ."

Ramsey gave her a black look.

Lucy smiled. "It ain't what you're thinkin'." She was relieved at Ramsey's look of relief. "I've got a bit of straightenin' up to do, and some cleanin'. And, I thought I'd go on over to the milliner's and buy a few things I need."

"I can take you there," Ramsey said bravely. The thought actually horrified him.

"Pshaw," Lucy snorted. "You want to go to a place where there's nothin' but a bunch of women?"

"Don't sound too bad to me," Ramsey said with a lecherous grin.

"You know what I mean," Lucy said, laughing.

"You sure you don't want me to walk you there and leave you while I go off on my own business?" he asked. Half of him wanted to be seen walking down the street with her. She was as pretty as a picture. On the other hand, most of the people in Jacksboro knew what she did—or rather, used to do, Ramsey chided himself—and he knew that walking down the street with her in broad daylight would be uncomfortable for him.

"I'm sure."

Something in the way she said it made Ramsey look at her intently. Then he realized she was having the same fears and doubts as he was, from the other side of the coin. And that knowledge made him angry. He was tempted for a moment to order her to accompany him, just to be perverse and to defy convention. Then the thought fled. Doing such a thing would be plumb foolish and would do neither of them any good.

"All right," he said quietly. "I shouldn't be gone long."

"Take your time." She smiled. "Stop off and have a beer at one of the saloons. There's a dozen of so in town. Might do you some good to be in a different place a bit."

He nodded. Without thinking about it, he pulled out his Colt and checked it to make sure it was loaded. He did not think he would need it, but it paid to be prepared for anything. He dropped it back in the holster, slipped the small loop over the hammer, and walked out.

Lucy, watching him, shuddered. Ramsey's actions had been so routine that he probably was not even aware he was doing them. It gave Lucy a chill of fright. Living with a man whose life was in jeopardy so often—a man whose life was lived so precariously that he performed such rituals automatically—would not be easy. In addition, she loved Matt Ramsey, and she thought she would die if anything happened to him.

She sat at the table and poured herself another cup of coffee. Wilkins had not come by to clear the breakfast dishes away yet. The coffee was getting cold, but she didn't mind too much. She thought as she sipped.

She wondered what she had gotten herself in for. All her life she had wanted to meet a man like Matt Ramsey. But now that she had, she had her doubts. He was tall and handsome, brave and tender, hard and yet soft. But he lived on the edge of life— and death—all the time. She didn't know if she could bear to see him ride off all the time on some adventure or another that might leave him hurt, maimed, or even dead. It would not be a life of ease.

Lucy smiled at that. What kind of life did she have now? A life that was hard and frowned on by most respectable people. A life in which she sold herself to any man who came along. She felt she was fortunate in that she plied her trade in a place like the Jacksboro Social Club, rather than in some of the low dives around town. The men who came to the Social Club were, for the most part, richer and of a better class than the common men who frequented the saloons and bawdy houses of Jacksboro. Still, she had to suffer the indignities of having lecherous, uncaring men paw at her, ravish her.

The worst of them all, she thought, was Calvin McIlvaine. The man was a grotesque figure. He seemed to know that, and out of perversity insisted on being entirely nude when she came to visit him. It was not bad enough, she thought, that she had to bed down with him; it was entirely too much for him to expect her to look at his grossly fat body, too.

Lucy finished her coffee and set the cup down. She hurriedly began to dress in her most modest outfit—a bright calico dress with high neck, tight bosom, and puffy sleeves. As she was pinning her hair up before putting on her hat, Wilkins knocked, entered the room, and began directing the two black youths in the clearing away of the table.

Just after Wilkins and his helpers left, Lucy did, too. She resolved as she walked down the stairs not to worry so much about what would happen between her and Ramsey. She would let life take its course. If they were destined to be together, they would be; if not, something would part them.

Ramsey strolled aimlessly down the street, looking in windows. A number of people greeted him politely, and he responded in kind. A few—farmers in wagons, mostly—scowled at him. He recalled seeing some of them while he was riding after the rustlers. He thought he understood now, after the cattlemen's offer two days ago, why they did so. They saw him as an exterminator—first the rustlers, then the sodbusters.

He shook his head, angry that the cattlemen had put him in such a position. He had nothing against the farmers, but they could not know that, and it bothered him.

After wandering around town a while, savoring the comfortable Indian summer temperatures and the warm glow of the sun, he turned toward Burkhardt's Livery. In the big stable, he found the black stallion. The horse's coat glowed with health and vitality. Ramsey patted the steed's strong neck and long, flowing mane. He was rewarded with a soft nickering and a friendly nuzzling.

"A magnificent animal, Mr. Ramsey," Burkhardt said, stopping on the other side of the horse from Ramsey and running a hand along the steed's glossy flank.

"Yep," Ramsey said. The pride in his voice was unmistakable. "You've taken good care of him, too."

"Such a horse deserves the best," Burkhardt said with a shrug. "Where'd you get him?"

"Down on the flats 'twixt the Bear River and the west fork of the Trinity."

"How'd you ever get somebody to part with him?" He half suspected the horse had belonged to an outlaw Ramsey had killed.

"Didn't."

Burkhardt was certain now that he had been right in his suspicions.

"Caught him. It's what I do." He paused. "What I used to do," he added sadly. "Used to catch mustangs and break 'em for sale. Caught this fellow five, six years ago, now, I guess. Had him half-broke, like the rest of 'em. Was all set to drive 'em all off to sell 'em." He smiled at Burkhardt. "But I couldn't bear to part with him. Best goddamn horse I ever had."

There was still a lingering sadness in his voice, but Burkhardt heard the affection there, too. The liveryman could tell that Ramsey loved the horse.

"There ain't many of them mustangs left, though," Ramsey said. "Too damned bad, too. And hell, I just couldn't see goin' out there tryin' to catch any more of 'em. I reckon others're still doin' it, but I hope those last ones remain free." He grinned. "Of course, there's always other places to go lookin'. I was out southwest of here some, lookin' over the Comanches' old lands. There's some mustangs left out there. I get my brothers, I just might have us mosey on out there and take up where we left off."

"You do," Burkhardt said seriously, "and you bring 'em here. I'll buy all the horses you can bring me." He grinned. "Except stolen ones." He laughed, an odd sound, since it was sharp and seemed to get cut off midway through.

Ramsey grinned back, not offended. He knew Burkhardt was just joshing. He squinted across the horse at the liveryman. "I expect you'll go and sell 'em to the army for twice what you paid for 'em. After me and my kin's done all the work."

Burkhardt honked out another abbreviated laugh. "I am a businessman," he said. He grew serious again. "But I won't rob you, Mr. Ramsey. You got my word on that. I might be in this business to make some money, but I couldn't ever take advantage of a man who knows and cares for horses as much as you do."

Ramsey nodded. He believed Burkhardt. And he even admitted a small burst of pride at the liveryman's words. He gave the black one more big slap on the neck. "I'll be back tomorrow to ride him some, Rudy. I don't want him gettin' fat and lazy."

"Yah, is good."

Ramsey felt pretty good as he headed down the side street that ran alongside the livery, up to the main street. He stopped in the first saloon he found. There was no name, just a broken sign that proclaimed the place served whiskey and beer. It was a dull, dingy place, looking like an outhouse compared with the shining Jacksboro Social Club. But he had been in worse places. There were only four customers, farmers all, Ramsey judged. He strolled to the bar. "Give me a shot of the best stuff you got," he told the surly, filthy bartender.

"Fifteen cent. Or two dollar if you want the whole bottle. Pay first."

"You always this friendly?" Ramsey asked sarcastically. "Or did I get you on a good day?"

"Fifteen cent. Or two dollar for the bottle. Pay first." The bartender had not even blinked.

Ramsey's face stiffened and his words were harsh. "I don't take kindly to bein' called a thief. Especially by some mangy-ass coyote like you." He pulled the Colt and cocked it. Then he jammed it against the bartender's forehead. "Now, set the bottle down here," he ordered, "or I'll drop the hammer."

"Pay first," the man croaked.

"Jesus, you are an idiot, ain't you," Ramsey said. He was somewhat in awe of the man's stupidity. "Just do like I told you. You'll get your money when I get my bottle."

The man turned as if he had two wooden legs. But he was scared, knowing that big-bore Colt was aimed at his back. He grabbed a bottle and a glass, turned, and set both down on the bar. Sweat coursed over his face as the Colt settled back against his forehead.

"That your best stuff, pal?"

"Yessir."

"Better not be watered down," Ramsey warned. Then he pulled the Colt away. He uncocked it, and dropped it into the holster. He poured a drink, keeping one eye on the bartender. He jolted the shot down and winced. It wasn't bad, but it wasn't the fine bourbon they served over at the Social Club. At least, he thought, it wasn't watered down too much.

"How come you're in here?" the bartender asked as Ramsey poured another drink.

"Something wrong with me bein' in here?"

"Suppose not." He licked his broken teeth. "But ain't many folks who stay at the Jacksboro Social Club come in here."

Ramsey shrugged. "Fancy-pants place like that sets my teeth on edge after a while," he said, less than truthfully.

The bartender grinned, an appalling sight.

Ramsey had had enough of this foul dive. He polished off the shot and reached into a pants pocket. He set a silver dollar on the bar. "Reckon that ought to cover it," he said easily. He spun on his heel and swaggered out.

Ramsey breathed deeply when he got outside. The sour smell of horse urine and manure was nowhere near as potent as the odor in the saloon. Ramsey was relieved to be out of there. Without haste, he wandered up to Flanagan's General Store and walked inside. It took a few moments for his eyes to adjust to the dimness.

He had been to Flanagan's several times to get supplies when he was after the rustlers, and he always liked the place. It was stocked with anything anyone could ever want. From cloth to coffee, from pails to pickles, from plows to pears, from horse tack to hardtack, from cans of whitewash to late-season watermelon.

Two men in eyeshades, white shirts, and sleeve garters were waiting on several chattering women. One of them was Flanagan himself, an elderly, bald, stocky man with a white mustache. He turned to Ramsey. "Be with you shortly, Mr. Ramsey," he said cheerfully.

"No rush." Ramsey wandered around, looking at the piles of pants and shirts, the rows of boots, and more. He was in a back corner when he heard the bell ringing, signifying that the door had opened. He glanced and saw three farmers, each wearing overalls, come in. Ramsey paid them little heed.

The three headed almost directly toward Ramsey, but stopped at a keg of nails. While one held a small burlap sack, the others began scooping nails from the keg and dropping them in the sack. As they worked, they talked. Their angry words attracted Ramsey's attention. He perked up his ears.

CHAPTER

★16★

"Goddamn night riders," one farmer said. He slammed nails into the sack twice, until the man holding the sack dropped it. Nails scattered on the floor. "Hell, they scared my family half to death comin' on us like that in the dead of night. Kilt two of my best hogs and tried to burn down my barn."

"Bastards," another said. "I heard they drove a herd of longhorns right through Barney McAuliffe's field t'other day till his crop was ground right into the soil."

The three shuddered. Trampling down a man's field like that was near about the worst thing could be done to these farmers, short of killing someone in the family.

"Who's gonna be next?" the second farmer mused, worry strong in his voice. "And how long's it gonna be before some one of us gets killed? Or someone in his family?"

"I don't know," the first one said, enraged, "but if those sonsabitches come on my farmland again, they're gonna get a dose o' buckshot."

"Same here," Hal Finn said defiantly. "This is gettin' to be too much for us to stand for. Them night riders've hit, what, five of us? And all in the past two nights. I don't understand it."

"Me neither," Ike Coughlan said. "But I'm fixin' to get back at those bastards some way."

"Who?" Uriah Wiggins asked, voice bouncing up and down the scale.

"Who the hell do you think, you stupid ass?" Coughlan demanded. "The goddamn Jack County Cattlemen's Association, that's who."

"We don't know it's them doin' all this," Wiggins whined.

100

"Well," Coughlan allowed, "I don't expect it's them directly, of course,'Riah." He sounded like he was talking to a four-year-old. He laughed harshly. "Hell, can you just picture that fat slob McIlvaine on a horse ridin' through the night?"

The others laughed a little, too, but there was no joy in it. And the laughter did nothing to mask the fear these men felt. Fear that they would lose everything they had worked all their lives for, fear that they would be the first to have a member of his family killed by the night riders.

"But those goddamn cattlemen are behind this, sure as I'm standin' here. Don't you ever doubt that none."

"But why in hell would they start comin' down on us now?" Finn wondered aloud. "They made it clear when we come here that they didn't want us around. But they never bothered us befo' this."

"I don't know," Coughlan said with a shrug. "It does seem purty suspicious."

It was not at all suspicious to Matt Ramsey, who stood in the shadows, holding a pair of denim trousers and listening in. It had started the night of the day he had refused the cattlemen's request to run the sodbusters out.

"Maybe they just brought in some of them gunslingers recent. Like that Ramsey fellah. Hell, for all I know, he's leadin' the riders."

Ramsey winced. No wonder the farmers had not looked at him with any favor. He suspected a good many of them had the same idea as Ike Coughlan. Ramsey swore mentally.

"Think we ought to go to the sheriff?" Wiggins asked. He sounded nervous. Ramsey couldn't tell who had spoken, but judging by the voice, he assumed it was the short, thin man with a large overbite.

"What the hell fo'?" Finn snorted. "Ol' Sheriff R. J. Laybe ain't about to help no piss-poor dirt farmers like us. Not 'less'n some'un gets killed dead fust. And even then I 'spect he won't do nothin' more than arrange for the buryin'."

"Hal's right, Uriah," Coughlan said. "That goddamn sheriff's as useful as teats on a boar hog."

"What're we gonna do then, Ike?" Wiggins asked.

Before Coughlan—a short, burly bear of a man—could answer, the door opened again, and another farmer entered. He stopped and looked around the store, frantic. He saw the three and hurried toward them. He was clearly agitated.

"What's gone wrong, Ernie?" Coughlan asked. He was worried. Ernie Hardesty was one of the steadiest men he knew. He was not easily frightened and few things disturbed him overly much.

"Night riders. . . . Mrs. Muldoon," he said, voice shaking. "Maggie . . . She was . . . Her and little Charity . . ."

"Tell it, damn you," Ike Coughlan snapped, voice rising in pitch and intensity. He grabbed Hardesty by the upper arms and shook him.

"Watch your language down there, you men," Flanagan snarled. "There's ladies present."

Coughlan glared at the store owner a moment before turning back to Hardesty. "Tell me, goddamn it," he whispered. "What happened?"

Hardesty took a rough breath to calm himself. As he did that, Ramsey edged closer, wanting to hear but still not be seen.

"Night riders come on Muldoon's place last night. They used their hosses to run through his fields. Liam run out to try to stop 'em. One of the bastards shot him. . . ."

"Is he . . . ?" Wiggins asked.

"No, he's alive. He'll be all right after a bit." Hardesty scowled and looked like he was going to cry at the same time. "Leastways his wound won't give him no trouble after it heals. Can't say as much about his mind."

He paused, breathing harshly. "The bastards set fire to . . ."

"I told you boys to watch your language here in my store," Flanagan said as he stormed up in a rage. "I've got ladies here tryin' to see to their buyin'. They don't need to listen to a bunch of foul-mouth louts like you. I'll thank you to get yourselves out of my store. Now!"

"Go to hell, Flanagan," Coughlan snapped. His tone made it clear he considered Flanagan a traitor to good Irishmen everywhere. "We got us a wagonload of trouble to hear about, and we need to hear it straight off. So go on back to sellin' your corsets and such." He turned back to Hardesty. "Go on, Ernie."

"The bastards," Hardesty started again, glaring a moment at Flanagan, "set fire to the house. Maggie and Charity were . . . were . . . inside." Hardesty began crying, unashamed. Maggie Muldoon was his sister. "Couldn't get out. . . ." Hardesty said, sobbing. "Liam hurt . . . couldn't help 'em. Dead. Both dead. . . ." He tried to stop the wracking sobs but could not.

"Those cow-humpin' sonsabitches," Coughlan roared, his voice quivering with emotion. It rattled the store's windowpanes with its volume. He was pale with rage.

"That's it!" Flanagan snarled. "Get out. All of you." He held an ax handle in his right hand, and he slapped it against his left palm several times for emphasis.

"We got buyin' to do," Wiggins said, voice quavering. "Things we need."

"Go and get 'em somewhere else," Flanagan said, his anger growing. He began to feel self-righteous.

"But there ain't no other . . ."

"GET OUT!" Flanagan raised the ax handle. He froze with the weapon in the air when the muzzle of a large pistol brushed across the nape of his neck and stopped.

"This's a hell of a way to conduct business, Flanagan," Ramsey said.

"That you, Ramsey?" Flanagan asked, trying to keep the fear out of his voice but not succeeding.

"Yep."

"Phew," Flanagan breathed in relief. Matt Ramsey wouldn't hurt him; he was sure of that. Not after Ramsey had gotten all his supplies here during three months of chasing outlaws for the Cattlemen's Association. "I'd be obliged if you was to help me get this riffraff out of my store. They can go down to some foul saloon and blaspheme there to their heart's content."

"I reckon not, Flanagan," Ramsey said coldly.

"You sidin' with these mangy sodbusters?" Flanagan asked incredulously. He wanted to turn and stare at Ramsey, to see if the gunslinger was in his right mind. But with the threat of the big Colt still pressing against his neck, he was not about to move. He did begin to sweat, though.

"I'm sidin' with these four gentlemen," Ramsey said calmly, emphasizing the last word ever so slightly. "It seems to me, from the little I overheard, that they've been hit with some hard times and might need a wee bit of helpin' out themselves. Mr. Blake over there will help them now. Those ladies over there can wait a spell. They've already occupied your time for half the mornin', I'd wager."

The women, who had been watching with frightened, fascinated interest, sniffed indignantly and waded out of the store, their noses in the air.

"See, you two ain't busy no more," Ramsey said tightly. "Now, have Mr. Blake get these folks what they need and they'll be on their way. Ain't that right, boys?"

"We don't need no help from the likes of you, Ramsey," Coughlan snapped.

Ramsey stared at him. It was quiet in the store now. Even Hardesty had stopped his sobbing. The silence was broken only by the men's breathing and Hardesty's occasional sniffle.

"You think you could take Flanagan, here?"

"No doubt," Coughlan said without hesitation. "Even now." He nodded toward the ax handle.

Ramsey grinned a little. The farmer was not tall, but he was big around. He looked to be strong as an ox. Ramsey suspected the man would have no trouble in stomping the daylights out of Flanagan, even if Flanagan did have an ax handle in hand.

"I don't doubt you, Mr.? . . ."

"Coughlan."

"I don't doubt you, Mr. Coughlan. Not the least little bit. In fact, I'm downright certain you could thump the bejesus out of Flanagan, even if he does have an ax handle. But I do have my doubts that you could take Mr. Blake and his scattergun over there."

The four farmers turned so fast that Ramsey was afraid one of them might break some body part. But they all seemed to come through it intact, and stared across the store. Miles Blake stood, leaning back against the counter, the scattergun raised to his shoulder.

"He wouldn't," Finn said. It was more of a question than a statement.

"Not while Flanagan here is occupied. Soon's Flanagan got out of the way, Mr. Blake would shred you and at least one of your friends here. And I suspect he's either got a belt gun or another shotgun within easy reach to take care of the other two of you. Ain't that right, Mr. Blake?" Ramsey did not look at the man.

"It is," Blake said, unconcerned.

"What're we gonna do, Ike?" Finn asked. "We can walk out of here. Or we can accept Mr. Ramsey's help and get our supplies."

"I don't cotton to takin' help from the likes of him." He jerked a big, square chin at Ramsey.

"Just 'cause we take his help now don't mean we got to take him to our bosom, Ike," Finn said reasonably. "We need those supplies."

Coughlan stood in thought. He often liked it when the men considered him something of their leader. But at times like this, when whatever decision he had to make would be at least partly wrong, he was not fond of his position. He weighed the options. But when he got to the thought of the wives and children back on the farms in want of supplies, whatever they might be, his mind was made up.

"All right, Ramsey," he said, "we'll take your help. This time. But don't expect no friendship from us over this."

"Considerin' your attitude, Mr. Coughlan, I'd not seek friendship with you under the best of circumstances." He paused. "Now, if you and your friends here are gonna get some supplies, you had best get to it. Before long, word of this is gonna be all over town. That'll bring Sheriff Laybe over here and then we'll all be ass deep in trouble."

Coughlan nodded, recognizing at once the wisdom of Ramsey's statement.

"Put the scattergun down, Mr. Blake," Ramsey said sternly, looking at the shopkeeper for the first time. "And help these gentlemen." At no time had he moved the muzzle of the Colt from the back of Flanagan's neck.

"No, sir." Blake seemed determined.

"Blake," Ramsey said wearily, "if you don't put that weapon down right now, I will blow the back of Flanagan's head off. Then I will shoot you right between the eyes."

"For pity's sake, Miles, put the gun down," Flanagan said urgently. "Do it."

Blake hesitated.

"These sodbusters are not worth so much trouble, Miles," Flanagan snapped, voice even more beseeching.

"Very well," Blake said. He started to lower the shotgun.

"Don't even think about it," Ramsey warned. He spun toward the side a little bit, drawing Flanagan up against him, holding the store owner with his left forearm around Flanagan's neck. Ramsey's right hand held the Colt at arm's length. The pistol was cocked and aimed at Blake's heart.

Time stood still. Ramsey was relaxed, Flanagan frightened. The four farmers were befuddled. They did not understand. The shopkeeper was in the process of putting the shotgun down. They wondered what Ramsey was up to.

CHAPTER

⭐ 17 ⭐

Blake was angry. He was a young man, rather handsome with his sweeping mustache and bright blue eyes. But his scowl of anger marred his face.

"Your move, Miles," Ramsey snapped. "But you got to the count of three to make it."

Ike Coughlan shuffled nervously. He was considering jumping Ramsey, but he couldn't decide if that would improve his situation or worsen it.

"Stand where you are, boys," Ramsey ordered harshly.

Coughlan froze.

"One," Ramsey said slowly. He waited a heartbeat. "Two." Another heartbeat. "Thr . . ."

"All right," Blake screeched wildly. He hastily pointed the muzzle of the shotgun toward the roof and very carefully eased both hammers down.

"Break it and pull the shells out," Ramsey ordered. "Toss 'em in the pickle barrel there. Drop the scattergun in after it."

Still scowling, Miles Blake did as he was told.

"Where's your backup piece?" Ramsey demanded.

"Ain't got one," Blake said blandly.

"That's real thoughtful of you, Miles," Ramsey sarcastically. "There ain't many men would be so considerate as to make their wife a widow at such a young age. Hell, she'll have the pick of the town."

Blake was enraged, but he knew he was helpless in this situation. He reached behind him and slowly pulled a .38-caliber Bulldog revolver from his back pocket.

"Set it on the floor and kick it over this way." After Blake had done so, Ramsey asked, "That all?"

"Yes."

Ramsey didn't believe him. "One of you boys go over there and check. But don't get between him and me. Pat Blake down to see if he's got another piece on him. Then check behind the counter. Best hurry, though, since I reckon those old bats are talkin' to Sheriff Laybe right about now."

"Go and do it, Hal," Coughlan said, patting Finn on the back.

"One of you others might want to turn the lock in the door."

Coughlan pointed, and Wiggins scurried to the front of the store. He turned the Closed sign outward and pulled the shades down over the windows in the door.

Finn found a Colt navy revolver behind the counter. He unloaded it and stuck it in his belt and dropped the cartridges in his pocket. "That's it," he announced.

"Good. Mr. Blake, if you would be so kind as to get these men what they need. And, lest you get the idea to try something, I'll be sittin' here with Flanagan. I figure he—and Mrs. Flanagan—will be most displeased was his head to get splattered all over the store."

The farmers seemed almost gleeful as they began voicing their list of needs. Blake dawdled at getting the items until Ramsey said with resignation, "Mr. Blake, I am gettin' just a tad weary of threatenin' you. There's nothin' you can do about this here situation. Stallin' in hopes that the sheriff will arrive and pluck your stones out of the fire will do no one any good. If the sheriff does show up and he decides to try'n settle this situation in a way that does not meet with my approval, there will be a heap of bloodshed. And yours will be the first blood to flow. I promise you that."

He paused just a moment. "Mr. Coughlan, if Mr. Blake here dawdles any longer, you have my permission to thump him once or twice. Don't take too long at it, but make him unconscious. Then you may get your own supplies."

Despite himself, Coughlan was beginning to like Matt Ramsey. He grinned harshly at Blake, who blanched. The shopkeeper was half a foot taller than the farmer, but was giving up close to forty pounds. And the farmer was strong, having spent most every day of his life on the hard work of the farm. Blake did little but keep shop. Blake moved considerably faster in the getting of supplies.

Ramsey perched his buttocks on the edge of a keg of nails. He twisted the back of Flanagan's shirt collar into a knot, giving him a good grip on the man. The Colt rested, cocked, atop his thigh.

Flanagan knew where the pistol was, and he knew Ramsey's reputation. He made no move; in fact, he was barely breathing.

"Go get the wagon, Ernie," Coughlan said. The wagon would be needed, but Coughlan also wanted to get Hardesty doing something, hoping it would take his friend's mind off his sister's death. Hardesty moved like he was wrapped in fog, but he left— through the back door.

It seemed like hours since the drama had begun to unfold. But it was less than fifteen minutes. Then came a banging on the door.

"Open up!" Laybe shouted. He rapped on the glass window in the store's door again. "Come on, open up in there. This is Sheriff Laybe. Open up!"

"Hold your horses, R. J.," Ramsey shouted back.

"That you, Matt?" the loud, disembodied voice sounded surprised.

"Yep."

"What in tarnation's goin' on in there, Matt?"

"Flanagan and Blake are fillin' a special order."

"Bull chips. Now come on and open this door."

"We're done, Ramsey," Coughlan said quietly.

"Best be on your way."

"We need to tote this up," Coughlan said sharply. "I aim to pay for these goods. I don't want nobody callin' Ike Coughlan a thief."

"I'll take care of it. Now get."

Finn and Wiggins hurried through the back room of the store and outside.

"Sheriff!" Blake suddenly shouted. "They're gettin' away. Go 'round the . . ."

Coughlan slammed a meaty fist into the side of Blake's head, knocking him down. The shopkeeper might not be unconscious, but he was incapable of speech or movement and would be for some time. Coughlan turned to leave.

"Ike," Ramsey called softly. When Coughlan looked at him, Ramsey said quietly, "I had no part in any of this night ridin' that's been goin' on. Your mentionin' it here was the first I ever heard of it."

Coughlan waved acknowledgment and then disappeared. A moment later, Ramsey heard a wagon creaking off, heading away from the street out front.

"All right, Flanagan, go on and let our guests in," Ramsey said calmly.

Flanagan walked stiffly, afraid Ramsey would shoot him in the back. He felt better when he reached the door safely. He unlocked it and opened it. Laybe and his two deputies strolled in. People crowded around the open doorway, peering inside, but knowing better than to attempt to enter.

Laybe wandered past Ramsey, who still sat on the edge of the keg, cocked Colt on his thigh. Laybe looked at him in wonder. The sheriff heard Blake groan, and he headed for the back of the counter. Along the way, he spotted the shotgun sticking butt upward in the barrel of pickles.

He found Blake behind the bar. "You all right, son?" he asked, kneeling at the young man's side.

Blake mumbled something the others could not understand. But the mumbling seemed to drag on and on.

"Think you can walk over to the doc's on your own, boy?"

Again Blake mumbled, but a moment later, with Laybe's help, he stood. He weaved a little, then steadied himself. He walked away, looking dazed. The people gathered around the door parted to make way for him.

"Well, Sheriff?" Flanagan demanded.

"Well, what?" Laybe had no liking for Flanagan. Hadn't had since that time nine years ago when Laybe needed a stake desperately to feed his wife and infant daughter, and Flanagan refused to give him some food and other essential supplies on credit. Laybe had managed to get a loan of some cash and gotten his supplies—riding eighty miles to another town so as to not spend his money in Flanagan's. But he had never forgiven Flanagan for that miserly snub.

"When're you going to arrest this thieving . . ." He pointed at Ramsey, unable to continue, he was so angry.

"Well, seein' as how he's settin' there with a cocked pistol in hand, no time soon," Laybe said humorlessly. He looked around. "What'd he steal?"

"Food, bullets, pots, God knows what else."

Laybe was looking at Flanagan, but asked over his shoulder, "You packin' all that stuff in your pants pockets, Matt?"

"Not last time I looked."

"Well, Flanagan?"

"It was those danged sodbusters. They took all that stuff with Ramsey's help. Never paid for a lick of it."

"That true, Matt?"

"Sort of. The farmers took a bunch of stuff. And I helped

'em by keepin' Flanagan and Blake from bein' too much of a hindrance to 'em."

"Was Flanagan paid?"

"Not yet. I did tell him, though, that I'd take care of it."

"If Ramsey pays you, would that shut you up, Flanagan?" Laybe asked roughly.

"I suppose. But there's more than just the goods. Damage and all, you know. . . ."

Laybe glanced around the room. "I don't see no damage here, Flanagan."

"The shotgun . . ." He stopped. Actually, there was little else in the way of damage, unless one counted the knot growing on Miles Blake's head.

"How much is owed?" Laybe said.

"It'll take me a minute to figure the total," Flanagan said stiffly. He walked to his counter, pulled a pencil from behind his ear, wet the tip, and then scribbled on an old piece of paper. Finally he straightened. "Sixty-three dollars and fifteen cents."

"That sound about right to you, Matt?" the sheriff asked, unconcerned.

Ramsey shrugged. "Got no idea. Don't much care, neither."

"Why?" Laybe asked, rather surprised. He turned slowly to face Ramsey.

Ramsey grinned. "I was just gonna have him put it on my bill."

Laybe chuckled. "The boys in the association are gonna shit adobe when they hear you charged them for a bunch of supplies for the goddamn sodbusters."

Ramsey stood, grinning. His features darkened. "Tell your deputies to take a hike, R.J."

Laybe sent his deputies off, and Ramsey uncocked the Colt, made sure the hammer was sitting on the empty chamber, and slid the pistol away. "Best tell Flanagan to keep his pencil wet. The reason I come in here in the first place was to get some new duds."

Laybe laughed. "Have at it." He grew serious. "We've got to talk about all this, Matt," he said quietly.

Ramsey stared at the lawman, whose mouth twitched in a sort of smile. "I ain't fixin' to arrest you. My word, Matt, I won't arrest you." Ramsey still stared hard. "Jesus Christ, Ramsey," Laybe snapped, "what more can I tell you?" He paused. "My word—nobody will arrest you. Even if our talk turns sour, I'll give you a chance to get out of town. I owe you that much."

Ramsey nodded. "I'll be over directly." He turned and walked off. He picked up two pairs of denim pants, three cotton shirts, two pairs of longhandles, a vest, new boots, several bandannas, a new hat, three boxes of cartridges, a wool coat, two blankets to make a new bedroll, a piece of canvas, and some food items that would pack easily and travel well. He was a little concerned that he might have to leave town in a hurry.

Flanagan scowled the whole time he got the items, stacking them in a box. Ramsey enjoyed the store owner's discomfiture immensely. When he had all he needed, Ramsey said, "Have somebody take this all over to my room at the Social Club. And send the bill to the Cattlemen's Association. It's been a pleasure doin' business with you."

Flanagan looked like he would choke on his rage and indignation. Ramsey laughed softly as he walked out. He headed straight for the sheriff's office. Just before entering, he glanced around. He spotted nothing untoward. Both deputies were far up the street, making their rounds. Resting his right hand on the Colt, Ramsey opened the door with his left hand.

Laybe was sitting with his back to the door, muttering under his breath as he threw old wanted posters into the open door of the iron stove. "That you, Matt?" Laybe asked, not looking up. He chucked a few more papers into the stove.

"Yep." Ramsey could see both Laybe's hands. He looked around, glancing in the back toward the cells. Only the prisoners he had brought in were there. He relaxed a little.

Laybe straightened after closing the stove door. "It's goddamn cold in here," he mumbled. He pointed to a chair. "Sit, Matt. Coffee?"

"Sure." Ramsey positioned the chair so that he could watch the front of the office, as well as Laybe. He sat, taking the tin mug of coffee that Laybe handed him. Laybe walked around his desk and flopped down in his chair. He sipped some coffee and then set the cup on the desk. "All right, Matt, what the hell went on over at Flanagan's today?" he asked.

Ramsey told it sketchily, as Laybe drank coffee, listening intently. The lawman's face changed with each new bit of information, running from anger to laughter to irritation and points between. Ramsey finally stopped talking.

"That it?" Laybe asked.

"Yep."

CHAPTER

⋆18⋆

Sheriff Laybe sat back in his chair, hands locked behind his head, staring at the ceiling. He didn't like this turn of events one little bit. It put him in one hell of an awkward—and potentially dangerous—situation. He sighed, half wishing he had never been elected.

Finally he fell forward, until his forearms were resting flat on the littered desk. "There's gonna be no end of trouble come from this, Matt," he said with conviction.

Ramsey shrugged. "Ain't my doin', R. J."

"Like hell."

Ramsey's eyebrows raised angrily. "Don't go layin' all this damnfool business on me."

"You shouldn't have helped those damned sodbusters, Matt. You should've just let things run their course. It would've all been taken care of sooner or later."

"Like you've taken care of the night riders," Ramsey commented.

"I had nothin' to do with any of that," Laybe said with equal heat. Guilt made him angry.

"But you ain't done anything to stop it, neither."

"If you hadn't of interfered, things would've come 'round after a spell."

"Bullshit. I couldn't just stand there and watch Blake blast a couple of farmers with that scattergun of his."

"Might've saved a heap of grief in the long run, Matt," Laybe said, tempering his anger. He was not a bad man in general, but he was taken in by the ranchers to whom he owed his job and livelihood. He had long ago come around wholeheartedly to their way of thinking. To him, the farmers were dirt-poor slobs who

112

were more trouble than they were worth. They filled up the land, fencing it off for their grubby crops, not allowing the ranchers to earn their living. And the ranchers were the ones with the money, the ones who kept the area afloat. The farmers contributed little but trouble, to his way of thinking.

Ramsey could not believe what he had just heard. He gaped in shock at the lawman.

"Look, a few deaths among the farmers is unfortunate," Laybe said, knowing he was not achieving the tone of reasonableness he wanted. "But people like them die every day, anyway." He shrugged, trying to assuage his own guilt. "A couple of 'em get killed, their fields get trampled down, and they'll move on out. Then there's no more problem."

"You don't know shit about such people, do you?" Ramsey asked harshly.

"Sodbusters? I know enough."

"You don't know shit about either farmers *or* night riders," Ramsey snapped. "Ain't many farmers I know of—and I was brought up amongst such people—are gonna run because of some night attacks. A few might turn tail, but most'll stick it out. My ma and pa fought Comanches and every other kind of Indians and never run. Neither did most of their neighbors. They stuck together and hung on through it all. They built and grew and had families. Now the Comanches ain't no more, and folks like mine're still there."

"They thrive on hard times, don't they?" Laybe said, a sneer in his voice.

"Not really," Ramsey said calmly. "But they've got the stones to stick it out when times get hard, because they believe in what they're doin'. Not because somebody's pushin' 'em one way or another." He glared at Laybe, who seemed to shrivel under the hot gaze.

"And as for the night riders," Ramsey said, spitting on the floor, "they're cowards. It's why they ride at night. Hell, most of those chickenshits even wear hoods most times. They like to kill, though, I'll give 'em that. And that's why they ain't a solution to this problem. You turn those bastards loose and they'll kill anybody they can get their hands on."

Laybe could say nothing to that. He knew it to be true for the most part. He had seen them before. He even agreed with their methods at times, especially when it came to driving undesirables out of the area. He wondered how things had come so far. Not long ago, Jack County was a peaceful enough place. But now, troubles arose on all sides.

"Goddamn it, Matt," Laybe snapped after a while. "You got to take some responsibility for what's goin' on."

"The hell I do. It wasn't me sent those night riders out there to plunder those farms. All I did was to help out a couple folks who were facin' uneven odds."

"Damn it, Matt, if you'd taken the job when the association offered it to you, none of this would've happened. I know you some, now. I've seen how you do things. You ain't the kind of man to go out there tramplin' some poor bastard's crops or shootin' folk indiscriminate like some of those others. . . ."

"What others?"

Laybe looked embarrassed. "Hell, you don't think these're local boys causing' all the ruckus, do you?" It did not require an answer. "The cattlemen made arrangements a week or so ago to have some outsiders come in here—just in case you turned them down. They never expected you to do that, but McIlvaine, especially, likes to cover his ass."

"And you agreed to them bringin' in a passel of hired guns to kill farmers?"

Laybe looked even more discomfited. "I never expected you to turn 'em down, either. I figured you'd take the job, handle it quietly, and nobody'd be the wiser."

Ramsey had taken a liking to the marshal in the short time he had been in Jacksboro, but now his opinion of the lawman plummeted. "Jesus goddamn Christ, R.J.," he snapped. He shoved up, knocking his chair over. He left it lying there as he paced the room, prowling like a caged cat. "How the hell can you just sit there while some poor dirt farmers are gettin' killed? Lord, it was a woman and a baby those bastards killed. How the hell can you let somethin' like that go by like it don't mean nothin'?" Ramsey was in a towering rage. It emanated from him like an aura.

Laybe looked stricken. "I don't like it none, Matt," he said weakly. "But it was an accident. It wasn't meant to happen. I'd never condone the killin' of women and kids." He looked adamant.

"Then do something about it, goddamn it!" Ramsey roared. He kicked the chair out of his way and glowered at Laybe.

The sheriff was nervous. Matt Ramsey was a big man and a deadly one under the best of circumstances. Now, with the gunman so enraged, Laybe began to think Ramsey might try something. And Laybe knew he would be no match for Ramsey.

"My hands're tied, Matt," he said in a strangled voice. Sheriff R.J. Laybe was basically a good man, and it twisted his guts to have such things happen. But like many basically good men, he was blind in some areas. He thought the farmers were wrong, and the ranchers right. The ranchers also controlled his pay, and he was too far in debt to cross them lightly. He felt helpless in this situation, though he didn't mind overly much, since he thought he was in the right. Still, he sat there wishing a couple of the farmers themselves had been the ones to die, rather than a woman and small child. That he could accept a lot more easily. The farmers would have gotten what they deserved. But the death of Maggie and Charity Muldoon gnawed at him.

He sighed. The more he thought about it, the more irritated he became over it. How dare the cattlemen hire men who would go out and slaughter women and children. His anger grew.

"Listen to me, Matt," he finally said. There was a note of urgency in his voice. "I know you take such things to heart. But I don't want you causin' no trouble in Jacksboro. I don't mind so much if you go after the night riders—if you do find out who they are. Just don't start gunnin' for folks you might suspect. You'd best be goddamn sure before you haul out that Colt."

Ramsey had gone back to pacing, but stopped again and grinned viciously at Laybe. "You could help me, R.J.," he said quietly.

Laybe shook his head. He was sad, but determined.

"You don't have to face 'em down with me, Sheriff," Ramsey said, his voice persuasive. "Just tell me who the hell they are. I'll go find 'em—and face 'em—myself."

"Can't do that, Matt," Laybe said evenly. "I just can't do anything to help you. In some ways, I wish I could." He shook his head, angry at the night riders. "We never suspected they'd resort to killin' women and kids. Still, that was an accident and . . ."

"Accident, bullshit," Ramsey snarled.

Laybe shrugged. "No matter. I can't help you, Matt. Not openly, anyway." He looked at Ramsey and added earnestly, "I won't go against you, Matt—unless it becomes necessary. But I won't help you none, either."

"Reckon that's somethin'," Ramsey said dryly.

The lawman looked back at him, unblinking. "Like I said, I don't mind if you go gunnin' for the night riders. They don't mean a damn thing to me. But I *don't* want you goin' after the members of the Cattlemen's Association."

Ramsey glared hard at Laybe. The sheriff grinned wanly back at him. "I might not've known you too long, Matt," he said quietly, "but I know you enough to know such a thing was on your mind. But I'm warnin' you now, goddamn it, if you go for any one of the cattlemen, I'll come for you—with all the hired guns, if needed. You won't stand a chance."

"Why're you protectin' those bastards, R.J.?" Ramsey demanded. "Hell, they're the ones hired the night riders. So they're the ones responsible for those two innocents gettin' killed."

"The cattlemen didn't want this to happen, Matt," Laybe said with little conviction. "They didn't hire them guns to go around murderin' women and kids. All they were supposed to do was throw a scare into those damned sodbusters. Trample some crops, kill a few hogs or milk cows or chickens. That was all." His voice faded. He did not sound convincing even to himself.

Ramsey stared at the lawman in disbelief. He could not believe Laybe was going to let these deaths go unpunished. He thought of urging the sheriff to go after the night riders, to throw a couple of them in jail for the deaths. He figured between him and the sheriff, they could convince the cattlemen that sacrificing a few of the night riders would go a long way to bringing peace back to Jack County. But he knew instinctively that Laybe would not go for it. And he knew that the cattlemen would not allow themselves to be convinced. So certain of their rightness, they would only hire more guns—probably wielded by even more vicious men than those already here.

No, Ramsey thought, he would have to handle this himself. He never gave a thought to the fact that no one had chosen him as the bringer of justice, nor to the fact that most of the farmers still would not trust him because of the position he had held with the Cattlemen's Association. None of that entered into it. He only knew what was right, and what needed to be done. So he was determined to do it. He turned toward the door.

"Matt," Laybe called softly.

Ramsey stopped with his left hand on the door handle. He looked back, right hand reaching instinctively toward the Colt.

"The trial for those rustlers you brought in will be in six days— the judge got delayed again. As soon as that's over, I want you out of Jack County. You got that long to do what you think you can with the night riders. But the minute the trial ends, I want you gone. Me and my deputies will escort you to the county line."

Ramsey nodded slightly and stepped through the door. His rage boiled just beneath the surface. It made him deadly. People seemed to see that, and gave him a wide berth as he stomped up the street. Thoughts banged around in his skull. He figured he could leave Jack County after the trial, then turn around and come right on back. Taking care of the cattlemen would not take him long.

But for now, there were other things to worry about. Like getting a new place to stay. He didn't figure the cattlemen would be overjoyed with him in the Social Club any more. Nor would he feel very comfortable. He didn't think the cattlemen would send their hired guns for him. Not now. Ramsey knew that without his testimony, the rustlers would walk out as free men, and the association would never allow that. No, Ramsey figured the cattlemen would wait until the trial was over before sending their hired guns for him.

Still, the cattlemen might send the night riders to pay him a visit to scare him, putting Lucy in danger. That thought bothered him considerably. And even if that did not happen, leaving Lucy in the Social Club would be dangerous and foolish. She deserved better.

Ramsey stopped at the Monarch Hotel—the finest in Jacksboro—and got a room. He paid for five nights in advance. The clerk was chilly toward him, and Ramsey grinned humorlessly as he left the hotel. Apparently the word had already gotten around that he had helped the farmers.

As he walked through the doors of the Jacksboro Social Club, he had the sudden urge to head into the association office and blast the cattlemen into oblivion. It would solve the problem, he figured. But he realized that the cattlemen were no fools. He suspected the office was empty, and the cattlemen all safely holed up in their homes out on their ranches already—or on their way there. And they would be protected by their ranch hands and the new hired guns.

Ramsey headed up the stairs toward his room, knowing McCafferty, the bartender, was watching his back.

CHAPTER

★ 19 ★

It took some time for Ramsey to explain to Lucy what had transpired, and what he thought about the situation. Lucy got more worried as the minutes passed. By the time Ramsey had finished, she was more frightened than she ever had been.

"I've got us a place over at the Monarch," he concluded. "If you want to come, that is." He looked at her, half in expectation, half in worry.

Lucy sat, trying to think. The fear made that difficult. She began to have doubts about her growing relationship with Matt Ramsey. On one hand, she still loved him; on the other, she was not sure she could live this kind of life, one constantly filled with fear and danger and violence.

She decided after a little while, though, that she would have to go along with him, at least for the time being. She did not see that she had much of a choice. She certainly could not stay here at the Social Club. Ramsey would not hurt her, but the cattlemen very well might send their gunmen to do so. Ramsey would protect her. Of that she was sure.

She also knew that Ramsey was an honorable man. If she should decide at some point that she could not live with him the way he was, he would let her go in freedom. But she was not sure she wanted to leave him anyway. She shrugged, deciding that she would let things work out as they would. With death seemingly coming at every turn these days, one could not be certain of anything. The future would be decided when it got here.

"I'll pack," she said quietly. She took in stride the momentous changes in her life that meeting Matt Ramsey had brought about. She was leaving a profession—if that's what one called it—that she had been involved in for almost a decade. It was not a profession she had taken any particular pride in or wanted to continue. But she had nothing to replace it as of yet. Except for her love of Ramsey. She figured she could live as his wife—if he ever proposed. If not, she had a few dollars put aside. She could go off on her own, seeking a husband elsewhere, or take up her old profession again in another place.

Nor did she worry about leaving the Jacksboro Social Club, where she had been living comfortably for quite some time. The Social Club was a fine place, the food good, the accommodations, even for the girls, first-rate. But the place had bad memories for her, too. The main one being the grotesque figure of Calvin McIlvaine grunting under her—she insisted she must be on top lest she smother under his gross weight—in his ever-so-brief passion.

"You sure you want this?" Ramsey asked. He was asking an awful lot of Lucy.

"Don't you want me?" she asked with a sudden sense of dread.

"Yes, ma'am, I do. But I don't want you to think I'm forcin' you into anything."

"I don't think that."

"Good."

Lucy rang the bell, and Wilkins appeared moments later. "Mr. Ramsey and I'll be leavin' for the Monarch shortly," Lucy said. "Would it be too much of a bother to have some of the boys help us move our things?"

"Not a bother, miss," Wilkins said politely.

"Would it bring you any trouble, Mr. Wilkins?" Ramsey asked. "Or harm?"

"No trouble," Wilkins said blandly.

"Harm?" Ramsey asked sharply, staring at the butler.

Wilkins shrugged. "Who can say," he asked rhetorically.

"You know why we're leavin'?" Ramsey asked.

"Yes, sir." He dropped his cultured act. "And I've got to say, Mr. Ramsey, that I'm all for you in this matter." He cracked a slight smile. "The owners of the club might be a little peeved, shall we say, that I offered even such small help as I can. But they'll not hold it against me much." His smile widened to a full grin. For him, it was an amazing achievement. "After all," he added, the rich tones and English inflections back, "where are they going to get a proper British butler to replace me?"

"Where, indeed," Ramsey said with a laugh. "All right, Wilkins. Get a small cart, if you can. Miss Lucy will be done here soon. As will I, since I have little. But Miss Lucy will have other things in her room. We'll need them all taken to the cart, brought to the Monarch, and carried to our room."

"Not to worry." The butler started for the door.

"And, Wilkins, thanks," Ramsey said quietly.

"It is my pleasure, sir," Wilkins said with great dignity. He sounded like he meant it.

Within an hour, Ramsey and Lucy were unpacking in their new room. As they worked, Ramsey wanted to talk to Lucy, to explain what all this might mean to both of them. But he knew she had already thought of most of it, and since there were no answers, such talk would be useless.

When they finished, they went to a restaurant for supper. Afterward, Ramsey brought Lucy back to their room. "I've got to go out," he said.

She nodded, afraid for him but knowing it was necessary.

"You know how to use a pistol?"

She shrugged. "A little."

"It'll have to do." From his coat pocket, he pulled the Bulldog revolver he had picked up from the floor of Flanagan's store after Blake had dropped it. He handed the snubbish little pistol to Lucy. "I've only got five of the chambers loaded," he said. "With the short barrel, it ain't very accurate at more than a few feet. But in a small room like this, it'll be deadly. Somebody ain't supposed to be here comes in, you blast him with that."

She nodded, worried. She was not sure she would be able to kill a man, but she was a little comforted by having the pistol.

Ramsey kissed her lightly on the lips. "I won't be long," he said.

He wandered through the lowering dusk, strolling up and down the street. Anyone seeing him would have believed him unconcerned about anything. But he was tense. Despite his certainty that he would not be gunned down until after the trial, he kept waiting for a bullet in the back. He hit several saloons, trying to stay as unobtrusive as possible, keeping his ears open.

But he learned little of value, and soon went back to his room. Before entering, he rapped on the door and called out. He would hate like hell to get gunned down by a nervous, Bulldog-wielding Lucy.

The next day, he got the mustang from the livery. Besides Wilkins, Burkhardt was the only Jacksboro resident he knew a little who did not act coldly toward him since he had backed the farmers in Flanagan's store. "You know where the Muldoon place is?" he asked.

Burkhardt looked around as if making sure no one as listening. "Find the stream four miles south of town," he whispered. "Follow it west almost two miles."

Ramsey nodded at Burkhardt in appreciation, knowing the liveryman had put himself in some risk by providing the innocuous information. He trotted away.

Ramsey spent the day riding the countryside. He started at the Muldoon place. He stopped a quarter of a mile away and looked through his telescope at the sod-and-wood shack the Muldoons had called home. He circled around the place, looking for signs. He found the track of the night riders and followed it past two other farms before he lost it in the jumble of prints left by cattle. He searched in ever-widening circles until he picked up the trail again. It led straight to the bunkhouse on Howard Crowell's place.

Ramsey nodded. Rage bloomed in him again, but he knew he must wait. Still, there was some satisfaction in proving that the cattlemen were behind the reign of terror. He turned his horse for Jacksboro, looking over more scattered farms as he did.

Throughout that day, he found signs of more night rider activity: a small pile of shell casings on a ridge a hundred yards from one place; the smoking rubble of a barn at another; several trampled fields; a wrecked windmill.

The black snorted and whinnied, wanting to run. Ramsey finally gave the horse its head, letting the powerful mustang race unfettered across the prairie. Ramsey thought perhaps he could outrun the troubles of late, but knew that was impossible. Within minutes he began enjoying the rhythmic pounding of the black's hooves, the rolling gait of the animal's back, the wind whipping across his face.

But finally he slowed the horse down to a trot and then a walk. He knew it had been dangerous to let the animal out like that, considering the number of chuckholes and other irregularities of the land that posed a threat. But they had been lucky, and the horse had wanted—maybe needed—the run more than the man did.

He rode into town just before dark fell. Burkhardt was not around, so Ramsey unsaddled the black and rubbed him down. Then he forked some hay into the trough in the corner of the stall and set a bucket of grain and one of water down inside the stall.

Soon after, he and Lucy were eating in a restaurant. Then he dropped Lucy off at their room and headed out again. Like the night before, he went from saloon to saloon, listening quietly. It was hard, considering his size and his reputation, to remain unobstrusive. But he managed fairly well. Twice, though, the saloon quieted when he walked in and remained that way while he had a drink. Behind him, as he left, he could hear the saloon erupt into noise again.

Both times that happened, he moved to a window or back door and listened for a while. As he suspected, those two places, like the others he had visited, were full of the talk of the night riders.

A number of farms had been hit by the riders the night before, and the farmers were nervous, worried, and angry. It was unusual for so many farmers to be in town at one time, since most were used to resting and rising early. But at times like these, Jacksboro and its saloons were the easiest places to gather.

Still, most of the farmers left early, worried about their families, and before another hour had passed, Ramsey found the saloons deserted of farmers. He went back to his room, where Lucy greeted him with relief. Ramsey knew the woman was scared to death and that she worried about him. But it could not be helped. He had to do these things.

The next morning, he rode out, heading north. As he entered the land claimed by Crowell, he pulled behind a small thicket. Tying the horse off, he walked around the thicket and sat. Through his telescope, he watched the bunkhouse. There was little activity, as he had suspected. The riders would be asleep after their night's work. Occasionally one of them would use the outhouse behind the bunkhouse and return.

Ramsey wished his brother Buck was here. The eighteen-year-old was the best shot with a rifle Matt had ever seen. To the younger Ramsey, a rifle was a natural extension of himself, much like the Colt was to Matt. If Buck was here, Ramsey thought, they could pop off a couple of the night riders and give them something to think about.

Ramsey brooded about it for much of the morning. Then he shrugged. There was nothing to be gained by doing nothing. He scrabbled down the slight hill, trying to keep the blank back wall of the bunkhouse between him and the main house. He stopped, back pressed against the back wall of the outhouse. And he waited, trying to ignore the stench of the latrine.

Half an hour later, a man entered the outhouse. He did his business, accompanying it with belches and other assorted bodily noises. Ramsey slipped around to the side of the outhouse, on the side where the door would open, shielding him to the last minute.

As the man opened the door of the outhouse and stepped out, Ramsey moved up behind him and stuck the muzzle of the Colt just under the man's ear. "Mornin'," he said politely.

"Howdy." The captured gunman was young, lean, and handsome. He had on a long suit coat that partially obscured the twin Colts he carried. He wore a hat with a high, round crown. He also wore knee-length black boots into which his pants were stuffed. He seemed unafraid, though a little surprised at what had happened.

Ramsey reached around and grabbed the man's two Colts, one at a time, and jammed them into the back of his own pants. Then he grabbed the man's collar with his left hand, and shoved him forward.

"Where're we going?" the captive asked. Still no fear in his voice.

"Have a little chat. Until then, you can keep your mouth shut."

The captive nodded and marched along.

At the thicket, Ramsey had the man lie face down. Ramsey tied his hands behind him and bound his ankles together, and then helped him to sit. "Who's responsible for firin' the Muldoon place the other night?" he asked bluntly.

"I got no idea what you're talking about."

"Farm six or seven miles southwest of Jacksboro. It was set afire couple of nights ago."

The man shrugged. He looked innocent. "Still got no idea of what you're talking about, mister. I'm just a ranch hand for Mr. Crowell."

"Ranch hands don't wear twin Colts with the front sights filed down," Ramsey commented dryly. He paused. "In case you don't know what happened after that Muldoon place was fired, I'll tell you. A woman and her little child were trapped inside. Both died."

Pain clouded the man's eyes a moment, then drifted off. He shrugged. "Still don't know anything."

Ramsey had had about enough of this kind of thing. He lashed out with one of the man's own Colts. There was a satisfying crack as it landed on the man's head. The man groaned and slumped.

CHAPTER

★ 20 ★

The saloon quieted down as soon as Ramsey walked in. Dozens of eyes glared at him. Not a one was friendly, though one or two were a little less hate filled than the others.

It had been a long day, and Ramsey was tired. After capturing the suspected night rider and knocking him out, Ramsey had snuck down to Crowell's corral and appropriated a horse. He tossed the captive over it, mounted the black, and rode away, towing the captured man's mount behind.

He rode steadily for five hours, heading almost due west. He stopped near a thick tangle of brush in a rocky wash. The captive was awake, though he did not appear to be in good spirits. Ramsey grinned nastily at him. He pulled the man down roughly. The man fell and Ramsey let him lie while he loosened the black's saddle.

Then he turned toward the prisoner. "You remember anything now?" he asked politely.

"No, goddamn it."

"That's a pity." Ramsey gathered some sticks and made a small fire. He heated some salted beef in a little water and cooked some coffee. He ate without hurry, not offering any to his prisoner. When he had finished and cleaned up, he asked, "Memory improved any?"

The man only growled.

"It's amazin', ain't it, how some young folks lose their memory these days."

"Piss off, Ram—"

Ramsey glanced sharply at him. So the man did know who he was. That confirmed, to some extent, Ramsey's suspicions that the man was one of the association's hired guns. Ramsey grabbed the man by the jacket and hauled him up. He ducked quickly, got a shoulder in the man's stomach and lifted.

"What the hell're you doin'?" the man asked. There was annoyance but no fear in the man's voice.

Ramsey ignored him. He walked toward the thicket. He waded into it as far as he could without getting torn to shreds and dumped the man unceremoniously. He started walking gingerly out of the thicket.

"What the hell? . . ." the man mumbled. "What're you doin'? Goddamn it. Hey, pard, come on back here and let me loose. Hey, where the hell do you think you're goin'?"

Ramsey swung up onto the mustang and rode away, leaving the man shouting behind him. He rode back to Jacksboro without stopping. After a testy supper with Lucy—who was not thrilled with the time she had been forced to spend alone lately, nor the lack or attention Ramsey had paid her—Ramsey had gone out from saloon to saloon.

Once again he overheard stories of raids on the farmhouses the night before. And, while there was still fear in many of the voices, there was a growing determination, too.

Ramsey spotted Sheriff Laybe, and nodded gruffly. Laybe crossed the street and stopped next to him. "Things're gettin' worse, Matt," Laybe said.

"Tell me somethin' I don't know."

"The sodbusters're gettin' restless, Matt. I expect they're gonna cause some trouble soon."

"Do you blame 'em for gettin' itchy?" Ramsey demanded.

"Reckon not," Laybe sighed. He was caught in the middle and didn't like it. No matter what he did, he would be an outcast with half the people in Jack County. He wanted to help the farmers, at least some. But they did not trust him, and would not allow it even if he offered. And if he did offer, it would mean neither side would put their faith in him.

"You learn anything, Matt?" Laybe asked.

"Not a hell of a lot. I thought I overheard that the farmers were plannin' a meetin' or something." He shrugged. It had been a rumor, a mere whisper. He didn't know how much credit he could give it.

Laybe looked around, making sure no one else was within earshot. "They're plannin' to meet in Plager's," he said. He snorted in derision. "They figure to band together or something and fight back."

"I wouldn't be makin' fun of them, R. J." Ramsey said softly into the chilly night. "They might be farmers, but at least some of them fought in the war. They live with death and hardship every goddamn day. They might not be such easy pickin's as you and the others think."

Laybe nodded. "Reckon you're right." He knew it would mean nothing but trouble for him, whether the farmers were bloodthirsty or not.

"When're they supposed to meet?" Ramsey asked.

"Now. I suppose they're just waitin' for everyone to show up. Damn fools."

"They might be damn fools," Ramsey allowed, staring up the gas light-brightened street, "but they're brave damn fools."

"Brave?" Laybe asked with a rough, scornful laugh. "You gone *loco,* Ramsey?"

"What else would you call a bunch of folks who've been under attack for a week by professional hired gunmen and who leave their farms unprotected to gather and plan a way to fight back?" Ramsey asked as he spun on his heel and stalked off.

Laybe stood and watched for a moment. He hated it when someone challenged his preconceived notions, and started him to thinking differently.

Ramsey drifted down toward Plager's Saloon. He didn't want to get there too early and have to avoid still-arriving farmers. But he didn't want to miss anything, either. He wasn't sure what he would do when he found the meeting. He just decided to see what happened.

He waited across the street from the saloon, in the shadows, until he was fairly certain no one else would be arriving. He stepped off the sidewalk and moved swiftly across the street. He stood just to the side of the batwing doors, where he could see inside a little and hear all that was going on. He was glad he had on his new coat, considering the coolness of the night air.

Ramsey listened for quite a while, as the farmers argued and shouted and made accusations. It was a typical meeting of any group that was fired up but had little vision. Ramsey grew bored, listening. He was tired, but that did not diminish his alertness any.

Ike Coughlan seemed to be trying to keep some order to the meeting, but he was having little success. Finally he bellowed at the top of his lungs. The voice, rising up from the immensely deep chest, boomed out, rolling over all the other voices. Silence came at last.

"We met tonight to come together to fight these night riders—and the cattlemen who hired them. We didn't come here to fight amongst oursel's. But that's what we been doin'. Now, let's see what our options is. Somebody come up with an idea."

"What about Sheriff Laybe?" one man asked.

"What's that walkin' pile of hog shit gonna do?" Coughlan roared. "He's bought and paid for by the Jack County Cattlemen's Association." Hate and scorn gave the words an ugly note. "He ain't gonna do a damned thing for us."

"The governor?" someone else offered.

"That idiot?" Coughlan scoffed. "Did any of you boys vote for him?" He got no answer. "Hell, no. 'Cause he's another one's been paid for by the rich cattlemen. You think he's gonna take our side against a bunch of fat-ass, money-spendin' cattlemen?" he asked rhetorically. "Good Lord, no."

The argument and debate rose again, with men shouting and almost coming to blows. This time, Coughlan let it go on for some time before he roared for silence again. When he had everyone's attention, he said, "This ain't gettin' us nowhere. I . . ."

"What about you?" Liam Muldoon demanded. "You got any ideas? All you're doin' is sittin' on your fat ass yellin' at folks and tellin' 'em how foolish their ideas are."

"And what about you?" Coughlan asked harshly. "You lost more'n any one of us so far. You got somethin' constructive to say to us, or are you just gonna keep pulin' about how hard life's been of late? What do you want to do?"

Muldoon's green eyes flashed in anger and it took some minutes before he could speak past the rage that choked him. "Why . . . you . . . goddamn . . . son . . . of . . . a . . . bitch," he gasped. "You know what I want to do with them. Kill 'em. Kill all of 'em. Rip 'em to pieces with my hands. Shoot 'em." He was frantic with his rage and quickly becoming incoherent.

With a mighty effort, he brought himself under control. He regretted his outburst, but he would not apologize. More calmly, he said, "I'd like to kill all those bastards. That's what I'd like to do."

"And how would we accomplish that?" Coughlan asked. There was no sarcasm in the voice.

"Fight back," another man said. "Fight back however we kin."

"We ain't no match fer them gunmen what the cattlemen hired," Coughlan warned. He looked out over the sea of angry faces. " 'Course we could form us our own little militia."

That seemed to meet with approval, as agreeing nods were seen around the saloon.

" 'Course, that means we'd be spendin' a heap of time away from our homes and families, leavin' 'em open to attack."

"That won't work," Uriah Wiggins offered in his squeaky voice.

A stunned, embarrassed silence fell over the small crowd. Then Barney McAuliffe stood and snapped his fingers. "Wait a minute," he muttered.

"Speak up!" someone in back shouted.

"I've got it!" McAuliffe said, nodding. The men waited expectantly. "We fight fire with fire."

Coughlan nodded, understanding right off.

Outside, Ramsey grinned. "Smart," he muttered under his breath.

"What?" Wiggins asked. "What's that mean? Huh? What?"

"We use the same basic tactics as them," McAuliffe said. He spoke slowly, as if he was still formulating the plan in his mind even as he spoke. "The cattlemen have hired gunmen. We should hire some guns, too. They're usin' night riders. Why can't we use some?"

The men sat in stunned silence for a few moments. And then every man there seemed to burst into speech at the same time. Though Ramsey could not pick out individual comments, the gist he got was that everyone agreed. The men finally began to settle down, and Coughlan stood.

"We're agreed? We hire our own gunmen to fight back against the cattlemen?" he asked.

A chorus of assent arose. Then a weak voice asked, "How will we pay for this? Hired guns aren't cheap."

That put a quick stop to the joy that had been building in the saloon.

"We all put in ten dollars," Coughlan said. "That ought to get us more than enough men."

"I can't afford no ten dollars," Wiggins whined.

Several others announced that they could not, either.

"Five dollars, then," Coughlan said. "That should still be enough."

"I can't afford no goddamn five dollars, neither," Wiggins snapped.

"Then what in hell do you suggest, 'Riah?" Coughlan demanded. "You want us to just bend over and offer ourselves up to those bastards? You want we should pull up stakes, turn tail, and go runnin' away?"

"No!" Muldoon roared. He jumped up. His face was flushed with anger. "I ain't runnin'!" He reached deep into his overalls and produced a battered cloth pouch. He plucked a gold coin out of the sack. "There's my ten," he announced. "Anyone can't afford ten can put in five. Or one. It don't matter, as long as you put somethin' in. Who's with me?"

Men pushed and shoved to get to the table where Coughlan and Muldoon sat and put down their money. Even Wiggins offered up five silver dollars.

"Now, let's open the bar," McAuliffe shouted, bringing forth a roar of approbation.

"No!" Coughlan shouted. With everyone looking at him in surprise, he said, "We still have one little problem."

Everyone looked at him blankly.

"Any one of you boys ever hired gunmen?" he asked.

The stunned crowd sat silently, most of the men with mouths agape.

Ramsey took a deep breath and pushed through the doors. He started walking toward the table where Coughlan looked out over his men.

"What do you want here, Ramsey?" one man growled. His voice seemed to reflect the general feeling of the group. The men's euphoria had gone, replaced by a creeping gloom.

"I come to help you boys out," Ramsey said coolly.

"We don't need your help, Ramsey," McAuliffe snapped.

"Let him talk, Barney," Coughlan said. He still did not know how he felt about Matt Ramsey, but he figured he owed the big, dark-haired gunslinger the benefit of the doubt for now. "Go on and speak your piece, Mr. Ramsey."

Ramsey nodded and stepped up to the table. He turned and faced the small crowd. He looked out over the faces. Most were filled with hate, though a few were interested, and even one or two somewhat sympathetic. "Maybe you boys don't want to hear this," he said evenly, "but I'd like to throw in with you. I reckon I could be of some service to you in such a matter as this."

CHAPTER

★ 21 ★

The crowd erupted in anger, and Ramsey calmly stood there while the rabid babbling raced around the room. When it rumbled to a halt, he said, harshly, "You boys're gettin' in over your heads here. You're facin' men who kill and pillage and plunder for a livin'."

"That's why we want to hire our own guns, Mr. Ramsey," Muldoon said tersely.

"And like Ike said a few minutes ago, there ain't a one of you ever done this before. First off, you're gonna have to send somebody to some big city. Someplace like El Paso or San Antone or Denver. Maybe even to Cheyenne. You'll have to trust that man not only to carry the cash with him but also to use it wisely. Then when he gets to wherever it is he's goin', he's got to figure out where to hire men—and be able to judge those men as competent guns, not just some snot-faced punk who likes to think he can handle Mr. Colt's revolver. Or did y'all think you could just walk up to any old damn fool wearin' a gun in some goddamn saloon somewhere and just hire him to come save your asses?"

He glared at the farmers, who looked none too happy. "And another thing, it'll take weeks for you to be able to find some hired guns and get 'em here. You boys can't afford that kind of time. You need men, and you need 'em soon.

"Besides, with what I saw collected here, you ain't gonna get but one or two. They had better be good, or they'll be dead in a real goddamn hurry. Or," Ramsey added viciously, "they'll get down here and the Cattlemen's Association will offer three times the money you did, and they'll go over to the other side. Most of those kind of men have no conscience."

"And you do?" someone asked bitterly.

130

"More than most others you'll find who make their livin' with a gun," Ramsey said honestly.

"What makes you think we'd ever trust you, Ramsey?" McAuliffe asked harshly. "You're workin' for the ranchers."

"I *was* workin' for the cattlemen. I ain't no more."

"You expect us to believe that?" Finn asked.

Ramsey shrugged. "I don't much give a hoot one way or the other. It's the truth. I turned down their offer to hire me to run you folks out of Jack County a few days ago."

"Was that just before our trouble started?" Coughlan asked from behind him.

"Yep," Ramsey responded without looking back.

"Why'd you turn 'em down?" Coughlan asked. He was beginning to warm to Ramsey again. But he still was not sure.

Ramsey looked at the faces arrayed before him, seeing in them many of the qualities—and faults—he had seen in the people he had grown up with. They were not handsome men, by and large, not with their weathered faces, scraggly beards, cracked hands, and dirty, torn clothes. But there was a determination in those faces that defied the gods to do their worst by them and they would still manage to somehow come out on top.

"My folks moved to Fannin County years ago, when the Comanches and Wichitas still held sway over the area," Ramsey said quietly. "They fought Indians, the weather, wild animals. They saw it all. Drought, floods, plagues of insects, carpetbaggers." He grinned ever so slightly at the last.

"But they built up their farm, kept it, made it fruitful. And they raised up a passel of good, strong children." He took a deep breath. "When the cattlemen asked me to run you folks out, I told them I wouldn't do it, and why. I thought that would be the end of it."

The silence in the room was almost palpable. Only one man's wheezy breathing and another frequent, choppy cough disturbed the quiet as the men waited expectantly for Ramsey to continue.

"Then I overheard Ike and some of the others talkin' over at Flanagan's place. I wasn't gonna stick my nose into their business, figuring you-all could handle things eventually. Until I heard of Mr. Muldoon's loss." Anger colored Ramsey's face. "I ain't fond of any men who kill women and children. At that point, I felt an urge to offer my services." He stopped and waited.

The men talked in agitation. From behind him, Coughlan said quietly, "Nice speech, Mr. Ramsey."

Ramsey was not sure, but he was fairly certain there had been no sarcasm in the statement. "Thanks." He turned and looked at Coughlan. "It was the truth. Just like I told you the truth the other day when I said I had nothin' to do with the raids on your farms. Whether you believe me or not . . ." He raised his hands.

"Why should we believe you?" Muldoon asked. "What makes you different from all the rest?"

Ramsey smiled. He knew he could never really explain that he was a rarity in the gun-for-hire business; that he was a man with a conscience and some sense of responsibility. But he had to try. "My folks were a prideful people. They passed that trait along to all their children. Me and my brothers don't take lightly insults to ourselves, our kin, or our friends. We don't believe in double-crossin' and backshootin'. Somebody hires me for a job, he best tell me the truth of it, or I'll turn against him."

"We are none of those things."

"True," Ramsey admitted. He rubbed a hand across his big jaw. "Like I said—or tried to say—my folks were just like all of you. Good, honest folk breakin' their backs to make a life from the land and God's bounty. That makes you sort of kin, or at least friends, even if I don't know you personal."

"I believe him, Liam," Coughlan said. "I seen him in Flanagan's. There was no call whatever for him to do that. He had nothin' to gain by it, and plenty to lose. But even if he had some secret reason for it, I saw the truth in his eyes then."

Muldoon shrugged. He was still grieving too much to think of such things.

Coughlan looked up at Ramsey and half smiled. "Trouble is, Mr. Ramsey, I don't think you'll ever be able to convince them." He jerked his chin toward the still-chattering group of men.

"I suspect you're right, Mr. Coughlan."

It came as no real surprise to Ramsey when the consensus went against hiring him. Too many men feared that his conversion was just an act to get them to let down their vigil. Coughlan shrugged in helplessness. Ramsey nodded at him and left.

But Ramsey was grim when he rode out the next morning. He suspected the night riders had been active. He was fairly certain that someone in town would have gotten word to the riders that virtually every dirt farmer in the county was in Jacksboro for their meeting.

Ramsey had planned to ride straight out to his prisoner, but as he saddled the black that morning, he changed his mind. Instead, he rode in a small circuit, checking some of the nearer farms. Several showed heavy signs of night rider activity. "Damn it all," he muttered. He kicked the horse into a lope.

When Ramsey dragged the young night rider out of the thicket by the rope around his ankles, he saw the man was in fair shape. Ramsey suspected the man's anger had kept him going. The man had soiled himself at least once and probably twice. His tongue was thick from dehydration and he was still shivering.

"A night out in the open jog your memory any?" Ramsey asked. He had wanted to make it a conversational tone, but it came out with all the anger that bubbled around in his insides.

"Water?" the man croaked, voice cracking with dryness.

Ramsey nodded and brought the canteen over. He held it to the man's lips. The man gulped greedily, though water splashed over his shirt. Finally Ramsey pulled the canteen away.

"You remember anything?"

"No, goddamn it." The man's voice was firmer.

Ramsey shrugged. He gathered sticks and cow chips and built a small, pungent fire. He placed a coffeepot in the snapping flames and then started frying a nice steak in a fry pan. The night rider looked longingly at the meat, and licked his lips. When the steak was cooked, Ramsey sat cross-legged and tore into the meat. The man watched with hunger widening his eyes.

Ramsey polished off the entire steak and the whole pot of coffee. He sat back against his saddle, feeling bloated. He lit a cheroot and picked his teeth with the back end of the match. "What's your name, boy?" he asked.

"None of your goddamn business," the man snapped.

Ramsey nodded. "Funny name, but who'm I to judge. Well, Mr. Goddamn Business, your memory gotten any better?"

"No. And my name ain't goddamn business. It's . . ." He clamped his mouth shut.

"Suit yourself, None. But it's a pity you still can't remember simple things." He shook his head in mock sadness. "Well," he said in resignation, "maybe another night out here in the fresh air will help you some."

The night rider knew with sudden dread that Ramsey would leave him out here another night, another week, if need be. Ramsey would, he knew, let him lie out here till he died of exposure or starvation or snakebite. Sonny Weeks wasn't afraid of dying, but he had always pictured himself going out fighting, his twin Colts blasting. Besides, he told himself, telling Ramsey what he wanted to know wouldn't mean anything. Ramsey would never be able to take all the cattlemen's hired gunmen anyway.

He licked his lips. "My name's Sonny Weeks. The men you want are . . . well, there was a bunch of 'em. We've been going out in a few groups—maybe eight, ten in each."

"Who was in charge of the group that fired the Muldoon place?" The words were sharp, biting.

"Newell Preston and Rusty Thompson."

"Now, that wasn't so hard, was it?" Ramsey asked flatly. He stood and pulled the big bowie knife from his boot. He quickly severed the ropes binding Weeks, who winced as blood began flowing back into his limbs.

Ramsey tossed the saddle blanket on the black and then the saddle. He paid Weeks no heed. It would be at least an hour before Weeks could even stand, he figured. Ramsey loaded his supplies into his saddlebags and pulled himself onto the horse. "Good day, Mr. Weeks," he said.

"Hey, where in hell's my gear? The horse and pistols?"

"The horse is enjoyin' his freedom somewhere out here on the prairie—if someone else ain't captured him. As for the pistols, well, I reckon you won't have need of them for a spell."

"You expect me to walk back to? . . ." He was incredulous.

"Unless you sprout wings and fly like a bird. *Adios*." Ramsey swung the black around and raced off, ignoring Weeks's bellowing as it grew dimmer behind him.

Ramsey spent the afternoon in the company of Lucy Tillman. He knew he had been neglecting her lately, and he felt badly about that. But it couldn't be helped. Still, he had nothing pressing this afternoon, and decided the best way to pass the time was with Lucy.

For her part, Lucy had been near about ready to throw Ramsey's things out into the hallway. It wasn't that she really didn't want him anymore, but she was not used to being left alone. She understood the necessity of Ramsey being away so much, but understanding did not mean she had to like it. This afternoon, spent idling away the hours with Ramsey, brightened her outlook quite a bit. She was not certain she would want to spend the rest of her life with this man. Still, he was better than anything else she had ever come across. She decided to keep her options open for the time being.

She bit back her disappointment when, just after their supper, Ramsey left again. She wanted to scold him, to order him to stay here, maybe give him an ultimatum—stay here or leave forever.

But she could not. If she told him she had a premonition that he would be hurt or killed, he would laugh at her. If she told him of her disappointment, he would tell her that he had a job of honor to perform, and there would be no standing in his way. Though she had only known Matt Ramsey a short time, she knew enough about him to be sure of his reaction—and his reasons. So she kept quiet, sitting in their room. She paced or wrung her hands. A few times she cried. And she often glanced out the window, hoping to see his big, reassuring figure heading back.

Ramsey walked rapidly down the street. He passed from one circle of yellow light cast by the streetlamps to another. He sidled up to the front door of Plager's Saloon and listened in for a while. There were not nearly as many men in there this night as there had been last night, but the stories told of more violence by the night riders. And the severity of the violence seemed to be growing.

From what Ramsey could hear, two farmers had been shot and wounded last night. Two houses were burned down, as was a barn. Several fields had been trampled, and an as yet uncounted amount of stock had been slaughtered.

Ramsey listened to it with a sinking feeling. It would, he knew, only continue to get worse. Unless he did something to stem the tide of the escalating violence.

Finally, he had heard enough. He wasn't learning anything of value. All he was doing was getting steamed up, and that could easily bring him trouble. He knew that from long experience. He shoved away from the saloon wall on which he had been leaning and walked slowly up the street.

As he was passing an alleyway, Ramsey heard a muffled thump. Without thinking, he pulled his Colt, turned into the pitch-dark alley, and trotted down it. As he passed the ends of the two buildings that formed the alley, someone hit him from behind. He fell and rolled. His pistol went flying off into the darkness.

CHAPTER

⋆ 22 ⋆

Ramsey came to his feet just in time to catch a fist full on the nose. As he stumbled backward, he thought he saw seven dark figures moving toward him menacingly. He grabbed the bowie from his boot top.

Before he could bring the knife into play, though, all seven men jumped toward him. One kicked him in the stomach, knocking the wind out of him. Ramsey had the brief thought that he was lucky, since the man had been aiming the boot at his groin.

Another kicked the hand with the knife in it, and that, too, went sailing into the night. A fist hit him in the forehead, and he grunted at the sudden pain. He found it hard to breathe.

But there was no way he would quit without a fight. He kicked out himself, pleased when his boot cracked on a bone. He punched and bit, kicked and swore. He didn't know how he did it, but he managed to get to his feet at one point and head-butt one of his attackers. That man stumbled away into the shadows and plopped down on his behind.

Ramsey wished he was more like Buck, or better yet, Luke right now. Either of those brothers was far better in a scrap like this. Matt was big, strong, and fearless, but he did not seem to have his two brothers' natural knack for this kind of thing.

Still, he tried to give as good as he got, and was satisfied that he had taken out three of his attackers, at least temporarily.

But the thumping he was receiving began to tell on him. A pistol barrel cracked against his head, and he went down. Looking up, the stars swirled rapidly in front of his eyes, and his ears were ringing. Three ghostly faces suddenly loomed over him. Ramsey gazed at the pale blobs with interest. He thought he recognized one.

"How's it feel now that the boot's on the other foot, Ramsey?" one asked.

It took a moment, but Ramsey finally realized Sonny Weeks had been the one who spoke. "Made it back all right, did you?" Ramsey asked, words garbled by his swollen lips, the blood in his mouth, and his dizziness.

"No thanks to you, you son of a bitch," Weeks snarled.

Ramsey blinked several times, trying to fight off unconsciousness.

"Well, you expressed some interest in a couple of the boys. These two fellahs are Rusty Thompson and Newell Preston."

"Don't come after me, Ramsey," the one identified as Preston said sharply. "I'll fry your ass good, you come for me or any of the others. Now, was it left up to me, I'd kill you here and now. But the cattlemen think you did some good work for them recently. That and they want you to testify at the trial of those goddamn rustlers." The blob of a head shook. "Goddamn fool. Should have just left them rustlers out there for the coyotes and buzzards. Would've saved everybody considerable time and trouble." He paused. "Anyway, the association just wanted us to warn you to keep your nose out of their affairs, except for testifyin' at the trial, of course."

Then the three faces were gone. Ramsey began to sigh in relief, when suddenly his head exploded as a boot slammed into his temple. "That's for leavin' me out there to shit my pants in a thicket, Ramsey," Weeks snarled.

Finally the attackers left. Ramsey lay there, letting the sharp pains ebb down to a manageable level. Unconsciousness threatened, and he was sure he blacked out a couple of times, but only for a few moments. He heard some people come, and he sucked in breath, trying to raise a little strength.

Strong hands grabbed him and started tugging at him. "Damn it," he muttered. He lashed out weakly with a fist. It had no effect on the burly man who held him. He passed out.

He awoke in his bed at the hotel. Every part of him hurt, but his head was the worst. It throbbed and pounded. His eyes were swollen almost shut, but he could see Lucy on one side of him and the physician on the other. "How am I, Doc?" he asked, voice a whisper. Even that hurt.

"You'll live." Doc Quigley was not one for long-winded speeches. "No broken bones. No vital organs hurt. You're lucky, Mr. Ramsey."

"Don't feel that way."

"I'll leave some medicines with Miss Lucy, and instructions for administering them. You'll be in plenty of pain a couple days. If it worsens, send for me." He left.

"How'd I get here, Luce?" Ramsey asked, voice fading.

She waved a hand. A shadowy figure stepped forward. "Me and Barney saw what happened, Mr. Ramsey. We was afraid to help. . . ." Ike Coughlan was ashamed of himself for the fear. "But after those hooligans left, we come got you and brought you here."

"Thanks, Ike," Ramsey whispered.

"It was the least we could do."

"Let him be now, you two," Lucy said, shooing Coughlan and McAuliffe out of the room.

In a few days, Ramsey was mostly recovered. His face was still a colorful thing to see, splotched with yellow and purple and bluish black. But he didn't feel too badly.

"What day is it, Luce?" he asked as he stood in front of the window.

"Monday, I think. Why?"

"Trial's tomorrow."

"So?"

"R. J. said he and his deputies were going to escort me out of the county as soon as the trial's over. I hadn't thought much on it before, since I was planning to leave anyway. But now . . ." He trailed off. He'd be damned if he'd be run out of anyplace.

"What're you gonna do about it?" Lucy asked, frightened. She was frightened almost all the time now. For him, for herself, for the farmers. All this bloodshed and violence spooked her.

"Talk to R. J. See if he'll listen to reason."

"Wouldn't it just be better to leave the county? Put all this behind us—you?"

"Too late for that now, Luce." Ramsey pulled on his shirt and buttoned it all the way up to the neck. He tucked it in his pants and then pulled on his boots. He slid the bowie knife into the sheath at the top of his boot. Then he strapped on his Colt. He didn't know it, but R.J. Laybe had found the weapons the morning after the attack and brought them to the room.

Ramsey didn't have to go far to find the sheriff. Laybe was waiting outside the Monarch. "Mornin', Sheriff," Ramsey said without enthusiasm.

"Mornin', Matt. How're you feelin'?"

"Right as rain." He paused, but there was no sense putting this off. "Trial's tomorrow." Laybe nodded acknowledgement. "I remember your warnin'." Laybe nodded again. "But I'm warnin' you now, R.J., that you better keep out of my way tomorrow, the next day, and every day until I finish my business here."

"Can't do that, Matt."

"Then you—and however many deputies you got—will be worm fodder."

Laybe stared into Ramsey's dark, hard eyes, and he saw no wavering of determination there. He almost shuddered. He would either have to let Ramsey have his way, or try to kill him. And he wasn't sure whether he and all his deputies combined could kill Matt Ramsey. He nodded slowly. "I still can't help you, though, Matt." It sounded feeble, and Laybe cursed himself.

"Just keep out of my way, is all I ask." He turned and walked away, heading for the restaurant. He began to feel better. The rage and thirst for revenge made his blood soar.

The courthouse was packed, and excitement buzzed through the air. With the prospect of six hangings so near to hand, the people were excited. Ramsey sat in the first row of seats, his new hat resting on his knee. He stared straight ahead, even when the six members of the Jack County Cattlemen's Association showed up and pompously took their seats in the first row on the other side of the center aisle from Ramsey.

Judge Charles Baldwin rapped the session into silence. "Let's get on with it," he ordered. This was another cut-and-dried case, he figured, and could see no reason for stalling. He checked the papers in front of him. "The six rustl . . . defendants here?" he asked. He peered over his half glasses at the crowd.

"They are, Judge," Laybe said. With a wave of his hand, he indicated the six manacled men sitting on a bench at one side of the courtroom, opposite the jury.

"Call your witnesses, then."

"Ain't got but one, Judge," Laybe said. "Matt Ramsey, come and be sworn in."

Ramsey walked up, still limping a bit. He swore on the Bible and then took a seat alongside the judge's bench.

"Tell us what happened, Mr. Ramsey," Laybe said confidently.

"Well, I was walkin' down the street and these seven mangy bast . . . fellers jumped me. I . . ."

Laybe looked apoplectic. "The rustlers, Matt," he muttered. "For God's sake. Tell us about the rustlers." He glanced meekly at the judge. "He was attacked and thumped on pretty good, Judge. Only a couple days ago." He hoped it would suffice as an excuse.

"Oh, the rustlers," Ramsey said. He stared at the cattlemen, who fidgeted under his hard gaze, even though several of the hired guns were there. "Sure. The Cattlemen's Association hired me to get rid of the rustlers in Jack County. I did that."

"What about these men?" Laybe asked, exasperated. He pointed at the six defendants.

"Never saw 'em," Ramsey said slowly. He kept his eyes locked on McIlvaine's.

Judge Baldwin almost swallowed his cud of tobacco. The rest of the court was stunned into silence. Lucy giggled softly.

"You mean to say, son, that you never saw any of them six before?"

"That's right, Judge."

"Then how'd they get here?"

"Beats the hell out of me."

Rodney Meers—the young lawyer who had reluctantly agreed to serve as the defense attorney—stood and in a soft, frightened voice said, "I move that we dismiss the case, Judge."

"You got any other witnesses, Sheriff?" Baldwin asked.

"No, sir." Laybe gulped. He was in deep trouble now, he thought.

"Then I got no choice. The case against all these men is dismissed." He looked over at the six incredulous rustlers. "I don't know why this happened, but I'd suggest that you boys move your tails a long way from Jack County, Texas. Soon. I'd further suggest you find a new—honest—way to make a living." He slammed the gavel down.

Ramsey still sat in the witness chair. He grinned tightly at each of the cattlemen. Then he looked into the hard, unforgiving eyes of Newell Preston. He made a gun of his fingers and "shot" Preston. Then, for the first time, he looked at the rustlers.

The six were having their shackles removed. All still looked dumbfounded. Grover Haynes grinned shyly at Ramsey, who nodded in return.

As Ramsey walked toward the door, he stopped in front of Preston. He stared at the gunman. Preston was as tall as Ramsey, but considerably less bulky. He had cold, flat eyes and a severely receding hairline. "Get your ass out of Jack County, Preston," Ramsey said tightly. "Today."

"Reckon not, Ramsey."

Ramsey shrugged. "It's your funeral." He walked out, arm in arm with Lucy.

That night, Ike Coughlan, Liam Muldoon, Hal Finn, and Ernie Hardesty visited Ramsey in his hotel room. Coughlan held his hat in his hand. "What we got to talk about is business, Mr. Ramsey," he said shyly. He glanced at Lucy.

Ramsey nodded. He looked at the woman, who nodded. She knew he would have to leave again. The men went to Plager's Saloon. When they had been seated and had drinks in front of them, Coughlan said, "We can't speak for all the farmers, Mr. Ramsey. But there's some of us think we owe you something, and feel bad for havin' treated you so poor in the past."

"It was understandable, Ike."

Coughlan shrugged and poured half his mug of beer down his throat. "Perhaps. Or not. But we'd like to help you. Or maybe we'd like you to help us. Whatever, we figure you'd like to get them that attacked you. We'd like to get rid of the night riders." He looked down, embarrassed. "Trouble is, ain't many of us good with a gun. We couldn't stand up to them face to face."

"What do you suggest, then?" Ramsey asked. He was still in a lot of pain. But he felt somewhat better since his performance this morning in court. He had come up with the idea the day before. What better way to get back at the cattlemen? he had figured.

"I ain't sure, exactly. But was you to consider bushwackin' those murderous bastards, we'd help you. A couple of us are good enough shots with a rifle. We wouldn't be no good against them in a pistol fight, but an ambush . . ."

"Where and when?" Ramsey asked, draining his own glass of beer. Another appeared before him, and he nodded thanks. "Those boys raid all over the place. They ain't gonna be easy to pin down. Besides, one of 'em told me, they usually go out in several groups."

"I don't know," Coughlan said, crestfallen.

Ramsey's mind was already working over the problem. He had a couple thoughts on solving it, none of them a certainty. "We'll think of somethin'."

"You'll help us?" Muldoon asked, a feverish glint in his eyes.

"Yep. Just be ready when I need you."

"We will be," Coughlan said.

The men clinked their glasses together in a salute that sealed their pact.

CHAPTER

⋆ 23 ⋆

Ramsey lay on a grassy ridge fifty yards from Ike Coughlan's farmhouse. The night was cold but clear, and a nearly full moon spread a considerable amount of grayish light over the landscape. Coughlan and Hal Finn lay to his right; Liam Muldoon and Ernie Hardesty to his left. Each of the five men had a rifle and a box of cartridges within easy reach.

It was three nights after they had made their pact. The day after, Ramsey had wrestled with the problem without coming to any solution. But the next day, he had an idea. He slept through most of the day, and in the late afternoon he rode for the Crowell ranch. He was waiting at the thicket when, two hours after dark, the night riders saddled up and rode out. Ramsey followed along as close as he dared. Several miles out, the men broke into smaller groups. He had spotted Preston, Weeks, and Rusty Thompson, and so he tagged along with that group.

Several times he got so close that he was almost a part of the group. He was dressed in dark clothing and had covered his face with dirt. Sitting on the black horse, he was almost a shadow. He managed, through some daring, to abort both raids on farms the group tried to make that night. With the first, he had stayed behind them a little. Just before they were to make their attack, Ramsey began firing his Winchester as fast as he could. He wasn't intending to hit anyone—though he did wing two. He mainly wanted them to think they were under siege by a posse. They raced off, Ramsey following along.

The next time, Ramsey figured out early on what farm they would hit. He raced ahead, rousing up the farmer. Within minutes, they had thrown up a hasty barricade of barbed wire around the man's garden patch. Ramsey hoped it would be enough.

The riders charged, unawares, and their horses ran right into the rolls and crudely stretched sections of barbed wire. The horses pulled up, squealing in pain. Ramsey, watching from the prairie a short distance off, winced. He hated to see horses treated in such a way. But, he figured, better that than a couple dead farmers.

Swearing, Preston had turned his men back for the Crowell ranch. Ramsey fell in behind. He caught snatches of conversation. Risking discovery, he rode as close as he dared to hear even more.

"Hey, it was just bad luck tonight," Rusty Thompson said. "Tomorrow'll be back to the same ol' shit." Thompson, Preston, and Weeks were plodding along near the back of the group. Their voices were notched with anger.

"I reckon," Preston growled.

"You figured out where we're gonna hit tomorrow?" Thompson asked.

Ramsey held his breath in anticipation.

"I figure it's about time we put that ringleader of theirs out of business for good," Preston snarled. "That Ike character. We'll start there tomorrow and take our time. We'll hit that dumb bastard hard. So hard he'll be out of Jack County with his tail between his legs before dawn." He laughed roughly.

Ramsey sighed in relief and stopped his horse, letting the others drift off. He realized they might have suspected someone was there, but he doubted it. They had talked too naturally. And he had been far enough away not to be spotted. He was just thankful that the wind was blowing toward him and that voices carried well on the prairie at night.

After several hours sleep, Ramsey rode out to Coughlan's farm. They made some plans and Ramsey rode back to town. He went to Flanagan's. The store owner and his clerk almost choked when he walked in.

"Get out," Flanagan hissed.

"I need a rifle," Ramsey said pleasantly.

"I said get out."

"Look, Flanagan," Ramsey said reasonably with but a hard underpinning to the words, "it's a fine, beautiful day out. Nice and cool, a fresh breeze. Don't go and ruin it by bein' such an ass." He didn't think he needed to make a threat.

"What do you want, then?" Flanagan asked.

"First thing I want is for your clerk there to stand still and keep his hands on the counter. And I want you to stay where I can see you at all times."

Flanagan backed toward the counter. Ramsey ended up buying a .44- caliber Ballard single-shot rifle with a thirty-inch octagonal barrel. Ramsey was not the best rifle shot going, and he was well aware of it. He thought a well-made single-shot rifle might give him a little more accuracy than the repeating Winchester.

He got several hours more sleep, and then ate supper with Lucy. Afterward, he went to Burkhardt's and rented a good-size farm wagon and big draft horse to pull it. He tied the saddled black behind the wagon and rode out to the Coughlan place. The four farmers were waiting. They were nervous, but determined. So they waited on the ridge.

Ramsey was beginning to think the night riders would never show up, that he had been somehow duped, when he heard horses. "They're comin'," he said. "Get ready."

Eighteen riders hove into view, wavering in the oddly gleaming silver moonlight. "Shit," Ramsey muttered. "They've all stuck together tonight."

"So?" Muldoon asked.

"Ain't gonna be easy to get all of 'em."

"We'll take what we can get," Muldoon said harshly. He hoped that the others would be scared enough to leave Jack County then.

The riders closed in. "Just hold your fire, boys," Ramsey said softly. "Wait. Wait." He brought the rifle to his shoulder. He had hoped to get Preston with his first shot, but the canny man was in the middle of the pack. Ramsey shrugged and set his sights on Sonny Weeks. " 'Bye, Sonny," he whispered when the riders were less than a hundred yards off. He fired. Weeks fell off his horse.

The farmers opened fire, and several riders fell. Ramsey had swiftly reloaded and fired, setting a pace. The farmers, once the initial volley was done, were shooting more haphazardly. But it didn't matter much, the night riders were charging off.

Muldoon leaped up and started whooping, dancing a crazy jig of victory on the little ridge. Ramsey stayed put, watching the battlefield, just in case. But he smiled at Muldoon's antics. The man had a reason to celebrate, Ramsey figured.

After waiting ten minutes to make sure the riders were not planning to return, Ramsey led the farmers down off the slight ridge. They checked all the men who had fallen. Seven were down, only one of them alive. Ramsey nodded. He had another idea and discussed it with the farmers.

"You boys did well tonight," Ramsey said as they piled the bodies in the back of the wagon Ramsey had brought. He helped the one wounded man up onto the seat and climbed up after him. "See you boys," he said. As he clucked the horses into motion, Ramsey turned to the pale man beside him and said almost cheerfully, "You pull any shit and you'll be ridin' in the back with your pals there." The man gave him no trouble.

Ramsey stopped in front of Quigley's and helped the wounded man off the wagon. "There's the doc's. You bang on the door enough, you might rouse him. If you can't, you'll have to wait till daylight."

Ramsey drove the wagon down to the undertaker's. He left it there, putting a nose bag on the big workhorse. He untied the black from the back, rode to the livery, left the horse there, and then walked back to the hotel. Lucy was waiting for him, awake and eager.

He felt a sense of satisfaction at the consternation with which Jacksboro went about its business the next day. When Ramsey went outside just after noon, the wagon was no longer in front of the undertaker's. He strolled down to Burkhardt's after eating and saw the wagon and horse. He nodded and left again. Word would be out already that he had been the one to rent the wagon the night before. And word of him renting it again tonight, which he planned to do, would be all over town before he had passed the city limits.

He met Coughlan, Hardesty, Finn, Muldoon, and McAuliffe two miles from the Crowell bunkhouse. He pulled the creaking wagon to a halt and greeted the others. It would be dark in only a few minutes. "You boys ready?" he asked. He was a little surprised to see McAuliffe, but he did not comment on it.

"Yes," they all answered with reserve and a tinge of fear. Ramsey was pleased to hear they were not eager. He did not want to turn these men into cold-blooded killers, or men who liked to kill.

They rode on another mile before stopping again. They staked their horses and walked forward. They took up positions at the thicket on the little hill overlooking the bunkhouse. They had less of a wait this night. An hour later, men began emerging from the bunkhouse and heading for the corral.

"Now?" Muldoon asked in a whisper.

"No," Ramsey answered in kind. "Too risky. Wait'll they're mounted. They'll most likely move out past us this way, up along the creek there. That'll be the time."

"If they don't?" Muldoon asked. He might not be eager to shoot men down, but revenge still burned hotly in his heart.

"Then we'll think of something else. Now shut up."

Within fifteen minutes, the horses were saddled and thirteen men were swinging onto them. They moved out as Ramsey had suspected, along the small, shimmering creek, right in the farmers' line of fire.

Once again Ramsey was frustrated in trying to pick out Preston, or even Thompson as a target. He saw neither man and figured both were acting as bodyguards for one or another of the ranchers. He picked another target. "Have at it, boys," he said softly.

The fusillade shredded the column of night riders. Five fell immediately. As the men on the hill quickly reloaded, the riders fought to control their mounts. Another volley raked the ragged column, and three more men fell.

The five farmers reloaded hurriedly and vollied again in grim-faced determination. There was no enjoyment in this for them, only a necessity, and they did it as well as they could. Ramsey fired again, too. He reloaded once more and then stood. Only two of the night riders were still mounted. The rest were on the ground, dead or wounded.

"You boys best make yourselves scarce in these parts," Ramsey bellowed.

The two night riders managed to regain control of their mounts.

"And don't ever come back," Coughlan added.

The two whipped their horses. They flew around the house and raced off into the night.

"All right, Hal," Ramsey said, "you, Barney, and Liam take the wagon down there and start loadin' the bodies on it. Me, Ernie, and Ike'll stay up here and keep our eyes peeled for any trouble. Just make sure you check all of them boys close beforehand. Might be a couple of 'em playin' possum."

The grim work was done soon enough, and Finn drove the wagon back up the small hill. "Three of 'em's still alive," he reported. "Don't none of 'em look bad."

Ramsey nodded. "You boys did well again. I think this'll end your problems."

"Amen," Muldoon mumbled.

"You gonna be all right by yoursel'?" Coughlan asked. He pointed his rifle at the three wounded men who sat on the back of the wagon.

"I suppose." He knew the three could jump him, but there seemed to be little he could do about it.

"How about if me and Hal ride along with you?" Coughlan asked. "Just in case."

"I'd be obliged."

So they did. And the three wounded men caused no trouble. Like the night before, Ramsey dropped the wounded off at Quigley's. Then he drove the wagon to the undertaker's and parked it.

Jacksboro was abuzz the next day. Ramsey had slept till noon, and then headed out with Lucy to take a meal. He could feel an excitement, an energy about the place. As he and Lucy passed Flanagan's he found out an added reason why. He grinned and pointed to the fluttering piece of paper in the store window. It said simply:

REWARD
$1,000 in gold
for
MATT RAMSEY
DEAD
Bring proof to
the Jack County Cattlemen's Association

Lucy grew pale. This was something she had never even considered. "Oh, Lord," she breathed.

"Don't fret over it," he said lightly. "It's just a desperate act by desperate men."

But Lucy was not appeased. She did not enjoy her meal, and Ramsey brought her back to their room right after it. Her mood had soured his day, and he was annoyed about that. He headed out again, hoping the fresh air, with the nip of autumn carried on the breeze, would revive his spirits.

He went to Plager's Saloon. It was about the only place he felt comfortable anymore. He was sitting at a table sipping a shot of whiskey when Sheriff Laybe entered, spotted him, and joined him.

"I suppose you've seen the signs the cattlemen have put up, Matt," Laybe said.

"Yep. I'm gettin' to be right popular." He grinned.

"Don't joke about it, Matt," Laybe snapped. "The cattlemen are serious."

"You come here to collect that reward money?" Ramsey asked harshly. His right hand dropped down to his side, near the Colt.

"Nope," Laybe said easily. "But Smitty over at the wire office showed me a telegram McIlvaine sent out this morning."

"And?"

"He's sent for four of the toughest gunslicks I ever heard of—Billy Joe Campbell, Bull McKinney, Tom Fisher and Lou Marsh. Preston and Thompson are still around, too. Blaine Yates, who ain't real fond of much of what the other cattlemen do, told me, the six plan to come after you together."

"Reckon I better start loadin' all six chambers in the old Colt," Ramsey said with a sloppy grin.

"Damn it, Matt . . ." Then Laybe shrugged. "It's your ass, Matt." He held the glass up in a salute.

CHAPTER

★ 24 ★

Ike Coughlan was hard at work, but he was not reluctant to stop for a few minutes to talk with Matt Ramsey. Coughlan was grateful for the respite, but he also owed Ramsey a lot.

"You heard any news from town, Ike?" Ramsey asked as the two shared a dipper of water. They were sitting in the shade of the dilapidated portico of the soddy. The cool wind whined around the corner of the house, whipping at their clothes.

"Only that the night riders seem to have disappeared from these parts," Coughlan said with a tight grin. He was not happy about all the bloodshed and killing, but he was proud that he and his friends had accomplished what was needed. "Is there something else I don't know about?"

"You ain't seen the posters the association has put up?"

"Nope. Ain't been into town since . . . since the other night." He was reluctant to mention the last trip, when he had accompanied a wagonload of bodies into Jacksboro. Sudden dread filled him. "Am I a wanted man now?" he asked, mulling the likelihood over in his mind. He was not afraid for himself, but he would hate for his wife and children to be tainted by such a thing.

"Nope," Ramsey said with a small grin. He leaned back, resting against the sod wall of the house. "Ain't nobody but those wounded riders knows you and the others were involved in that excitement the other night. And they ain't talkin' much."

"Why ain't they talkin'?"

"Somebody convinced them of the wisdom of silence," Ramsey said dryly.

"You?" Coughlan asked, not surprised.

Ramsey shrugged. There was not much credit to it. He had

figured the wounded men would concoct a story of how they were innocent and how they had been set upon by a bunch of ruffian sodbusters, angry and on the prowl for some reason only God knew. With feelings running against the farmers anyway, it would be believable. Judge Baldwin, who was still in town and still smarting at having rushed to return to Jacksboro for a trial that had fizzled, would be inclined to issue warrants for the arrest of the farmers.

Ramsey had figured all that, and had made a stop at Doc Quigley's, where the four wounded men were recovering. He had addressed them as a group, out of the doctor's hearing. With little effort, he had managed to impart the knowledge that if they opened their mouths against the farmers, they would not live long enough to see the next sunset. Ramsey had even been persuasive in telling the men that their health would be vastly improved if they were to go someplace else as soon as they were able to travel. One had left that morning.

"I see," Coughlan said. He was relieved. But something tugged at his mind, worrying him. Suddenly he looked at Ramsey sharply, with understanding. "You?" he asked again. "You're the one has a wanted poster out on him, ain't you?"

"Sort of." He grinned at the puzzled look on Coughlan's face. "I ain't wanted by the law. But the association has put out a reward on me. A thousand bucks for my hide. Dead." He stared out over the farm. Coughlan had been lucky in having gotten most of his late-season crops in before the night riders had appeared. He was set for the winter, and the fields were mostly harvested now, awaiting the snow.

"That's trouble, ain't it?" Coughlan asked. He had a sinking feeling. Ramsey was in trouble because he had sided with the farmers.

"Well, if word gets around, it'll draw every gun-totin' idiot for miles around. There ain't anyone in Jacksboro I need to concern myself about overly much."

"But? . . ."

Ramsey grinned at Coughlan. The man might be illiterate, and would never be anything more than a poor dirt farmer, but he was no fool. "But, I got word that McIlvaine and the others have sent for four top gunmen. He plans to have them join Preston and Thompson to come for me all at once."

"Oh?" Coughlan's mouth was dry. He was afraid for Ramsey, whom he now considered a friend. But he also knew Ramsey would need help. It was help Coughlan could not give, and that bothered him.

Ramsey sat silently for some moments. It was not in him to ask for help, but he had to. The four new gunmen would not be long in arriving, he assumed. He could not avoid them forever. And it would be suicidal for him to face six hired guns all at once. He had three options—face them by himself, and die; get some help from the farmers; or leave Jacksboro.

The first was not the best, the last almost not an option. His pride and honor would not let him run from any man—or group of men. His best hope was getting help from the farmers. He wished he had more time. If he did, he could get word to his brothers. With Buck and maybe Kyle, the odds would be almost even—two or three to one, rather than six to one. The Ramseys had faced such odds before. But he did not have the time to get word to Buck, who should be back in Texas by now, or Kyle, up in Colorado.

"I can use your help, Ike," he said, stomach twisting into knots at having to do this.

"To face those hired guns?" Coughlan asked. He, too, felt sick.

"Yep." Ramsey looked out over the farm. He was fairly certain Coughlan would turn him down, and he did not want to put any more pressure on the farmer. So he did not stare at Coughlan.

"Can't do it, Matt," Coughlan said, voice strangled by guilt. He wanted to explain, to tell Ramsey how he and his farmer friends would be all right in an ambush but they would freeze up or shake with fright when facing down six hired killers. But he had told that to Ramsey a long time ago, and he knew Ramsey knew these things as well as he himself did.

Still, Coughlan was sick with guilt. Ramsey had helped him and his friends so much, putting his life on the line. Now that Ramsey needed help, the farmers should be more than happy to help their benefactor in any way they could.

"I understand," Ramsey said. He pushed himself up. He had expected the response, and truly believed the farmers were incapable of helping him right now. But he had felt it necessary at least to try. "Well, you take care, Ike," he said. There was no rancor in his voice.

"You, too, Matt," Coughlan said quietly. He kept his head bowed, saying a prayer for Ramsey, until he was sure Ramsey was riding away. He stood and watched the black mustang walk off past the field, with the wind rustling the old corn stalks. Coughlan tried to assuage his conscience by remembering that Matt Ramsey was a hired gun himself, and therefore used to such predicaments. And that Ramsey was strong, sure of shot, and resourceful. None of it helped make him feel any better, though.

Sadly he turned, thinking he had seen the last of Matt Ramsey. His wife, Ethel, was watching him from the doorway. He thought he saw accusation in her eyes. But it was tempered by relief, too. He tore his eyes away from hers and went back to his work.

Ramsey leaned against the corner of Flanagan's store and watched as four hard-looking men stepped down off the Overland Stage. They were almost indistinguishable from each other.

They were uniformly tall, lean, almost elegant. Each had long hair, two of them stringy; one frizzy; the fourth with gentle waves flowing onto his shoulders. And they had long mustaches that curled around the mouth and crept past the bottom of the chin. They were elsewise clean-shaven.

Each wore striped wool pants tucked into high black boots; a white silk shirt; string tie; tail coat that reached the knees, with only the top two buttons fastened; flat-crowned hats with wide brims and long strings dangling on their chests.

Their only differences were in way they wore their armaments. Each carried two pistols that Ramsey could see. One had twin ivory-handled Colts in a shoulder rig, barely seen under the coat; one had two plain-grip revolvers stuck into his belt; another wore his pistols—Ramsey believed them to be Remingtons— in cross-draw holsters; and the last had his white-handled Colts worn in a traditional manner.

They were, Ramsey decided, a professional—and deadly— looking group. They saw him and stopped to stare for some seconds. Ramsey touched his hat brim at them in acknowledgement. At least two of the four nodded almost imperceptibly in return. Southfield, the servant, was ushering them away, toward the Social Club.

Ramsey shoved away from the wall and headed toward the Monarch. It was a week since he had spoken to Coughlan. He had been wondering how long it would take the gunmen to arrive in Jacksboro.

Lucy was pulling on a pair of thin gloves. She was dressed sedately in an embroidered two-piece bustle skirt with a soft blouse and a flowered bonnet to match. She looked demure and virginal. Her belongings were piled on the bed and the floor in neatly stacked boxes. Ramsey's heart sank.

Lucy looked sad when she turned toward him. She smiled wanly and turned to face him. "I think it best if I stay out of the way a while," she said. The tip of her tongue probed the corners of her mouth nervously.

Ramsey nodded, heartbroken. "Reckon it would," he said, voice cracking with emotion. "Where'll you go?"

"The Plainsman."

Ramsey nodded again, feeling stupid. He wanted to ask if she was planning to go back to her old profession, but he could not bring himself to do so.

She read the question on his face. "I've got enough money to live on for a spell . . . till this is cleared up and done with," she said quietly. "I don't need to work." She looked down, her pale face flaming pinkly.

"Need help gettin' your things over there?" Ramsey asked glumly.

"No. I hired two boys to do it. They ought to be here soon."

"Want me to escort you over there?"

"It might be best if you didn't," Lucy said, discomfited.

"All right." He opened the door for two youngsters who rushed in and began grabbing boxes. Ramsey sat at the table staring moodily out the window.

When the boys had carried out the last of the boxes, Lucy walked over and gently ran a gloved finger along Ramsey's stubbled cheek. "You'll come see me, won't you?" she asked, frightened.

"I reckon." Ramsey would not look at her. "If that's what you want."

"Oh, it is."

"I'll stop by." He did look at her then. She was crying quietly. She bent and brushed her full, tender lips against his. Still crying, she turned and hurried out, slamming the door behind her.

Ramsey sat at the table for a long time, thinking. *You really messed up this time, Matt Ramsey,* he told himself silently. *Ain't you ever gonna learn?* He wanted nothing more than to go get drunk; drown his heartache in bourbon. But he knew the six gun-men would be coming for him sooner or later. He just didn't know when, so he would need to be alert and prepared at all times.

It was dark when he finally stood. He grinned suddenly as he thought of what Kyle would think of him sitting here so morosely,

mooning over some soiled dove. And Buck! Lord, Buck would
ride him unmercifully, ribbing him until he couldn't stand himself
anymore. He missed Kyle and Buck. His other brothers, Amos and
Luke, too. He vowed that he would go visit Kyle up in Colorado
as soon as this was over.

"If I live that long," he said quietly to himself. He chuckled
and headed for the door. He was hungry, and he could no longer
stew in his self-pity. After all, he told himself firmly, Lucy was
not lost to him. She just wanted to be out of the cross fire, and
she was preparing herself for his demise, which appeared to be
an almost certain thing, considering the odds he faced.

He ate a good meal and then headed to Plager's Saloon. There
he nursed a few shots of redeye before leaving. *No need to tempt
fate,* he thought.

He spent the next three days wandering around town, neither
looking for trouble nor hiding from it. He had, though, started
wearing his spare Colt again, stuffed into his gunbelt at the
small of his back. People had begun to shun him once more.
He thought perhaps they were afraid to be associated with a
soon-to-be corpse. He laughed to himself over that one.

He visited Lucy once and spent the night. She was still warm
and loving, but at the same time reserved. He left in the morning,
feeling unsatisfied and still disturbed by the woman.

That afternoon, he went down to Plager's again. It had become
his favorite hangout, and the bartenders and customers were among
the few people in town who were not avoiding him. As he had since
the gunslingers arrived in Jacksboro, he stood at the right corner of
the bar, which ran along the back wall of the saloon. That way he
could keep an eye on the door and the solitary window in the wall
opposite him.

He had just finished a mug of beer when the batwing doors
creaked opened. They hung that way for a moment, as if by magic.
Then six lean, well-armed men filtered into the dark saloon and
spread out. The sunlight of the fading afternoon behind them put
halos around their upper bodies.

"You didn't think you could hide from us forever, did you,
Ramsey?" one snarled. Ramsey recognized the voice as Newell
Preston's.

"I ain't been hidin' from anybody," Ramsey said, straightening,
anger flooding through him. He remembered Preston's pale face
hanging over him in a dark alley. "Least of all some hog-wallowin'
drunk like you."

The men moved farther into the saloon, about halfway acros[ ]
and stopped. Ramsey could make out faces now.

"Enough of the talk, Ramsey," another said. "Time for action[ ]

"Who's your friend, Preston?" Ramsey asked, tensing.

"That 'un is Bull McKinney," Preston said. He sounded like h[ ]
was enjoying himself. "The others, startin' on the far end ther[ ]
are Tom Fisher; Rusty, you already know; Billy Joe Campbel[l]
Mr. McKinney; me, of course; and Lou Marsh here on my left[ ]

Ramsey listened to drumming hoofbeats outside that fade[ ]
down the street and then stopped.

"Got any last words, Ramsey?" McKinney asked.

"You're in a godawful hurry, ain't you."

"Can't see no reason for delayin'. We finish here, we g[o]
business elsewhere."

Ramsey nodded. "You can wait long enough for these oth[er]
folks to leave, can't you?" Ramsey asked reasonably. There w[as]
no fear in his voice; there was a bit of condescension. "No reas[on]
to go spillin' innocent blood."

McKinney shrugged.

"Go on, you damned sodbusters," Campbell said. "Get the he[ll]
out. But be quick about it."

The few customers and the bartender raced for the doorway.

"Make your play, Ramsey," McKinney said.

CHAPTER

⋆ 25 ⋆

The time had come; stalling would not change Ramsey's fate. He took a deep breath. Then he jerked out the Colt and fired three times, as fast as he could thumb the hammer.

He dived behind the bar to his right, noting with satisfaction that Preston was down and Marsh was holding a bloody right arm.

Ramsey popped up near the center of the bar, slapping his right arm across the bar to brace it, and fired the last two slugs in his pistol. He paid no attention to the bullets that tore up chunks of bar along its length. Billy Joe Campbell was hit, but still standing. Marsh was wielding a pistol in his left hand.

Ramsey flopped back down, behind the bar, ejecting shells as quickly as possible. As he shoved six new brass cartridges into the cylinder, he squatted and craned his neck up. The angle was terrible, but he could see the five men still standing advancing slowly, crouched, pistols out.

Colt reloaded, Ramsey scooted down the bar a little, spun, took a deep breath. He jumped up, firing as he had before. He emptied the Colt, oblivious to the return fire, though knowing it was there. He knew that Billy Joe Campbell was down, legs cocked at an odd angle. Ramsey figured him to be dead.

He dropped behind the bar again, slid his Colt into the holster and yanked out the spare. He did not expect the others to wait on him this time. He slid several feet down the bar and then popped up, firing again.

Guns roared in the small saloon, and a bluish haze covered the place. The acrid smell of powder smoke was thick. Ramsey thought he heard another gun, different from the rest, but he was not sure. He was sure, though, that his opponents were dropping faster than could be accounted for by his firing. He had the fleeting thought—or maybe it was a hope—that some the farmers had come to help him.

Sweating, he slipped behind the cover of the bar and beg knocking shells out of the Colt and jamming fresh ones in. F crawled to the end of the bar opposite where he had started th battle, and poked his head around, pistol ready.

This low to the ground, the smoke was not as heavy. He sa several bodies lying near the door, and only one pair of le, standing. They were not clad in high black boots or striped wo pants. Cautiously, he ducked behind the bar and then straightene Colt at arm's length.

The pall of gun smoke had cleared a little, and Ramsey cou see the figure at the far end of the saloon more clearly. A smi began to stretch over his face.

"Looks like I showed up just in time," Kyle Ramsey sai Matt's one-armed brother stood just inside the saloon doors, big grin on his face and his smoking LeMat in hand.

"I reckon," Matt allowed. He made sure his Colt and the spa were reloaded and stuck them away. He looked away, not wantin to embarrass his brother as Kyle worked with his one hand reload his LeMat. While Kyle was doing that, Matt checked (the six gunmen. They all were dead.

By the time he had done that, Kyle had finished his reloadi and slipped the odd-looking pistol into the cross-draw holste Matt looked at his brother and grinned. He stepped up and gav Kyle a bear hug. Kyle returned it joyfully.

"Damn, I do believe I am pleased to see your ornery ol' hid big brother," Matt said with a laugh after he stepped back. Neithe paid attention to the fact that Matt was the bigger man by a littl Kyle was the older, and to Matt he would always be his b brother.

"I suppose I can see why," Kyle said, looking around at th carnage. He had seen far, far worse in the war. And a few tim afterward. He could stand to laugh with joy at the reunion whi standing amidst it; so could Matt.

"It brings to mind the question, though, just what the hell a you doin' here?" Matt asked, as the oddness of the situation bega to really hit him.

"Well, it's the damnedest thing. I was sittin' at Amos's whe out of the blue this wire . . ."

"At Amos's?" Matt asked, his incredulity growing. "What th hell were you doin' at Amos's?"

"Oh, yeah, that's right, you don't know any of this," Kyle said with a chuckle. "Hell, if you stayed home once in a while, 'stead of ashayin' all over the countryside, stirrin' up the people, creatin' messes wherever you . . ."

"Jesus, Kyle, shut up!" Matt said, laughing. "Damn, you ain't said that much at one time since you were eight. Just tell me what happened."

Before Kyle could begin telling his story again, Sheriff Laybe entered the saloon. "Good Lord almighty," he whispered, looking around. Behind him, people jostled for a look through the doors. He stared at Matt. "Who's your friend?" he asked.

"My brother Kyle," Matt said. He managed to keep the anger out of his voice. "Kyle, Sheriff R. J. Laybe."

Each man nodded at the other.

"I'll have to take you and your brother in, Matt," Laybe said, reluctantly, weakly.

"He suicidal, Matt?" Kyle asked. He wore a half smile, but there was little humor in it.

"I reckon," Matt said easily. He looked at Laybe. "The only reason I don't knock you on your ass right here and now is 'cause you've helped me a little when you could. But had you had the stones to back me from the start, none of this would've happened. Now you get to clean it up. Come on, Kyle."

Matt shoved past Laybe, bumping his shoulder, and headed out. Kyle fell into step alongside. The people moved aside to let these two big men, so different in looks, so alike in deadliness, go by. They spoke in awed whispers.

As they walked, Kyle announced that he was hungry, so Matt led the way to a restaurant. Kyle ordered, and Matt sat back. "All right, big brother, spill it."

Kyle grinned. "Hell, those two pests of little brothers up and convinced me to go back to Texas. That's what I was doin' at Amos's. Me and Luke got back a couple weeks ago."

"Buck?"

"We had us a couple of adventures, and found ourselves out in the flats of Colorado. What with bein' so close, Buck decided to go on off and visit that girl he was sweet on a couple years ago. Eula Mae. You 'member her. I never met her." He grinned. "His skirt chasin' is gonna bring that boy trouble."

Matt laughed bitterly, thinking of Lucy Tillman. "We've all had troubles from that," he said.

Kyle looked at him in surprise, but nodded, understanding. Hi' food came, and he tore into it, talking around the bites of por' chop and boiled potatoes.

"Anyway, I was just settin' at Amos's, mindin' my own busi' ness, when this wire came. Sent to any of the Ramseys who migh' be in Fannin County, Texas. It came in at the wire office over i' New Liberty. Boys there saw the name and run it straight on ou' to Amos's. Amos, being the oldest, looked at it, handed it to me and said, 'This looks more along your line.'" Kyle laughed.

"Damn thing said you was up to your ass in gun-totin' sonsabitches and could use some help, was any available." He grinned. "I was of no mood to go, but Amos mad' me." His grin widened and laughter bubbled up. "Actually it weren't Amos at all, it was Rose Margaret." He laughe' heartily. For the first time in some years, Kyle Ramsey felt goo' about life.

"So here I am," Kyle said when his laughter had dwindled.

Matt sat, stunned, wondering who would have done such thing. "That wire have a name attached to it?" he asked.

"Yep. Some feller named Ike Coughlan. You know him?"

Matt nodded. "Farmer I helped out just a bit ago." He shook his head amazed. "I'll be damned." He thought for a few min' utes. "But how? Anybody sends a wire out of Jacksboro, it' be known by the sheriff. And if he knows it, the Jack Count' Cattlemen's Association would know about it. It would've take' you some days to get here. If folks here knew help might b' comin' for me, those gunslicks wouldn't have waited befor' comin' after me."

"How long did they wait?"

"Just a couple days, actually, once they arrived. I knew earlie' on that they were headed this way, though. I figure they give m' them couple days to worry and sweat some."

"Damn fools don't know you very well, do they?"

"Reckon not." He paused and stole a spoonful of his brother' peach cobbler and ate it. "But I still don't know how Coughla' managed it. He couldn't have sent the wire from here, like said, and I know he ain't left the area long enough to ride ove' to somewhere in Wise County to send it."

"If you'd shut that flappin' hole in your face a minute, I'll tel' you." Kyle finished off his supper and pulled the dish of cobble' toward him. "The wire said that if help was to be comin' a reply should be sent to the wire office in a place called Park Springs ddressed to 'Former Rustler.' " He gazed at Matt with a question n his eyes.

Matt looked blank.

Kyle shrugged. "It also said he'd wait a week for someone to how up and ask for this 'Rustler' feller. I sent a wire back and hen hauled butt fast as I could. Some scraggly boy was waitin' or me. He was a pretty closed-mouth young dude, but as we rode ellbent for here, he explained things some."

Kyle finished off the cobbler and leaned deeper into his chair, vhich creaked under the broadness of his back. Kyle dexterously olled a cigarette with his one hand, lighted it, and puffed. "Said is name was Grover, and that this was a payback." He questioned is brother with his eyes.

Matt nodded, an understanding smile on his face. "I was origially hired by the damned Cattlemen's Association to get rid of some rustlers. I buried a few and captured a few others. One of 'em was a boy didn't look like he belonged with those other losers. I treated him decent."

"Just like you to be so softhearted," Kyle muttered, grinning. "Anyway, he said this Coughlan feller felt bad about not bein' able to help you out none, so he concocted this scheme. He'd heard you talk of some tough brothers, ones who'd be able to pull your fat out of the fire." He puffed out his chest, and then burst out laughing. "This kid Grover was wanderin' around Jacksboro, apparently, and hooked up with Coughlan, lookin' for a job. Coughlan had him ride over to Park Springs."

"Jesus," Matt muttered. He was pleasantly surprised at the help he had received. He would have understood if Grover Haynes had just ridden on out for parts unknown, and if Coughlan had stuck to his farming. But they had taken a considerable risk in trying to help him. He was impressed. He went on to fill in the pieces of information that Kyle had lacked.

When Matt had finished speaking, Kyle asked, "So what do we do now?"

Matt shrugged.

"Shit, you ain't fixin' to let those damn cattlemen get away with all this crap, are you?"

"Would be bad business, wouldn't it?"

"Sure as hell would. Besides, you don't fix it now, the minute you ride out of here, those cattlemen're gonna be all over them farmers again. And I ain't about to let that happen." His chin jutted as he challenged his brother.

Matt grinned. "Lord, you are a tough one, ain't you?" he said in false mockery. They both laughed. "I aim to fix it before we leave." He paused. "There's some other loose ends need tendin', too."

Kyle nodded. "Then let's get to it."

CHAPTER

★ 26 ★

The two Ramseys strolled to the Jacksboro Social Club and across the saloon floor, toward the back.

"Hey, you can't go back there," McCafferty roared. Ignored by the Ramseys, he shouted, "They ain't there."

Matt and Kyle continued to ignore him. They slammed through the door, surprising the six members of the Jack County Cattlemen's Association. "Evenin', boys," Matt said cheerily. He marched into the room until he was standing in front of the desk. Kyle stopped just inside the door, where his eyes could command the sweep of the entire room.

Calvin McIlvaine sat in ponderous obesity behind the desk. Jasper Pomeroy had pulled up a chair and was next to him. "What do you want here, Ramsey?" McIlvaine demanded. But his fear sparkled on his face.

"A little chat with you and the others."

"Get the hell out."

"Listen to me, you fat pile of hog shit," Matt snarled. "I have had it up to my eyes with your nonsense. Your days of runnin' Jack County are over."

"Don't cross us, Mr. Ramsey," Pomeroy said in deadly tones.

"Or what?" Matt demanded. "You gonna send more hired guns after me? You got six good ones layin' over at the undertaker's now."

Pomeroy seemed to shrink, though McIlvaine still blustered. "What do you want?" Pomeroy asked quietly.

"Your word that you'll leave the farmers be, that you'll not send no more night riders after them, that you'll not cut down their fences or trample their crops. Your promise to live in peace with all the folks in the county."

"All right," Pomeroy said meekly.

"No! Never!" McIlvaine roared, his flab quaking in outrage.

"Shut up, Cal," Pomeroy said quietly but forcefully. "We've been beaten fair and square. It's time we cut our losses."

"You sure?" Tobe Walker asked. He sounded skeptical.

"I'm sure," Pomeroy said. He looked up at Matt. "That suit you?"

"I reckon." Matt turned and walked away. Kyle went through the door a moment later.

When they reached the street, Kyle asked, "You don't believe that festerin' compost heap, do you?"

"Not as far as I could throw my horse."

Kyle nodded, doubts fleeing. He thought Matt had given in too easily. "What next?"

"A little visit with the sheriff."

Laybe was sitting at his desk, feet on it, looking shocked. "Christ, not you two," he moaned when the Ramseys entered and grabbed seats.

"Have fun cleanin' up that mess over at Plager's?" Matt asked mildly.

"Hell, no!" Laybe said emphatically.

"Good," Matt said, surprising the lawman. "I know how you can keep from havin' to do it again."

"How?" Laybe asked. He wasn't sure he liked where this might be heading.

"Do your goddamn job!" Matt barked.

"I have been," Laybe retorted, just as vehemently.

"Had you been doin' your job 'stead of ass kissin' the cattlemen, then the gravediggers and undertaker wouldn't be workin' 'round the clock. You know that and I know that. Hell, everybody in Jacksboro knows that." He paused to collect himself. "You've helped me out some of late, R.J., but precious little. Otherwise you've caused me more trouble than you saved. I don't cotton to such things."

Matt patiently explained Kyle's and his visit to the Social Club, and his certainty that the cattlemen would not abide by the word they gave. "So, R.J.," Matt concluded, "the reign of the Jack County Cattlemen's Association is over." He glared with hard, dark eyes at Laybe. "Everybody knows it 'cept them—and maybe you. So you best listen. It's time you did your job, like I said. You ain't—or shouldn't be—at the beck and call of those bastards no more. They caused a lot of bloodshed and a lot of pain and sufferin'. It's got to end, and you got to do your share in stoppin' it."

"What can I do?" Laybe asked, almost plaintively.

"Stop whinin', for one thing," Kyle offered.

"And stop worryin' about your goddamn job in the next election. Just 'cause you won't have the cattlemen's money behind you don't mean you'll lose the election. You do your job the way it's supposed to be done and you'll have no trouble winnin' the goddamn thing."

Matt paused and then said, "I expect the cattlemen will try somethin' else. I ain't sure of what or when. But they will. I want you to stop it before it gets out of hand. And arrest those bastards—all six of 'em—if necessary. Or you'll answer to us."

Laybe nodded glumly. He was caught in a vise, he figured. Either way he went, he would be in trouble with somebody. He sighed. There was no use in fighting it. He could see that the cattlemen were done with as a power. Maybe the farmers would become the next power. A few large farms, and a couple years of good crops, and there'd be some rich farmers. Besides, he thought, if he was going to be in trouble anyway, he might as well do what was right. "Okay, Matt," he said.

Four days after their talk with both the cattlemen and the sheriff, Matt and Kyle Ramsey were crossing the street when Kyle said, "Company." His hand moved smoothly toward the LeMat and gripped the handle without pulling the weapon.

"I see 'em."

The three men who had stepped from behind wagons or horses moved with well-practiced smoothness. They simply cleared the obstacle they were behind, drew their pistols, and opened fire.

Kyle dropped to one knee and yanked the LeMat. He fired the barrel of buckshot. The charge hit both men flanking him. One fell; the other stood, dazed a little, and then started to raise his pistol again. Kyle hastily flicked the small lever on the hammer and fired twice more from the nine-shot revolver, punching two bullets into the man who was standing. The bullets knocked that man down in a heap. Kyle swung toward the other side.

Matt needed no help. He had drawn his Colt and brought the gun to arm's length. He heard the heavy cough of buckshot from Kyle's LeMat and then the two sharper cracks. He smiled, cold and deadly, as he plugged the gunman twice in the heart.

He turned and saw Kyle walking toward two men on the ground. One still moved. Kyle loomed over him and thumbed back the hammer of his pistol. *"Adios,"* he said quietly.

"No!" Matt shouted.

Kyle stopped and looked at him in surprise. He wondered if his brother had lost his mind.

Matt strolled up and looked down. "Don't kill him," he said. "He might be of use to us." The germ of an idea had formed, and he wanted to see what would grow from it. He reached down and grabbed the man's bloody shirt. Bunching the material in his hand, he lifted. The man's torso came up, though his head lolled. The man moaned. Matt marched off, carting the gunman rather easily. The man's spurs left odd little trails in the dirt.

He brought the gunman to Quigley's. The physician began working on the man. "How're your other patients?" Matt asked, referring to the wounded night riders he had brought in almost two weeks ago.

"Two're still here. One left the other day. Why?"

"Can they be moved?"

"Sure."

Matt herded the two night riders to the jail, ordering Laybe to lock the men up, saying he would explain it later. Then he and Kyle went back to the doctor's. "How's that feller?" Matt asked.

"Not bad. Took a load of buckshot in the chest, but nothing penetrated too deep. You want him, too?"

Matt nodded and helped the gunman to the jail, too. The man moaned, but Matt didn't think he was as badly hurt as he was putting on. Once at the jail, Matt stood in front of the cell containing the gunslick and the two night riders. A wondering Laybe and puzzled Kyle stood behind him, leaning against the wall.

"Sheriff Laybe's agreed to let you boys go," Matt lied, though he was sure he could convince the lawman. "If you testify at a trial against the cattlemen."

"Go to hell," one of the night riders snapped. "I ain't tellin anybody a damn thing."

"Then you'll swing from the gallows, you fractious little snot," Matt snapped roughly. "You've got no more help in Jacksboro from the cattlemen."

"What do you want us to do?" the other night rider asked.

"Tell the truth," Matt said simply. "Testify how the six members of the Cattlemen's Association hired you, and why."

"It was Mr. Pomeroy hired me," the second night rider said.

The other night rider sighed. He knew he was in serious trouble. He'd hate like hell to have overcome a bullet wound only to die at the end of a rope. "Him and Mr. McIlvaine hired me."

"The others didn't have nothin' to do with it?" Matt asked sharply.

"No," the two answered in unison.

"How about you?" Matt asked, addressing his remark to the gunman. When the man only moaned, Matt pulled his pistol and fired once. The sound was deafening in the small jail, and the gunman jumped when the bullet plowed into the wall inches above his nose where he lay on the cot. "Don't play possum with me, boy. I asked you a question."

The man groaned but sat up. He wasn't in the best of shape, but better than he had been pretending. "Both was there," he said quietly. "McIlvaine was all bluff and bluster, makin' demands and givin' orders. But it was Pomeroy who paid out the cash and spoke to me quietly afterward to tell me just how he wanted things done." The man shrugged and winced.

"You'll testify to that in court?" Matt demanded. "All three of you?"

"You're gonna let us go, Sheriff?"

Matt gave him a hard glance, and Laybe swallowed hard. "I'll do everything I can."

All three agreed to testify, and Laybe, with intestines knotted in annoyance and fear, went to the Social Club to arrest Jasper Pomeroy and Calvin McIlvaine. The other cattlemen, scared, watched.

The trial was held three days later. The two night riders and the hired gunslinger testified loudly and without reserve. When it came his time to testify, McIlvaine blustered and roared, threatening the judge, the sheriff, the Ramseys, and everyone else in Jack County. Pomeroy was smooth and suave on the stand, simply stating that the three outlaws were liars and that he had never seen them before. He smiled benignly, but some of the jurymen caught his unctuous smirk at times.

It seemed as if the entire town of Jacksboro tried to cram into the courtroom as word passed that the verdict was to be tendered. The Ramseys and Laybe sat in the front row, facing the bench. McIlvaine and Pomeroy, with their lawyers, sat at a table nearby.

The jury came in and sat down. The foreman gave a sheet of paper to a court officer who handed it to Baldwin, and the judge announced the verdict: Both men were guilty. Into the silence that followed the chaos, Baldwin announced that both would hang in a week.

"No!" McIlvaine shouted, pushing ponderously to his feet. His fat face was red, and sweat rolled down his flabby jowls. "No! It was all Jasper's doing," he shouted. "I only went along."

"Sit down, Mr. McIlvaine," Baldwin rebuked him.

"No!" McIlvaine screamed. He scrabbled at his chest, and Matt thought the man was having heart spasms. Suddenly a derringer appeared in McIlvaine's fat fist and he was aiming it toward the judge.

Three shots rang out, and McIlvaine collapsed into his chair, mouth flapping open. His arm fell uselessly to his side, and the derringer, unfired, fell to the floor. It landed with a clunk.

Laybe and the two Ramseys stood behind a cloud of gunsmoke, slipping their revolvers away, as order began to fall over the court once again.

"Ain't you ready yet?" Matt asked roughly.

"Us cripples need a little more time than you regular folks," Kyle said as he pulled himself onto his horse. He looked at his brother solemnly. "You get it all settled?"

"Yep." Matt would be glad to be shed of Jacksboro, but there was an undercurrent of sadness, too. He had gone to talk with Lucy after the trial was over. He was not sure he wanted to marry her, but he wanted to keep that option open. And he thought that if that was the only way to keep her, well, that would be all right, too.

But Lucy had had plenty of time to think in the time since she had left Matt Ramsey's room at the Monarch. And she had concluded that she could never live with a man like Matt Ramsey. Love him, yes; live with him all the time, no. She wanted a man who was going to be there for her. Not someone who was going to run off every time she turned around, trying to help somebody somewhere, getting in gunfights. She could not live with the uncertainty of his never coming home again, of thinking of him gunned down in some cheap dive somewhere.

He offered to give up that life, but she knew he would never be able to do it. A friend would need help, and he wouldn't be able to resist that "one last" job. Besides, he was no farmer. The only other thing he could do was catch and break horses, and she wanted little part of that life, either.

And she realized even if he didn't, if he really gave up the life he was used to living, he would be a different man than the one she had fallen in love with.

"That your final word, then, Luce?" he asked. He had a deep aching in his heart.

"Yes," she said, barely in a whisper. She looked up at him and offered a pale smile. "I'd be obliged if you was to think about me of a time."

"I will."

"And maybe come to see me someday?"

Ramsey nodded. He kissed her and headed out the door. By the time he was outside and walking swiftly across the street, he began to feel a little better. He realized with some relief that he really didn't want to be married. Not yet, anyway. Still, he would miss that raven-haired beauty.

The next day, Matt and Kyle visited the four remaining members of the Cattlemen's Association and extracted a written promise that they would not cause trouble with the farmers. Then it was time to leave.

"Well, let's go," Kyle said impatiently.

Matt touched his heels to the black's sides and, with Kyle beside him, trotted toward home.

RICHARD MATHESON

Author of DUEL

is back with his most
exciting Western yet!

JOURNAL OF THE GUN YEARS

Clay Halser is the fastest gun west of the Mississippi, and
he's captured the fancy of newspapermen and pulp writers
back East. That's good news for Halser, but bad news for
the endless army of young tinhorns who ride into town to
challenge him and die by his gun. As Halser's body count
grows, so does his legend. Worse, he's starting to believe
his own publicity—which could ultimately prove deadly!

Turn the page
for an exciting chapter from

JOURNAL OF THE GUN YEARS

by
Richard Matheson

On sale now,
wherever Berkley Books are sold!

BOOK ONE
(1864-1867)

It is my unhappy lot to write the closing entry in this journal.

Clay Halser is dead, killed this morning in my presence.

I have known him since we met during the latter days of The War Between The States. I have run across him, on occasion, through ensuing years and am, in fact, partially responsible (albeit involuntarily) for a portion of the legend which has magnified around him.

It is for these reasons (and another more important) that I make this final entry.

I am in Silver Gulch acquiring research matter toward the preparation of a volume on the history of this territory (Colorado), which has recently become the thirty-eighth state of our Union.

I was having breakfast in the dining room of the *Silver Lode Hotel* when a man entered and sat down at a table across the room, his back to the wall. Initially, I failed to recognize him though there was, in his comportment, something familiar.

Several minutes later (to my startlement), I realized that it was none other than Clay Halser. True, I had not laid eyes on him for many years. Nonetheless, I was completely taken back by the change in his appearance.

I was not, at that point, aware of his age, but took it to be somewhere in the middle thirties. Contrary to this, he presented the aspect of a man at least a decade older.

His face was haggard, his complexion (in my memory, quite ruddy) pale to the point of being ashen. His eyes, formerly suffused with animation, now looked burned out, dead. What many horrific sights those eyes had beheld I could not—and cannot—begin to estimate. Whatever those sights, however, no evidence

173

of them had been reflected in his eyes before; it was as though he'd been emotionally immune.

He was no longer so. Rather, one could easily imagine that his eyes were gazing, in that very moment, at those bloody sights, dredging from the depths within his mind to which he'd relegated them, all their awful measure.

From the standpoint of physique, his deterioration was equally marked. I had always known him as a man of vigorous health, a condition necessary to sustain him in the execution of his harrowing duties. He was not a tall man; I would gauge his height at five feet ten inches maximum, perhaps an inch or so less, since his upright carriage and customary dress of black suit, hat, and boots might have afforded him the look of standing taller than he did. He had always been extremely well-presented though, with a broad chest, narrow waist, and pantherlike grace of movement; all in all, a picture of vitality.

Now, as he ate his meal across from me, I felt as though, by some bizarre transfiguration, I was gazing at an old man.

He had lost considerable weight and his dark suit (it, too, seemed worn and past its time) hung loosely on his frame. To my further disquiet, I noted a threading of gray through his dark blonde hair and saw a tremor in his hands completely foreign to the young man I had known.

I came close to summary departure. To my shame, I nearly chose to leave rather than accost him. Despite the congenial relationship I had enjoyed with him throughout the past decade, I found myself so totally dismayed by the alteration in his looks that I lacked the will to rise and cross the room to him, preferring to consider hasty exit. (I discovered, later, that the reason he had failed to notice me was that his vision, always so acute before, was now inordinately weak.)

At last, however, girding up my will, I stood and moved across the dining room, attempting to fix a smile of pleased surprise on my lips and hoping he would not be too aware of my distress.

"Well, good morning, Clay," I said, as evenly as possible.

I came close to baring my deception at the outset for, as he looked up sharply at me, his expression one of taut alarm, a perceptible "tic" under his right eye, I was hard put not to draw back apprehensively.

Abruptly, then, he smiled (though it was more a ghost of the smile I remembered). "*Frank*," he said and jumped to his feet. No, that is not an accurate description of his movement. It may well have been his intent to jump up and welcome me with avid hand-shake. As it happened, his stand was labored, his hand grip lacking in strength. "How *are* you?" he inquired. "It is good to see you."

"I'm fine," I answered.

"Good." He nodded, gesturing toward the table. "Join me."

I hope my momentary hesitation passed his notice. "I'd be happy to," I told him.

"Good," he said again.

We each sat down, he with his back toward the wall again. As we did, I noted how his gaunt frame slumped into the chair, so different from the movement of his earlier days.

He asked me if I'd eaten breakfast.

"Yes." I pointed across the room. "I was finishing when you entered."

"I am glad you came over," he said.

There was a momentary silence. Uncomfortable, I tried to think of something to say.

He helped me out. (I wonder, now, if it was deliberate; if he had, already, taken note of my discomfort.) "Well, old fellow," he asked, "what brings you to this neck of the woods?"

I explained my presence in Silver Gulch and, as I did, being now so close to him, was able to distinguish, in detail, the astounding metamorphosis which time (and experience) had effected.

There seemed to be, indelibly impressed on his still handsome face, a look of unutterable sorrow. His former blitheness had completely vanished and it was oppressive to behold what had occurred to his expression, to see the palsied gestures of his hands as he spoke, perceive the constant shifting of his eyes as though he was anticipating that, at any second, some impending danger might be thrust upon him.

I tried to coerce myself not to observe these things, concentrat-ing on the task of bringing him "up to date" on my activities since last we'd met; no match for his activities, God knows.

"What about you?" I finally asked; I had no more to say about myself. "What are you doing these days?"

"Oh, gambling," he said, his listless tone indicative of his regard for that pursuit.

"No marshaling anymore?" I asked.

He shook his head. "Strictly the circuit," he answered.

"Circuit?" I wasn't really curious but feared the onset of silence and spoke the first word that occurred to me.

"A league of boomtown havens for faro players," he replied.

"South Texas up to South Dakota—Idaho to Arizona. There is money to be gotten everywhere. Not that I am good enough to make a raise. And not that it's important if I do, at any rate. I only gamble for something to do."

All the time he spoke, his eyes kept shifting, searching; was it *waiting*?

As silence threatened once again, I quickly spoke. "Well, you have traveled quite a long road since the War," I said. "A long, exciting road." I forced a smile. "*Adventurous*," I added.

His answering smile was as sadly bitter and exhausted as any I have ever witnessed. "Yes, the writers of the stories have made it all sound very colorful," he said. He leaned back with a heavy sigh, regarding me. "I even thought it so myself at one time. Now I recognize it all for what it was." There was a tightening around his eyes. "Frank, it was drab, and dirty, and there was a lot of blood."

I had no idea how to respond to that and, in spite of my resolve, let silence fall between us once more.

Silence broke in a way that made my flesh go cold. A young man's voice behind me, from some distance in the room. "So that is him," the voice said loudly. "Well, he does not look like much to me."

I'd begun to turn when Clay reached out and gripped my arm. "Don't bother looking," he instructed me. "It's best to ignore them. I have found the more attention paid, the more difficult they are to shake in the long run."

He smiled but there was little humor in it. "Don't be concerned," he said. "It happens all the time. They spout a while, then go away, and brag that Halser took their guff and never did a thing. It makes them feel important. I don't mind. I've grown accustomed to it."

At which point, the boy—I could now tell, from the timbre of his voice, that he had not attained his majority—spoke again.

"He looks like nothing at all to me to be so all-fired famous a fighter with his guns," he said.

I confess the hostile quaver of his voice unsettled me. Seeing my reaction, Clay smiled and was about to speak when the boy—perhaps seeing the smile and angered by it—added, in a tone resounding enough to be heard in the lobby, "In fact, I believe he looks like a woman-hearted coward, that is what he looks like to me!"

"Don't worry now," Clay reassured me. "He'll blow himself

out of steam presently and crawl away." I felt some sense of relief to see a glimmer of the old sauce in his eyes. "Probably to visit, with uncommon haste, the nearest outhouse."

Still, the boy kept on with stubborn malice. "My name is Billy Howard," he announced. "And I am going to make . . ."

He went abruptly mute as Clay unbuttoned his dark frock coat to reveal a butt-reversed Colt at his left side. It was little wonder. Even I, a friend of Clay's, felt a chill of premonition at the movement. What spasm of dread it must have caused in the boy's heart, I can scarcely imagine.

"Sometimes I have to go this far," Clay told me. "Usually I wait longer but, since you are with me . . ." He let the sentence go unfinished and lifted his cup again.

I wanted to believe the incident was closed but, as we spoke— me asking questions to distract my mind from its foreboding state—I seemed to feel the presence of the boy behind me like some constant wraith.

"How are all your friends?" I asked.

"Dead," Clay answered.

"*All* of them?

He nodded. "Yes. Jim Clements. Ben Pickett. John Harris." I saw a movement in his throat. "Henry Blackstone. All of them."

I had some difficulty breathing. I kept expecting to hear the boy's voice again. "What about your wife?" I asked.

"I have not heard from her in some time," he replied. "We are estranged."

"How old is your daughter now?"

"Three in January," he answered, his look of sadness deepening. I regretted having asked and quickly said, "What about your family in Indiana?"

"I went back to visit them last year," he said. "It was a waste."

I did not want to know, but heard myself inquiring nonetheless, "Why?"

"Oh . . . what I have become," he said. "What journalists have made me. Not you," he amended, believing, I suppose, that he'd insulted me. "My reputation, I mean. It stood like a wall between my family and me. I don't think they saw me. Not *me*. They saw what they believed I am."

The voice of Billy Howard made me start. "Well, why does he just *sit* there?" he said.

Clay ignored him. Or, perhaps, he did not even hear, so deep was he immersed in black thoughts.

"Hickok was right," he said, "I am not a man anymore. I'm a figment of imagination. Do you know, I looked at my reflection in the mirror this morning and did not even know who I was looking at? Who is that staring at me? I wondered. Clay Halser of Pine Grove? Or the *Hero of The Plains*?" he finished with contempt.

"*Well*?" demanded Billy Howard. "Why *does* he?"

Clay was silent for a passage of seconds and I felt my muscles drawing in, anticipating God knew what.

"I had no answer for my mirror," he went on then. "I have no answers left for anyone. All I know is that I am tired. They have offered me the job of City Marshal here and, although I could use the money, I cannot find it in myself to accept."

Clay Halser stared into my eyes and told me quietly, "To answer your long-time question: yes, Frank, I have learned what fear is. Though not fear of . . ."

He broke off as the boy spoke again, his tone now venomous. "I think he is afraid of me," said Billy Howard.

Clay drew in a long, deep breath, then slowly shifted his gaze to look across my shoulder. I sat immobile, conscious of an air of tension in the entire room now, everyone waiting with held breath.

"That is what I think," the boy's voice said. "I think Almighty God Halser is afraid of me."

Clay said nothing, looking past me at the boy. I did not dare to turn. I sat there, petrified.

"I think the Almighty God Halser is a yellow skunk!" cried Billy Howard. "I think he is a murderer who shoots men in the back and will not . . . !"

The boy's voice stopped again as Clay stood so abruptly that I felt a painful jolting in my heart. "I'll be right back," he said.

He walked past me and, shuddering, I turned to watch. It had grown so deathly still in the room that, as I did, the legs of my chair squeaked and caused some nearby diners to start.

I saw, now, for the first time, Clay Halser's challenger and was aghast at the callow look of him. He could not have been more than sixteen years of age and might well have been younger, his face speckled with skin blemishes, his dark hair long and shaggy. He was poorly dressed and had an old six-shooter pushed beneath the waistband of his faded trousers.

I wondered vaguely whether I should move, for I was sitting in whatever line of fire the boy might direct. I wondered vaguely if the other diners were wondering the same thing. If they were, their limbs were as frozen as mine.

I heard every word exchanged by the two.

"Now don't you think that we have had enough of this?" Clay said to the boy. "These folks are having their breakfast and I think that we should let them eat their meal in peace."

"Step out into the street then," said the boy.

"Now why should I step out into the street?" Clay asked. I knew it was no question. He was doing what he could to calm the agitated boy—that agitation obvious as the boy replied, "To fight me with your gun."

"You don't want to fight me," Clay informed him. "You would just be killed and no one would be better for it."

"You mean *you* don't want to fight *me*," the youth retorted. Even from where I sat, I could see that his face was almost white; it was clear that he was terror-stricken.

Still, he would not allow himself to back off, though Clay was giving him full opportunity. "*You* don't want to fight *me*," he repeated.

"That is not the case at all," Clay replied. "It is just that I am tired of fighting."

"I *thought* so!" cried the boy with malignant glee.

"Look," Clay told him quietly, "if it will make you feel good, you are free to tell your friends, or anyone you choose, that I backed down from you. You have my permission to do that."

"I don't need your d——d permission," snarled the boy. With a sudden move, he scraped his chair back, rising to feet. Unnervingly, he seemed to be gaining resolution rather than losing it—as though, in some way, he sensed the weakness in Clay, despite the fact that Clay was famous for his prowess with the handgun. "I am sick of listening to you," he declared. "Are you going to step outside with me and pull your gun like a man, or do I shoot you down like a dog?"

"*Go home*, boy," Clay responded—and I felt an icy grip of premonition strike me full force as his voice broke in the middle of a word.

"Pull, you yellow b——d," Billy Howard ordered him.

Several diners close to them lunged up from their tables, scattering for the lobby. Clay stood motionless.

"I said *pull*, you God d——d son of a b——h!" Billy Howard shouted.

"No," was all Clay Halser answered.

"Then *I* will!" cried the boy.

Before his gun was halfway from the waistband of his trousers,

Clay's had cleared its holster. Then—with what capricious twist of fate!—his shot misfired and, before he could squeeze off another, the boy's gun had discharged and a bullet struck Clay full in the chest, sending him reeling back to hit a table, then sprawl sideways to the floor.

Through the pall of dark smoke, Billy Howard gaped down at his victim. "I did it," he muttered. "I *did* it." Though chance alone had done it.

Suddenly, his pistol clattered to the floor as his fingers lost their holding power and, with a cry of what he likely thought was victory, he bolted from the room. (Later, I heard, he was killed in a knife fight over a poker game somewhere near Bijou Basin.)

By then, I'd reached Clay, who had rolled onto his back, a dazed expression on his face, his right hand pressed against the blood-pumping wound in the center of his chest. I shouted for someone to get a doctor, and saw some man go dashing toward the lobby. Clay attempted to sit up, but did not have the strength, and slumped back.

Hastily, I knelt beside him and removed my coat to form a pillow underneath his head, then wedged my handkerchief between his fingers and the wound. As I did, he looked at me as though I were a stranger. Finally, he blinked and, to my startlement, began to chuckle. "The one time I di . . ." I could not make out the rest. "What, Clay?" I asked distractedly, wondering if I should try to stop the bleeding in some other way.

He chuckled again. "The one day I did not reload," he repeated with effort. "Ben would laugh at that."

He swallowed, then began to make a choking noise, a trickle of blood issuing from the left-hand corner of his mouth. "Hang on," I said, pressing my hand to his shoulder. "The doctor will be here directly."

He shook his head with several hitching movements. "No sawbones can remove me from *this* tight," he said.

He stared up at the ceiling now, his breath a liquid sound that made me shiver. I did not know what to say, but could only keep directing worried (and increasingly angry) glances toward the lobby. "Where *is* he?" I muttered.

Clay made a ghastly, wheezing noise, then said, "My God." His fingers closed in, clutching at the already blood-soaked handkerchief. "I am going to die." Another strangling breath. "And I am only thirty-one years old."

Instant tears distorted my vision. *Thirty-one*?

Clay murmured something I could not hear. Automatically, I bent over and he repeated, in a labored whisper, "She was such a pretty girl."

"Who?" I asked; could not help but ask.

"Mary Jane," he answered. He could barely speak by then. Straightening up, I saw the grayness of death seeping into his face and knew that there were only moments left to him.

He made a sound which might have been a chuckle had it not emerged in such a hideously bubbling manner. His eyes seemed lit now with some kind of strange amusement. "I could have married her," he managed to say. "I could still be there." He stared into his fading thoughts. "Then I would never have . . ."

At which his stare went lifeless and he expired.

I gazed at him until the doctor came. Then the two of us lifted his body—how *frail* it was—and placed it on a nearby table. The doctor closed Clay's eyes and I crossed Clay's arms on his chest after buttoning his coat across the ugly wound. Now he looked almost at peace, his expression that of a sleeping boy.

Soon people began to enter the dining room. In a short while, everyone in Silver Gulch, it seemed, had heard about Clay's death and come running to view the remains. They shuffled past his impromptu bier in a double line, gazed at him and, ofttimes, murmured some remark about his life and death.

As I stood beside the table, looking at the gray, still features, I wondered what Clay had been about to say before the rancorous voice of Billy Howard had interrupted. He'd said that he had learned what fear is, "though not fear of . . ." What words had he been about to say? Though not fear of other men? Of danger? Of death?

Later on, the undertaker came and took Clay's body after I had guaranteed his payment. That done, I was requested, by the manager of the hotel, to examine Clay's room and see to the disposal of his meager goods. This I did and will return his possessions to his family in Indiana.

With one exception.

In a lower bureau drawer, I found a stack of Record Books bound together with heavy twine. They turned out to be a journal which Clay Halser kept from the latter part of the War to this very morning.

It is my conviction that these books deserve to be published. Not in their entirety, of course; if that were done, I estimate the book would run in excess of a thousand pages. Moreover, there are many entries which, while perhaps of interest to immediate family (who will, of course, receive the Record Books when I have finished partially transcribing them), contribute nothing to the main thrust of his account, which is the unfoldment of his life as a nationally recognized lawman and gunfighter.

Accordingly, I plan to eliminate those sections of the journal which chronicle that variety of events which any man might experience during twelve years' time. After all, as hair-raising as Clay's life was, he could not possibly exist on the razor edge of peril every day of his life. As proof of this, I will incorporate a random sampling of those entries which may be considered, from a "thrilling" standpoint, more mundane.

In this way—concentrating on the sequences of "action"—it is hoped that the general reader, who might otherwise ignore the narrative because of its unwieldy length, will more willingly expose his interest to the life of one whom another journalist has referred to as "The Prince of Pistoleers."

Toward this end, I will, additionally, attempt to make corrections in the spelling, grammar and, especially, punctuation of the journal, leaving, as an indication of this necessity, the opening entry. It goes without saying that subsequent entries need less attention to this aspect since Clay Halser learned, by various means, to read and write with more skill in his later years.

I hope the reader will concur that, while there might well be a certain charm in viewing the entries precisely as Clay Halser wrote them, the difficulty in following his style through virtually an entire book would make the reading far too difficult. It is for this reason that I have tried to simplify his phraseology without— I trust—sacrificing the basic flavor of his language.

Keep in mind, then, that if the chronology of this account is, now and then, sporadic (with occasional truncated entries), it is because I have used, as its main basis, Clay Halser's life as a man of violence. I hope, by doing this, that I will not unbalance the impression of his personality. While trying not to intrude unduly on the texture of the journal, I may occasionally break into it if I believe my observations may enable the reader to better understand the protagonist of what is probably the bloodiest sequence of events to ever take place on the American frontier.

I plan to do all this, not for personal encomiums, but because I hope that I may be the agency by which the public-at-large may come to know Clay Halser's singular story, perhaps to thrill at his exploits, perhaps to moralize but, hopefully, to profit by the reading for, through the page-by-page transition of this man from high-hearted exuberance to hopeless resignation, we may, perhaps, achieve some insight into a sad, albeit fascinating and exciting, phenomenon of our times.

Frank Leslie
April 19, 1876

If you enjoyed this book, subscribe now and get...

TWO FREE

A $7.00 VALUE—

If you would like to read more of the very best, most exciting, adventurous, action-packed Westerns being published today, you'll want to subscribe to True Value's Western Home Subscription Service.

Each month the editors of True Value will select the 6 very best Westerns from America's leading publishers for special readers like you. You'll be able to preview these new titles as soon as they are published, *FREE* for ten days with no obligation!

TWO FREE BOOKS

When you subscribe, we'll send you your first month's shipment of the newest and best 6 Westerns for you to preview. With your first shipment, two of these books will be yours as our introductory gift to you absolutely *FREE* (a $7.00 value), regardless of what you decide to do. If you like them, as much as we think you will, keep all six books but pay for just 4 at the low subscriber rate of just $2.75 each. If you decide to return them, keep 2 of the titles as our gift. No obligation.

Special Subscriber Savings

When you become a True Value subscriber you'll save money several ways. First, all regular monthly selections will be billed at the low subscriber price of just $2.75 each. That's at least a savings of $4.50 each month below the publishers price. Second, there is never any shipping, handling or other hidden charges—*Free home delivery*. What's more there is no minimum number of books you must buy, you may return any selection for full credit and you can cancel your subscription at any time. A TRUE VALUE!

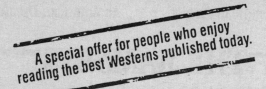

An American Family   An American Dream

THE RAMSEYS
Will McLennan

Bound to the land and united by their blood, the Ramseys have survived for generations. Brave, sturdy, and strong-willed, they have forged out a rugged new life in North Texas, overcoming drought, disease, and the mayhem of the Civil War. Every Ramsey is born to fight for justice and freedom on the American Frontier.